MURDER AT HONEYCHURCH HALL

When Kat Stanford abandons a successful television career to help her mother, Iris, move into a rustic carriage house in Devon, she quickly discovers that, behind the well-trimmed hedgerows, Honeychurch Hall is populated by more eccentrics than Kat ever met in all her time in London. The Dowager Countess, Lord and Lady Honeychurch, their precocious seven-year-old heir, his missing nanny, a brooding stable manager, a housekeeper with an extensive designer shoe collection... Everyone seems to harbour a secret – and Kat's mother may be hiding the darkest of them all...

MURDER AT
HONEYCHURCH HALL

MURDER AT HONEYCHURCH HALL

by

Hannah Dennison

Magna Large Print Books
Long Preston, North Yorkshire,
BD23 4ND, England.

British Library Cataloguing in Publication Data.

Dennison, Hannah
    Murder at Honeychurch Hall.

    A catalogue record of this book is
    available from the British Library

    ISBN   978-0-7505-4317-0

First published in Great Britain in 2014 by Constable

Published in Large Print 2016 by arrangement with
Little, Brown Book Group

Magna Large Print is an imprint of Library Magna Books Ltd.

Printed and bound in Great Britain by
T.J. (International) Ltd., Cornwall, PL28 8RW

This book is dedicated with heartfelt gratitude to my boss, Mark Davis, Chairman of Davis Elen Advertising. I am forever indebted to your gracious support of my writing endeavors.

Acknowledgments

The idea for setting the Honeychurch Hall series on a country house estate was sparked by my widowed mother, Brenda Dennison, who decided to live in her dream house when most women of her age would be heading for a retirement village. Mum, your zest for life and spirit of adventure, together with an insatiable curiosity and wicked sense of humor, are qualities I am thrilled to immortalize on paper.

Inspiration for the Hall itself comes from Hillersdon House, where I was lucky enough to keep my horses as a teenager. I'm indebted to Mike Lloyd, the new owner, who is passionately restoring the entire estate to its former glory. Thank you for sharing historical anecdotes, juicy dark secrets, and ghostly happenings that will keep me busy writing for years.

A huge thank-you must go to Rachel and Leigh Gotch, Toy & Doll specialists for Bonhams in London, who very generously gave me a tour of the warehouse. Their knowledge is nothing short of jaw dropping. Little did they realize that the visit would mark the beginning of an expensive hobby! Speaking of toys, I'm very grateful to Peter Hall, for entrusting me with his two vintage Merrythought 'Jerry' Mice, who play a key role in solving the mystery. May Jazzbo Jenkins live on!

Writing is a lonely profession, which is why I am thankful for the support of my kindred spirits in the trenches – Elizabeth Duncan, Clare Langley-Hawthorne, Kate Carlisle, and Daryl Wood Gerber. Also, Mark Durel, Andra St. Ivanyi, and Carola Dunn deserve a special mention for story suggestions and spotting plot snafus.

I feel incredibly lucky to have Dominick Abel as my literary agent. It's such an honor to have him in my corner. His help, support, and guidance are beyond measure. I also must thank Marcia Markland, senior editor at Thomas Dunne Books, without whose enthusiasm this book would still be just a wish-upon-a-star. It is such a delight and a privilege to be under your wing. I am also grateful to Kat Brzozowski, associate editor at Thomas Dunne. Books, for her seamless multitasking and ever-ready smile.

As always, I am thankful to my family, especially my daughter, Sarah, who has been with me on this writing journey from the very beginning.

And, last but always foremost in my heart, my husband, Jason – who continues to amaze me with his endless patience, sweetness, and infinite support. You are my hero.

Chapter One

'Mum!' I exclaimed. 'Thank God you've called. I've been so worried.'

'I hope you're not driving, Kat,' chided my mother on the other end of the line.

'I *am* driving,' I said as my VW Golf crawled through the heavy stream of London traffic along the Old Brompton Road. 'And don't change the subject.'

'If you're not wearing a headset, you'll get a ticket–'

'Which is why I am pulling over,' I said. 'Do *not* hang up. Let me stop somewhere.'

Mum gave a heavy sigh. 'Quickly then. This call is expensive.'

I turned into Bolton Place, a quiet residential street divided by two graceful crescents that encircled communal gardens. Spotting a space outside the church of St. Mary's, I parked and switched off the engine.

'Where did you get to last night?' I demanded. 'I was about to call out the cavalry.'

'You sound tense,' said my mother, deliberately avoiding the question. 'Is everything alright with Dylan?'

'You know very well my boyfriend is called David,' I said, annoyed that she always knew how to hit a nerve. 'God, it's boiling.' I wound down the window, taking in the heat of a hot August day and the smell of freshly mown grass.

'You're too old to have a boyfriend–'

'*Man* friend then. And I'm not tense,' I said. 'I was concerned when you didn't come to my leaving party last night. Did you have another migraine?'

'No. I was in denial,' said Mum flatly. 'I was hoping you weren't going to go through with giving up *Fakes & Treasures*.'

'I want my life back, Mum. Have you any idea what it's like to be constantly in the public eye?'

'Such a pity,' she went on. 'I loved seeing you on the telly. You always looked so nice. Are you sure you're not making a mistake?'

'You sound just like David–'

'Oh dear,' said Mum. 'In that case, I'm *delighted* and I'm sorry I didn't come.'

Ignoring the barb, I said, 'Good, because I'm *delighted* that we're going into business together. Speaking of which, I thought we could look at some properties this weekend.'

'That may not be possible–'

'And I must show you what I bought at Bonhams saleroom this morning,' I said. 'Two boxes of Victorian toys and vintage teddy bears that I got at a bargain price – our first stock items. I can't wait to show them to you.'

There was a long pause.

'Did you hear what I said, Mother?'

Another even longer pause and then, 'I've broken my right hand,' she said bluntly.

'Oh Mum,' I cried. 'Are you okay?'

'I am now.'

'Why didn't you tell me?'

'I'm telling you now.'

'How bad is it?' I said. 'Can you cook? Dress yourself?'

'With one hand?'

'Well, you do have the other one.'

'Very funny.'

'I'll drive over straight away,' I said.

'What about Dylan? Won't he mind?'

'*David* is away this weekend.'

'Your father wouldn't like me gadding off without him,' said Mum. 'Did you know that we never once spent a night apart in all our fifty years of marriage?'

'Yes I did know and it was forty-nine years, not fifty,' I pointed out. 'And if you are going to be unkind about David, I won't come.'

'When did you say his divorce from that Trudy woman is final? I keep forgetting.'

'It's complicated,' I muttered.

'Have you watched Trudy's new television show?' Mum said, hitting another nerve. 'Very amusing – *Walk of Shame! Celebrity Family Secrets Revealed.*'

'Mum ... I'm warning you. I do not want to talk about Trudy Wynne,' I said. 'Do you want me to come or not?'

'Yes, yes,' said Mum wearily. 'I do have a little project that needs finishing. Some typing.'

'I didn't know you could type.'

'Of course I can type,' said Mum with scorn. 'I use Daddy's Olivetti.'

'That's a collector's item. I'm surprised you can still buy the ribbon,' I said. 'I'll stop by my place to pick up a few things and should be with you in under an hour.'

'I doubt it,' said Mum. 'I've moved – now, don't get all cross and silly.'

'Moved? Where? When?' I cried. 'What about our business plans?'

'I've changed my mind. What do you need me for anyway?'

'The whole idea was that you'd help me run *Kat's Collectibles*,' I said, exasperated. 'We'd find you a lovely flat above a shop–'

'Whilst you moved in with David,' said Mum. 'You know your father would never have approved of you living in sin.'

'It's the twenty-first century, Mother,' I said. 'And anyway, Dad wanted me to look after you. He didn't want you to be lonely.'

'I'm not lonely.'

'When did you make this momentous decision?'

'Let me see, about a month ago.'

'A *month?* But...' I was beginning to feel light-headed. 'We speak every day. Sometimes two or three times a day.' Then I remembered that recently Mum was always the one ringing me. 'I thought I didn't recognize the phone number. Where are you calling from?'

'My mobile.'

'You have a *mobile?* Seriously?' I said. 'And when did you put the house up for sale?'

'All these questions,' said Mum. 'That nice man who runs the dry cleaners made me an offer I couldn't refuse.'

'Mr. Winkleigh?' I gasped. 'Dad would never have sold to Mr. Winkleigh. He couldn't stand him.'

'Well, your father's not here so he won't find out, will he?'

I tried to absorb yet another piece of disturbing information. Even the thought of shopping for groceries would guarantee to bring on one of my mother's 'turns' and yet somehow, she'd managed to move house. 'You can't have done it all by yourself.'

'I'm not an invalid, you know,' said Mum.

This was rich coming from someone who spent all my school holidays with a migraine lying down in a dark room.

'And besides,' she added. 'Alfred helped.'

'And Alfred is whom? Your Spanish boyfriend?' Nothing would surprise me at this point.

'Alfred is hardly a Spanish name, dear. A Spanish name would be Juan or perhaps Pablo,' said Mum mildly. 'Alfred is my brother.'

I swear I stopped breathing. 'I didn't know you had a brother.'

'Well, I do,' said Mum. 'As a matter of fact I had two – though Billy's dead and gone. Aneurism on Blackpool Pier. He died young. So very sad.'

'So I must have cousins. I'd love to have cousins.'

'You wouldn't like them.'

'I would like them.' I could feel my temper rising as I remembered envying my friends' big families, especially at Christmas. I hated being an only child. 'Did Dad know you had brothers?'

'Of course he *knew*. He just didn't like them so we didn't see them,' said Mum. 'Does it matter?'

'Actually, it does matter,' I said. 'I always thought you and Dad were orphans.'

'Really? I wonder why?'

17

'Because that's what you told me,' I shouted.

'Well, never mind all that,' said Mum briskly. 'You'd better get cracking if you want to be here in time for tea.'

'Wait a moment,' I said. 'What did you do with all my things?'

'Oxfam,' Mum declared. 'And before you throw another wobbly don't worry – I put all your furry friends in a suitcase. I have it right here–'

'And my dressing-up box?' I said, recalling the iron trunk full of dozens of beautifully handmade costumes. Mum had always been very nifty with the needle. 'I want my children to have those.'

'You'd better get a move on in that department or it will be too late.'

'Thanks for reminding me, Mum,' I said.

'I was just joking.'

But I knew she wasn't.

'Do you have a pencil?' Mum went on. 'I'd better give you the address.'

'Wait,' I said. 'I need something to write on.' I pulled the sale catalogue out of my tote bag and found a pen. 'Ready.'

'The Carriage House, Honeychurch Hall Estate–'

'Honeychurch?' I snorted. 'How very *Winnie-the-Pooh*.'

'Don't snort. It's so unattractive,' said Mum. 'Honeychurch is all one word.' There was a long pause. 'Little Dipperton.'

'Little what?' I said.

'Dipperton, like the Big Dipper only little. With t-o-n on the end.'

'Where the hell is Little Dipperton?'

18

'Devon.'

'*Devon?*' I sputtered.

'Near Dartmouth. Very pretty little fishing port. You'll love it. I'll take you there for a cream tea.'

'Devon!' I said again. 'That's over two hundred miles away.'

'Yes, I am aware of that. I just moved here.'

'But you don't even like the countryside.'

'Your father didn't but I do,' said my mother cheerfully. 'I love the countryside. I've always hated city life. Now I wake up to the sound of the birds, the smell of fresh air–'

'But ... Devon.' I felt dizzy at yet another revelation. 'What about Dad's ashes? I thought we agreed we'd put him in Tooting Crematorium? You'll never be able to visit him.'

'I changed my mind about Tooting Crematorium. He suffered from claustrophobia, you know.'

'Mum, he's in an orange Tupperware container right now,' I exclaimed. 'What's the difference?'

'It's too final.'

I tried a different tack. 'What about all your friends?'

'Your father worked for HM Revenue & Customs,' said Mum. 'We didn't have friends.'

'You don't even drive.'

'I've always been able to *drive*. I just liked your father driving *me*.' Mum chuckled. 'In fact, I've just bought myself a nice MINI Cooper in Chili Red.'

'How can you afford a new car? A house – and a grand house by the sound of things – in the country?' Alarm bells began to ring in my head.

'How, did you hear about this *carriage* house in the first place?'

'I have contacts.'

'But you must have viewed it? How? When?'

'I don't have to answer any more questions from you,' Mum said. 'I can do what I like.'

Another ghastly thought occurred to me. 'You've spent all of Dad's money, haven't you?' There was an ominous silence on the other end of the phone. 'He said you would.'

'Katherine, there's something I need to tell you–'

'You *have* spent it!' I exclaimed. 'You only call me Katherine when you're about to give me bad news.'

'Does the name Krystalle Storm mean anything to you?'

Thrown for a moment, I said, 'No. Why? Who's she when she's at home?'

'Critics say she'll be even bigger than Barbara Cartland.'

'Who?'

'The romance writer. Barbara Cartland.'

'What's that got to do with Dad's money?'

'Her books are everywhere. Over half a million sold worldwide,' Mum enthused. 'I'm surprised–'

'You know I don't read that kind of rubbish, Mum. What did Dad call it? "Penny Dreadfuls for pathetic old ladies",' I said. 'And don't try to change the subject again.'

'Fine,' Mum snapped. 'You know what, I don't think I need your help after all. I can manage on my own.'

'Now *you're* throwing a wobbly. I'm happy to

come. In fact, I quite fancy a cream tea.'

'No,' said Mum coldly. 'I don't want you here. I already have someone who is *longing* to lend me *his* hand. He's very kind. Very kind indeed.' And before I could utter another word, my mother hung up.

I was deeply perplexed. It was clear that Mum's grief had made her rash and impulsive. What had possessed her to move so far away from London? The fact that she'd managed to get into my father's carefully protected pension fund was extremely worrying. My mother was notoriously hopeless with money. It was a family joke. Dad and I had gone to great lengths to make sure that she'd just receive a monthly income so she couldn't spend it all at once. I felt I'd let him down and he'd only been gone four months.

There was nothing else for it. I'd have to drive to Little Dipperton, wherever that might be, and make her see sense.

Chapter Two

I made a quick stop at my garden flat near Putney Bridge to throw a few things into a suitcase including brochures of some properties I was determined to show Mum. I also decided to take the two boxes of vintage teddy bears and Victorian toys that I'd purchased that morning.

'Ready Jazzbo Jenkins?' I said to my lucky mascot, a six-inch-tall Merrythought 'Jerry' toy mouse from the 1940s that I kept on my car dashboard. It had been given to mum as a child, and she had given it to me. 'Let's go and sort out my mother.'

It was a gloriously sunny day in August and – according to the temperature gauge inside my car – a stifling eighty-five degrees. Everything in England always seemed ill equipped to deal with heat waves and my car was no exception. The cold-air fan just sucked in the hot air from outside. Even with all the windows open, sweat trickled down my back. It was going to be a long, sticky drive.

Traffic was heavy as holidaymakers headed for the West Country for the official last week of the school summer holidays. I trailed behind lines of slow-moving caravans and the occasional sight of a car pulled onto the hard shoulder with an over-heated engine.

Along the roadside I saw a sign STRAW-BERRIES HALF A MILE.

Tears unexpectedly stung my eyes as I recalled family outings when I'd beg Dad to stop for strawberries but we never did because I always spilled food, drink – or anything really – on my clothes. I slowed down to look at the table filled with punnets of strawberries under a large umbrella and decided to pull over.

Feeling rather guilty, I bought two – one for Mum and one for me to eat right this second. I devoured mine in five minutes flat. The straw-berries were sweet, plump, and delicious and unfortunately, the juice dripped onto my white capris. Dad had been right.

By the time I'd driven past Stonehenge on the

A303, the sun had vanished and the sky was heavy with dark storm clouds rolling across Salisbury Plain. With a loud crash of thunder, rain started to come down like stair rods. Traffic slowed to a crawl and ceased altogether. Then, just as quickly as it had fallen, the rain stopped and an exquisite rainbow straddled the distant hills.

I pulled into a petrol service station to pick up some flowers and a bottle of Blue Nun for Mum.

Queuing at the register I noticed *Gypsy Temptress* by the author Mum had mentioned – Krystalle Storm – on a revolving stand of paperbacks. Against the backdrop of a church, a scantily clad gypsy girl with raven hair and masses of bracelets leaned against a vast oak tree trunk looking seductive in her low-cut dress. I picked up a copy and read the back cover. *'He was a man of the cloth. She – an outcast from her kin. Can love...'*

'It's good,' said a young woman in her late twenties. 'It's the first in the Star-Crossed Lovers Series – oh! Excuse me. Are you Kat Stanford from *Fakes & Treasures?'*

I smiled politely. 'Yes.'

'I love that show!' she said. 'It's your hair.'

Unfortunately television personalities are pigeonholed with certain character traits – Gordon Ramsay and his famous temper; bra-less Charlie Dimmock from the TV show *Ground Force;* and me, nicknamed Rapunzel because of my mane of hair.

'Thanks,' I said. 'Maybe I will buy this for my mother.'

'Be careful,' she said with a chuckle and pointed to a warning at the bottom of the cover. 'See there? It's categorized as a "sizzler." Racy stuff.'

'I'm not sure if my mother could handle sizzling,' I said and put it back. Then, on impulse I grabbed it, after all. It would be a peace offering of sorts. Maybe I'd even give it a try.

My spirits lifted as I barreled down the M5. Wiltshire turned into Somerset and then – at last – I flew past a road sign featuring a jaunty tall-ship logo announcing WELCOME TO DEVON and the sun came out again.

The countryside was breathtakingly diverse. There were vast expanses of lush rolling fields dotted with sheep and cattle, rushing streams bounded by thick woods or, ancient low stone dry walls, gullies, and crags lined with the rich red earth that Devon was famous for. And, amongst all this beauty was another kind – silhouetted on the horizon, stood the dark, sinister tors of Dartmoor with its shifting mists and treacherous bogs.

With a last look at the detailed directions I'd carefully jotted down courtesy of Google Maps, I turned off the dual carriageway and onto a quiet two-lane road flanked by thick pine forests on one side and a low stone wall fronting a bubbling river on the other. Dartmouth was signposted twelve miles and from there, Little Dipperton just two miles farther.

I checked my watch. It was almost four. I'd made excellent time and was feeling thoroughly pleased with myself.

Two hours later I was hopelessly lost and incredibly frustrated.

It would appear that Google Maps had no knowledge of the myriad of tiny, interconnecting, twisting lanes that spread across Devon – 90 percent of which had no signposts at all or if they did, ended in impassable tracks. Picking up a mobile phone signal was erratic, too, and when I finally got one and rang my mother, she didn't answer.

By six o'clock all my good humor had completely evaporated. At last a church spire appeared in the distance so I headed for that.

Navigating a series of dangerous hairpin bends, I narrowly missed following in the footsteps of an earlier vehicle that had smashed through a stone wall and into a drainage ditch. And then, out of the blue, I came upon a small village consisting of whitewashed, thatched, and slate-roofed cottages with a handful of shops and a pub called the Hare & Hounds. There was also a church, an abandoned forge, a greengrocer, a tea shop, and a general store that doubled up as a post office. Outside the latter stood a dirty blue Ford Focus.

At first, I thought everything was closed until I noticed the door to the general store was ajar. Parking behind the Ford Focus, I went inside.

'Hello?' I cried. 'Anyone home?'

There was no reply. Pushing my sunglasses on top of my head, I moved deeper into the gloom and tripped down a step. It was like descending into the black hole of Calcutta.

The place was jammed to the gunnels with items ranging from tiny sewing kits to flyspray killer. Shelves were haphazardly stacked with pliers, tinned goods, jigsaw puzzles, and hemorrhoid cream. A revolving wire display stand offered picturesque postcards of Devon for sale – three for two pounds.

In one corner a Plexiglas window encased a small cubbyhole that bore the sign POST OF-FICE. A notice board was covered with colored flyers and handwritten cards offered a variety of services and local events – 'Babysitter Wanted!' 'Need Someone to Wash Your Car?' 'Women's Institute Jam Making Competition.'

Behind the counter and along the back wall were shelves filled with large glass jars containing sweets that I thought went out with the ark – Sherbet Pips, Fruit Chews, Blackjacks, and the kind of treacle toffee that removed dental fillings in one bite.

Strolling over to the counter I noted the old-fashioned cash register and a brass bell. In front stood a low bench spread with a selection of trashy magazines and national newspapers. To my dis-may, the store carried this month's *Star Stalkers!* My photo was in the bottom right-hand corner on the cover. It had been taken at a charity event and the article was written by my nemesis, Trudy Wynne. The caption said, GOOD-BYE RAPUN-ZEL, HELLO LADY GODIVA! TO SEE WHAT HAPPENED NEXT – TURN TO PAGE 5.

Of course I knew what happened next. It was the deciding factor in my decision to quit *Fakes & Treasures* and escape the public eye.

Quickly, I covered the offending magazine with the local newspaper, the *Dipperton Deal*. I swept my hair up into a coil and wondered not for the umpteenth time if I should just cut the lot off.

'Anyone home?' I called out again, now aware of voices coming from behind a red-and-white plas-tic fly curtain that presumably led to a storeroom.

'She was a tart and a thief, Muriel,' cried a female voice. 'I knew she was trouble the moment she arrived.'

'I find that hard to believe,' came the reply. 'Gayla seemed such a nice girl.'

'Well she wasn't.'

'I thought Gayla came through one of those posh London agencies?' said Muriel. 'Don't they do background checks?'

'Why don't you just go ahead and say it?' There was a pause and then, 'You think this has something to do with my Eric, don't you?'

'Vera, dear, when it comes to the two of you, I don't know what to think anymore.' There was a heavy sigh. 'Come along, I really want to lock up and–'

I gave a loud cough. 'Hello? Hello?'

The two women emerged through the curtain. One was in her late sixties with a tight gray perm and wearing a sleeveless floral dress. She was holding a paperback book. The other was in her mid thirties, with blond hair that was in dire need of a root touch-up, scraped back into a ponytail. She was dressed in a pair of tight leather trousers, a scarlet V-neck T-shirt with matching acrylic nails that grasped the handles of a bulging plastic carrier bag.

'Enjoy the private conversation, did you?' the younger woman said, swaying slightly due to excessively high heels – Louboutins, I recognized the signature red soles.

'Vera, don't be rude.'

I felt embarrassed. 'I just got here. I heard voices.'

27

Vera looked me up and down, taking in my stained white capris. 'Had an accident, did you?'

'I'm rather fond of strawberries and they're rather fond of me,' I said with an apologetic smile.

'I'm afraid we're closed,' said Muriel.

'I don't want to buy anything,' I said. 'I'm lost. There don't seem to be any signposts around here.'

'They were all taken down during the war and never replaced, luv,' said Muriel.

'That was over sixty years ago,' I exclaimed.

'We're a bit of a forgotten corner down this way and that's the way we like it,' said Vera. 'We don't take kindly to strangers.'

I noticed Muriel was holding a copy of *Gypsy Temptress*.

'I love Krystalle Storm,' I said desperately.

'Vera told me to read it,' said Muriel. 'She said it might liven up my marriage though frankly, I'm not sure whether my husband would remember what to do.'

'You should.' I smiled again. 'It's a bit racy though, isn't it, Vera?' Sensing Vera thawing a little I added, 'Apparently, Krystalle's got a new book coming out in the–' I wracked my brain. 'Star-Crossed Lovers Series.'

'That's right,' said Vera. 'Did you enter the competition?'

'Was there one?'

'Call yourself a fan?' Vera cried. 'It's all over her Web site. I'm going to win. I'm already through to the semifinals.'

'What's the prize?' I asked.

'A long weekend for two in Italy and dinner

with Krystalle Storm herself. All expenses paid –
flight, hotel, the lot,' said Vera. 'I'm going to take
my Eric.'

'And I'm sure you'll both have a lovely time,'
Muriel said wearily and turned to me. 'Where are
you going, luv?'

'Little Dipperton.'

'This is Little Dipperton,' said Muriel.

'Thank God!' I said. 'Actually, I'm looking for
Honeychurch Hall.'

'Honeychurch Hall?' Vera's face reddened and
she and Muriel exchanged looks. 'You're not the
new nanny, are you?'

'No,' I said. 'Why?'

'Vera's the housekeeper, that's why,' said Muriel.
'And she hires the nannies.'

I took in Vera's youth and leather attire with surprise. Housekeepers had come a long way since
the drab black uniform worn by Mrs. Hughes in
Downton Abbey.

'My mother bought the Carriage House,' I said.

'It's *your* mother, is it?' said Vera. 'She'll find it
hard to settle here. We all grew up on the Honeychurch estate and we don't take kindly to folks
coming in from outside of Devon – especially
when they gazump my husband who'd been
promised the Carriage House by his lordship.'

Muriel put a restraining hand on Vera's arm.
'Vera–'

'Well, it's true. It's not fair you London folk
coming in with all your money and buying up our
properties.'

'I honestly don't know anything about the
circumstances,' I said quickly.

29

'I'll close up now if you don't mind.' Muriel gestured to the plastic carrier bag. 'Now Vera, you make sure you give your mother my love. I hope she enjoys the care package. There's no need to return the magazines.'

Vera barely acknowledged the comment. She was too busy staring at me. 'Have we met somewhere before?'

'I don't think so,' I said.

'I know who you are!' Vera's eyes widened. 'You're that antiques woman on the telly! *Fakes & Treasures!*'

'I'm not, actually.' The lie was out before I could stop it. Vera seemed just the type of person to call Trudy's *Star Stalkers* hotline and claim the hundred-pound 'finder's fee.'

'You look just like Kat Stanford,' Vera persisted. 'Take down your hair–'

'Oh for heaven's sake,' said Muriel. 'Leave the poor woman alone and tell her how to get to the hall so we can all go home.'

Vera muttered something disparaging under her breath but grudgingly obliged. 'Go back to the main road. When you pass the entrance to Ruggles Farm–'

'Is there a sign saying Ruggles Farm?' I asked.

'It's a farm. Do you know what a farm is?'

I gave a polite smile. 'Of course.'

'It'll be on your left,' said Vera. 'You'll come to a T-junction next to Cavalier Copse–'

'Does *that* have a signpost?' I said hopefully.

'No. It's a copse. You do *know* what a copse is?' Seeing my blank expression, Vera rolled her eyes. 'You city folk. A copse is a small wood. On second

30

thought, it's better if you take the shortcut through Cavalier Lane. That'll take you straight to the Hall.'

'Can you point me in the right direction?' I said.

Vera rolled her eyes again. 'There is only one direction. The lane is very overgrown but it can take a small car. The entrance to the Hall has big stone pillars topped by stone hawks. You can't miss it.'

'Thank you.'

'Wait!' Muriel hurried over to the counter and pulled a clipboard and pen out from under. 'Will you sign the petition?'

'I don't live here.'

'It's to stop the government building a high-speed railway line to Plymouth,' said Muriel. 'They say it'll cut fifteen minutes off the travel time to Paddington.'

'Bastards,' muttered Vera.

'I don't usually sign petitions.' I'd learned the hard way that anything with my name on it could be misconstrued.

'The railway line will slice through this here,' persisted Muriel. 'It's an area of natural beauty. It will destroy a lot of farmland and homes. *Please.* It's just a name but every name counts.'

I hesitated. 'Yes, of course. That's terrible. I'm happy to.' I signed J. Jenkins and put my address down as London.

Muriel studied it. 'London addresses really help. They give us national recognition. What's your first name?'

'Jazzbo,' I faltered. 'It's a nickname.'

'Yeah right,' Vera said with a sneer. 'Thanks, *Jazzbo.*'

Moments later I was back in my Golf and turning into a narrow lane flanked by high hedge-banks. Vera had not exaggerated. Grass grew down the center and a profusion of foxgloves, cow parsley, and old man's beard brushed both sides of my car. I prayed I wouldn't meet any oncoming traffic.

The lane snaked up the hill. Rounding yet another hairpin bend I came upon two equestrians thankfully moving in the same direction as me.

The pair made a curious sight. The woman on the handsome chestnut horse with white socks was riding sidesaddle dressed in a full habit and top hat. Her little companion was astride a small black pony.

I slowed down and crawled along behind them. Only the boy seemed to care that they were holding up the traffic – or rather, me. He turned around to stare and I couldn't help but laugh and wave.

Wearing a pair of old flying goggles and a white scarf wrapped around his neck, the boy was simply adorable. I guessed at once who he was supposed to be.

Among David's many antiquarian collections were first editions of *Biggles* by W. E. Johns, chronicling the heroic adventures of the fighter pilot during World War I. Biggles's trademark look was flying goggles and a white silk scarf.

But after crawling behind them for the next couple of miles, I was growing tired of playing peekaboo with Squadron Leader James Bigglesworth – especially when the unexpected arrival of a tan-and-white Jack Russell shot through a hedge and tore around my car, barking manically at the wheels.

Still, the rider on the chestnut horse didn't notice despite 'Biggles' repeatedly shouting, 'No, Mr. Chips, no!' Mr. Chips dashed about in circles, steaming past the riders and back to my car again.

Finally, the lane widened by a few feet and a narrow grass verge materialized in front of a five-barred gate opening onto a public bridleway marked TO CAVALIER COPSE. The horses pulled in and at last I could squeeze by. To my surprise, the rider on the chestnut horse was a bone-thin woman sporting a scarlet slash of lipstick who looked to be in her early eighties. I offered a smile of gratitude and was rewarded by a dismissive hand gesture from her and a military salute from 'Biggles.'

Leaving the riders behind, I began a steep hill climb that opened out along a ridge running the length of a long range of hills. The view was spectacular. On my right stood the distant moors of Dartmoor. On my left, far below, the River Dart sparkled in the evening sun.

I could also make out a huge country house nestled amongst the trees, a vast walled garden, and several outbuildings and barns.

But that was about it. There was no other sign of civilization other than a dozen sheep and a few cows.

I thought of Mum dressed in her neat outfits from Marks & Spencer, kitten heel shoes, and perfectly coiffed hair. I just couldn't imagine her embracing country living.

After yet another hairpin bend I came upon two towering granite pillars topped with statues of hawks with their wings extended. Etched into one pillar was HONEYCHURCH HALL. I'd made it!

A pair of eighteenth-century gatehouses stood at either side of the entrance. They were severely run-down with cracked leaded pane windows, broken guttering, and roofs gaping with holes. Each arched front doorway bore the family crest and motto carved in stone: *ad perseverate est ad triumphum* – To Endure Is to Triumph.

A large sign warned TRESPASSERS WILL BE PROSECUTED. POACHERS WILL BE SHOT.

As I pulled into the entrance a young woman in her early twenties stepped from the shadows pulling a fuchsia-pink rolling suitcase behind her. Dressed in black jeans and a white ruffled long-sleeved shirt, she flagged me down.

I stopped and opened the window. 'Hello?'

She seemed agitated. 'You are the taxi? Yes?'

I detected a foreign accent. Even with no make-up she was beautiful with large blue eyes and shoulder-length blond hair swept off her face with a turquoise bandana.

'I'm afraid not,' I said. 'Where are you going?'

'To Plymouth railway station.' She kept glancing over her shoulder as if expecting someone. 'I must catch the seven-thirty-seven train to Paddington. I have to!'

I hesitated. Plymouth was miles away and I'd been driving forever. 'Have you tried calling the taxi company?'

'They said thirty minutes.' She checked her watch. 'Now, they are ten minutes late and I cannot telephone them because there is no mobile phone signal here.'

'Give them a little longer but I'm happy to call for you when I get to a landline,' I said. 'Do you have the number?'

'Please.' She handed me a business card for Bumble-Bee Cars.

'Who shall I say called?'

'Gayla Tarasova.'

I recalled the conversation I'd overheard earlier between Muriel and Vera inside the general store and guessed this woman had to be the disgraced nanny.

'You are very kind,' said Gayla. 'You know Lady Edith?'

'Not yet. My mother has just bought the Carriage House.'

'You are Kat!' Gayla broke into a smile. 'Your mother is a nice lady. Please tell her–' Gayla's expression grew earnest. 'She must go back to London. She *must!* She is in great danger here.'

'Danger?' I said sharply. 'What do you mean?'

'Listen to me. Rupert is a wicked man who must be stopped!'

Beep! Beep! Beep! The sound of a car horn startled us. Gayla's eyes widened with terror. 'Oh! It's him! It's Rupert! He mustn't see me here. I must go.'

Gayla's fear was contagious. 'Wait,' I cried. 'I'm blocking the entrance. Hold on.'

But Gayla dragged her suitcase back into the shadows just as a black Range Rover came barreling toward me. *Beep! Beep! Beep!*

'Oh, for heaven's sake!' I muttered and reversed tight against the gatehouse wall. The Range Rover barely slowed down to make the turn into the lane.

Without so much as an acknowledgement, the driver swung left – thankfully in the opposite direction from the horses. I caught a glimpse of a tweed flat cap, a neat military mustache, and a brown-and-white English setter in the front passenger seat.

'And thank you, too,' I shouted at the disappearing vehicle.

I called Gayla's name but she remained hidden, probably worried that the Range Rover – driven by the 'wicked Rupert' – would return. *It's none of your business, Kat,* I told myself. Even so, I waited for a few more minutes.

When Gayla still didn't reappear I shouted, 'I've got to go. I'll call the cab company!' and set off down the long tree-lined drive.

As I rounded a corner, the dense thicket on my left broke briefly to reveal a rusted, wrought-iron archway straddling a pair of wrought-iron gates topped by a metal cast of a galloping horse. The land beyond fell away and once again I caught a glimpse of the river.

Ahead, I spotted soaring chimneys and mullioned windows disappearing and reemerging between the trees. Another break in the shrubs on my left revealed glorious parkland where a handful of horses grazed alongside – good grief – were those llamas?

Just yards from the grass verge stood an ornamental lake covered with lily pads and framed with scattered clumps of pampas grass. At the top of a shallow bank that led down to the water's edge stood a tall angel, arms reaching heavenward, carved in white marble surrounded by a sea of red roses – presumably a family memorial.

Although I had been keeping an eye open for any sign directing me to the Carriage House I realized I'd gone too far up the drive. It split in two with the right-hand fork turning uphill into a newly paved road lined by post-and-rail paddocks. One side harbored a small outdoor sand dressage arena; the other was laid out with cavalletti jump poles. Ahead was a range of redbrick buildings with neat white trim and green roofs. An impressive archway with a clock tower in Roman numerals registered the right time – six-thirty-five – and marked a grandiose entrance to the stable yard. A large silver horse lorry with living accommodations over the cab and a hunter-green Land Rover were parked against an outside wall.

I took the left fork that ended in a turning circle in front of Honeychurch Hall. In the center stood a large empty stone fountain featuring rearing bronze horses marooned in a sea of weed-infested gravel.

I slowed to a stop under a bank of overhanging trees that bordered a wood. The house felt intimidating and unwelcoming. The architecture could be described as 'classic revival' with its Palladian front and, judging by the four banks of tall chimneys topped with decorative, octagonal pots, I suspected it encased a much older building – most likely a Tudor manor house. The main entrance was a central porte cochere with Tuscan columns.

Compared to the immaculate stable yard I'd just seen, the house was a shambles.

The twelve-pane casement windows on the ground and first floors were shuttered. Paintwork was peeling and many of the cornices had fallen and lay broken and abandoned on the gravel. A forest of weeds and small holly trees emerged through the exposed roof on the east side of the building where sheets of black plastic had lost the battle to keep out the elements.

Scaffolding had been erected up the side of the west wing where a section of the roof was partially hidden under a huge dark green tarpaulin. Tiles were stacked along the front of the house.

Roof repairs to grand homes such as these ran into the hundreds of thousands of pounds. Often, the staggering cost of a new roof marked the beginning of the end for these country estates especially if they were listed buildings and had to comply with all kinds of complicated codes. I'd attended many estate sales and it was heartbreaking to see magnificent old properties such as this one, abandoned and left to their fate, slowly disintegrate.

Turning my attention back to my own disintegration, I knew I had to change my stained, white capris before meeting my mother. I'd changed clothes in the backseat of the car before and, with no signs of life coming from the house, felt the coast was clear.

Unfortunately, this was not the case. As I was squeezing between the front seats, a hammering on the window revealed 'Biggles' in leather flying helmet and goggles with his face pressed against the glass.

I wound the window down a crack. 'Hello.'

'Please get out of the car,' he said. 'You're trespassing and I'm afraid I'm going to have to shoot you.'

Chapter Three

The boy, who appeared to be about seven years old, stood with his hands clasped behind his back. 'Name, rank, and serial number!' he demanded.

'I'm Kat Stanford. And you are–?'

'Harry.'

'Really? I must have been mistaken,' I said. 'I could have sworn you were Squadron Leader James Bigglesworth.'

Harry broke into a huge smile. 'Yes! I am! How did you know?'

'Your fame is legendary, sir,' I said. 'I believe all your friends call you Biggles. May I call you Biggles?'

Harry grinned, 'Yes, please.'

'And my friends call me Kat.'

Harry reverted to his alter ego and gave me a frosty look. 'You do know that you could have been shot. There *is* a war on.'

'I'm afraid I got lost, sir. I was looking for the Carriage House.'

'I can show you the way but first, I must inspect your cargo.' Harry pointed to the boot of my car. 'Open up, please.'

Catching sight of the cardboard boxes of vintage teddy bears and Victorian toys in the boot, Harry gasped. 'Wow! Bears!' He reached in and pulled out a tattered Steiff cinnamon bear. 'This chap looks suspicious,' he said. 'I'm going to have to take him away for questioning.'

'He's a bit fragile for questioning,' I said. 'He's already been interrogated. Can't you see what happened to his paw?'

Harry put him back. 'Are you building an army?'

'No, I collect them and sell them to nice people who will take care of them.' I moved Harry gently aside and closed the hatchback. 'Do you have a special toy?'

'I'm not allowed,' said Harry. 'Mummy says I'm too old for silly toys.'

'We're never too old for bears.'

'Do you have a special toy?' asked Harry.

'Yes. Do you want to meet him?'

Harry nodded.

I whipped around to the passenger door and grabbed Jazzbo Jenkins off the dashboard.

'Meet Jazzbo Jenkins,' I said. 'He's my lucky mascot.'

Harry frowned. 'Why is he wearing a blue cardigan?'

'I don't know,' I said. 'He always has.'

'And where are his badges?'

'What kind of badges?'

'Places he's visited. Seaside piers.'

I regarded Harry with curiosity. 'Do mice visit seaside piers?'

'Of course they do! I need a mascot for one of my secret missions,' said Harry, reverting to his alter ego. 'I need to borrow him. There is some-one he must meet.'

'Why don't you show me where the Carriage House is first and then we'll see.'

'Alright,' said Harry. 'But we have to go in the car.'

'I can't take you in my car,' I said. 'What would your mother say?'

'She won't mind. We'll only be a minute.' Before I could stop him, Harry had opened the passenger door, jumped inside, and buckled up.

'Where *is* your mother?' I added as I joined him. 'I suspect that wasn't who you were riding with today.'

'No!' Harry gave a snort of laughter. 'That was Granny. Granny and William are putting the horses to bed.'

Glancing at my watch I saw it was almost seven. The evenings stayed much lighter in the West Country than in London. 'Shouldn't you be in bed, too?'

'It's the school holidays, silly.' Harry gave Jazzbo a squeeze. 'Anyway, Jazzbo says he wants me to come – just in case we're attacked by Germans.'

'How far is it?'

Harry gestured back down the drive toward the gatehouses. 'That way.'

I turned the car around and we set off in companionable silence.

'What a lovely place to grow up,' I said at last. 'Were you born – at the Hall?'

'Yes,' said Harry. 'But in twenty – no, nineteen days – I'm going away to boarding school.'

'Good heavens!' I exclaimed. 'How old are you?'

'I'm going to be seven on September the first.'

'Seven!' I never saw the point of having children if they were going to be shipped off to boarding school. 'That's awful, Harry. I am sorry.'

'Why?'

'Well– you'll miss your family, won't you?'

Harry didn't answer. Stealing a glance, I noted he was holding Jazzbo so tightly that his knuckles were white. Cursing my lack of tact I added, 'On the other hand, just think of all the new friends you'll make. What school are you going to?'

'Blundells, then Stowe, then Cambridge,' said Harry. 'Father went there, too, and my grandfather and my great-grandfather and my great-great-grandfather. And my great-great-great-grandfather and–'

'And then you'll come back here and run the estate just like they did?' I suggested.

Harry frowned. 'I don't know. Mummy says yes, but Father says it's a white elephant. I don't see how a house can be a white elephant. I mean, where is its trunk?'

'Do you have brothers and sisters?'

He shook his head. 'Mummy says I'm an only child and very special.'

'I'm an only child, too,' I said. 'And yes, we are *very* special.'

As we drew alongside the white marble angel, a tall blond woman in jodhpurs and shirt picked up one of the floral arrangements.

'Who's that?' I asked Harry.

'That's Mummy!' He slithered down in his seat and ducked under the dashboard. 'Quickly! She mustn't see us! Drive fast!'

To my astonishment, Harry's mother carried the roses down the bank to the water's edge and hurled them in – vase and all. 'Your mother just threw the roses in the lake!'

'Mummy didn't like Kelly,' said Harry. 'She's glad she's dead.'

'Oh dear,' I said. 'Was Kelly a dog?'

'No, silly! Kelly was a tart,' said Harry cheerfully. 'She was attacked by killer bees who stung her to death with deadly venom.'

'Goodness. Poor Kelly.' I glanced over at Harry dressed in his Biggles gear and wondered if his parents worried about their child having such a vivid imagination. I'd certainly worry if he were mine.

'Stop!' cried Harry as we drew alongside the wrought-iron archway. Pointing at the dense cluster of thicket and overhanging trees opposite, he said, 'The Carriage House is through there.'

'Are you sure?' I said doubtfully.

'It is, it is!' Harry insisted. 'See? Look!'

The entrance was barely visible. Nestled in the undergrowth was a weatherworn signpost that confirmed he was right – TO CARRIAGE HOUSE.

'No one has been down here for years.' I eyed the partially cobbled track with dismay. 'There has to be another entrance.'

'Yes, but that's *miles* away and I'm not allowed to leave the park,' said Harry. 'Anyway, this is a shortcut.'

I groaned. 'Not another shortcut.'

With deep misgivings I nosed my car through the undergrowth and – minutes later – realized it was a big mistake. In bygone years this almost certainly had been a service road linking the main drive to the Carriage House – but not today. The cobbled track soon fizzled out leaving nothing but deep furrows filled with muddy water.

Every time we plunged into a rut, Harry squealed, 'We're flying! Turbulence! Whoa! Hold her steady!'

'Is it much farther?' I asked desperately as my car struggled to move through cloying mud while filthy water splashed up the sides of the windows.

'No. It's over there,' said Harry. 'See?'

Praise the Lord, indeed it was. Peeping through the trees was a chimney top and horse weather-vane.

We rounded a corner and I gave a cry of alarm. Immersed in another deep rut was my mother's MINI in Chili Red. There was no sign of her. 'Oh, no,' I groaned again.

'Oh, bugger. That car is *still* stuck,' said Harry happily. 'It's been there for *days!*'

'I'm not sure you should say that word, Harry,' I said. 'But yes, oh bugger. We're stuck, too.' There was no way forward and no chance of reversing or turning around.

Exasperated, I cut the engine and clambered out sinking in glutinous mud. 'I think I'd better walk you back to the house.'

'No. Leave it to Biggles!' said Harry, scrambling out of the car – wisely wearing Wellington boots. Still clutching Jazzbo he added, 'I've got a jolly good idea. We'll go and get William.'

'Harry–'

'William is the strongest man in the world,' he

44

said. 'He used to work in the circus.'

'Harry, don't–'

But Harry had vanished into the woods.

'Oh great.' I stood there, perplexed. My poor car looked as if it had gone through a rally driving competition – and failed.

I didn't hold much hope for Harry's return. With a heavy sigh, I retrieved my overnight case from the boot of the car and picked up the flowers, wine, and strawberries for Mum.

Squeezing between the MINI and the bushes, I peered through the mud-smeared windows. The glove box and half the dashboard were covered in yellow Post-it Notes. I could make out a few words in Mum's neat handwriting – 'cherry red lips,' 'grotto,' and 'gas man.'

Five minutes later, after walking through more mud, I reached a dilapidated five-bar gate propped against a dry stone wall. A pair of granite pillars marked the entrance to the cobbled courtyard of my mother's new abode.

So this was the famous Carriage House.

There was no doubt the place had charm but ... was my mother insane? Its condition was a hundred times worse than the main house.

It was built in a quadrangle with a range of outbuildings forming two sides and a ruined barn stretched along the other. I use the word 'barn' generously. It was missing half its roof, the upright wooden girders slanted at dangerous angles, and I suspected that the first good gust of wind would blow the whole thing down. Tucked in between the outbuildings and barn stood three metal dustbins overflowing with household rubbish. Next to one of the outbuildings was a latch-gate that led into a pine forest.

The cobbled courtyard was peppered with buttercups and ragwort. Two planks of wood lay over an open drain with an orange traffic cone serving as some kind of warning. In the center stood an old wishing well, a water pump, and a stepped mounting block.

On the fourth side stood the Carriage House. Bearing the date 1830, it was a two-story redbrick building half-hidden under swathes of wisteria and Virginia creeper. The slate roof had gaping holes patched very much like that of the main house. Along the ridge and straddling the roof pitch ran a skylight smeared with green moss.

Even though the place was run-down the architecture and attention to detail was exquisite. There were lunettes in the clerestory and small hatches led to a hayloft. An arched double carriageway door spanned both stories and carried a heavy iron bar and padlock rusted from years of neglect and disuse.

Above the carriageway door was a small window trimmed in peeling blue paint – presumably the old grooms' quarters – and above that, a timber cupola topped with an ogee dome and the horse weathervane I'd seen through the trees.

I consider myself a practical person and up until this moment, had believed my mother to be so, too. Our house in Tooting had been almost sterile in its neatness. Dad's love of Do-It-Yourself ensured the entire interior was repainted a bland magnolia every second year.

I just couldn't imagine Mum living here. I also

wondered if she was aware that buildings such as this were usually listed and that structural alterations had to be approved by the district council.

Hammering on the carriageway door I shouted, 'Mum! It's me! Hello?' But there was no answer.

Putting down my suitcase and goodies, I stood back and surveyed the property. No windows faced the courtyard. Access to the grooms' quarters would most likely be at the rear.

I followed the line of the building and turned the corner. To my dismay, just a mere fifty yards farther on stood *another* set of granite pillars that marked the original tradesman's entrance. A hideous makeshift corrugated iron gate had been erected between the pair with razor wire running along on top. Spray-painted in crimson was another warning, TRESPASSERS WILL BE PROSECUTED. POACHERS WILL BE SHOT.

It was obviously the official entrance to the Carriage House and for some reason it had been closed off.

Suddenly the corrugated iron gate shuddered and began to jerk open. Harry stepped into view followed by a brand-new, shiny, red Massey Ferguson tractor. A heavy chain swung from the three-hitch axle behind.

On the seat in the open cab perched a burly man with a weather-beaten face and the bushiest eyebrows I'd ever seen. He was dressed in jeans, a checked shirt, and wore a knitted woolen cap. Harry trotted along, waving madly at me.

'Hello!' I shouted above the din of the engine as the man drove by. 'Thanks so much for coming.' But the driver paid no attention. He simply made a sweeping turn in the courtyard – neatly flattening the orange cone – slammed the gears into reverse, and bolted backward through the granite pillars and out of sight.

Harry joined me, beaming from ear to ear. 'Biggles to the rescue!'

'Brilliant,' I said. 'And that must be William?'

'No, that's Eric,' said Harry. 'William can't come. He visits Mrs. Stark at Sunny Hill Lodge every Friday. He tried to get me to go with him once but it smells of wee and cabbage.'

'Oh,' was all I could say. Noting Harry was empty-handed, I asked, 'Where's Jazzbo?'

'He's being debriefed,' said Harry.

'Promise you'll return him,' I said. 'He's very special to me.'

'He'll report in tomorrow morning.'

We hurried over to Mum's MINI to find Eric clambering back onto the tractor. To my alarm, he had attached the end of the chain to the front fender of the MINI.

'Wait!' I shrieked. 'Don't pull–'

But it was too late. Eric slammed his foot on the accelerator and, with a violent jolt, the tractor lunged forward catapulting the MINI out of its muddy grave – along with the fender that flew off, bounced along the grass, and came to rest just a few feet away from my own.

'Oh bugger,' groaned Harry.

'Yes, bugger indeed,' I muttered.

Eric seemed unconcerned. He pulled on the brake, cut the engine, jumped down from the tractor, and, giving his machine an affectionate pat, sauntered back to disconnect the cable.

Trying to keep my temper, I joined him.

'They don't make cars like they used to,' said Eric, giving the fender a kick. 'The stuff in my yard is worth twenty of this modern rubbish.'

'Will you be able to repair it?' I said putting the emphasis on *you.*

'Not my problem, luv,' he said turning on his heel.

'Excuse me,' I said following after him. 'It *is* your problem. You did this. You need to repair it.'

'Keep your hair on,' he said with a snigger. 'I've got a friend in the village who'll do it for a good price.'

'I don't see why we should have to pay for your mistake,' I fumed.

'Just trying to be neighborly and that's all the thanks I get. Nice.'

'Excuse me, hello there!' cried a voice speaking with the strangled vowels of the upper classes. A woman emerged from a narrow path in the forest. The last time I'd seen Harry's mother she'd been throwing floral tributes into the ornamental lake. Up close she had hat-hair and a long, hard face with a regal aquiline nose. 'Have you seen Harry, Eric?'

I looked around, not surprised to find that Harry had vanished.

'No, your ladyship,' said Eric, touching his cap but not seeming remotely servile.

'Because I've told you before,' said the woman, 'Harry is *ab-so-lute-ly* forbidden to go to your yard. It is *not* safe with all that equipment. Am I clear?'

'Gayla not doing her job?' Eric said with a sneer.

'Gayla is on her way back to Russia,' Harry's mother said coldly. 'Vera caught her stealing.'

Eric's jaw dropped. 'When?'

'I'm sure Vera will tell you all about it – oh.' Her ladyship suddenly noticed me standing there. 'Have *you* seen my son?'

'As I said, m'lady,' Eric cut in quickly, 'we've not seen him.'

Eric glowered at me so I thought it best to keep quiet for the time being and just shrugged.

Her ladyship formally extended her hand revealing short, grubby nails. 'Forgive my *frightful* manners. Lavinia Honeychurch. How do you do.'

'Katherine Stanford,' I said, taking her hand and wondering if she expected me to kiss it or curtsey. 'My mother lives at the Carriage House.'

'Oh yes, what a *nightmare*. I am so sorry. Such a *frightful* muddle.'

I felt a twinge of alarm. 'A muddle? What do you mean?'

'Of course she'll have to move,' said Lavinia. 'My mother-in-law – the dowager countess – made a *ghastly* mistake.'

'I should, say so,' muttered Eric. 'His lordship promised the Carriage House to me and Vera.'

'It's not his to promise,' Lavinia snapped. 'And you know very well that Lady Edith would *never* permit you to live there.' She turned to me. 'Perhaps your mother will take Sawmill Cottage instead?'

'I thought my mother *bought* the Carriage House,' I said. 'How could there have been a mistake? Either it was for sale, or it wasn't.'

'I don't get involved in estate matters,' said

50

Lavinia airily. 'You must talk to my husband about such things. Goodness, what on *earth* are these automobiles doing here? No one has used this thoroughfare for years.'

'The proper entrance to the Carriage House was closed off,' I said.

'You mean the *tradesman's* entrance?' Lavinia frowned. 'Surely not.'

'It's barricaded with razor wire.' I gestured to my Golf that had sunk a good six inches in the mud and my mother's MINI. 'That's why we had to use this track.'

'Is this true, Eric?' demanded Lavinia.

'It's my land,' said Eric belligerently.

'Despite what you may like to think, it is *not* your land,' said Lavinia. 'It belongs to the estate and you are our tenant. I'm afraid I shall have to tell his lordship about this.'

'Go ahead,' said Eric. 'Be my guest.'

'I – I – shall.' Lavinia reddened. 'Mrs. Stanford–'

'It's Katherine and I'm actually a Ms.'

'Cropper will telephone tonight to arrange a time for you to meet with my husband so we can sort out all this nonsense.' Lavinia shot Eric one last frosty look, turned on her heel, and vanished into the woods.

I braced myself for another altercation but Eric said, 'Thanks for not giving Harry away. He's a good lad.'

'It seems there have been misunderstandings all around,' I said firmly. 'Shall we start again?'

'How did your mother know the Carriage House was for sale in the first place?' he asked.

51

'I have no idea,' I said. 'So it *was* for sale?'

A *James Bond* themed ringtone erupted from Eric's jacket pocket.

'MI-6 calling?' I joked.

Eric gave a sheepish grin and scrambled to answer his mobile from his top pocket. His smile of greeting swiftly changed to an expression of fury. 'Stupid bitch!' he shouted. 'Right. Yes. Don't worry, m'lord. I'll take care of it.'

Without so much as a good-bye, Eric jumped into his cab, started the engine, slammed his foot on the accelerator, and drove off.

I tramped back to the Carriage House, retrieved my suitcase, and finally located a paint-peeled front door down a narrow alley sandwiched between a feed shed and an old henhouse.

Picking up a handy brick, I hammered on the door, shouting, 'Mum! Hello? Hello!'

As I waited for what seemed like forever, the door opened and I gasped. I barely recognized her.

Mum's hand was in a plaster cast up to the elbow. A black eye and an angry bruise on her jawbone marred her normally immaculate appearance. Her lip was swollen and her left foot was bandaged.

Mum's perm had turned frizzy and bore an unattractive gray skunk stripe down the center part. She was wearing elasticized red tartan pajama bottoms that had belonged to Dad, an orange hand-knitted poncho, and a pair of penguin-head slippers I'd worn as a teenager.

There wasn't a scrap of makeup on her face although Mum had attempted to apply lipstick across her mouth.

'What are you doing here?' she asked crossly. 'I told you not to come.'

'I've come to look after you,' I said, looking her up and down. 'And by the looks of things, you need it.'

'I don't want your help.' Mum peered at my trousers. 'Why are your feet so muddy? Is that jam?'

'It's strawberry juice.'

'Really, Kat. You do look a mess.'

I was incredulous. '*I* look a mess? By the way ... nice slippers.'

Mum looked at her feet and then up at me.

We began to laugh. 'You'd better come in,' she said. 'I'm so happy you're here.'

Chapter Four

'I'll give you the grand tour later,' said Mum, ushering me inside. 'Now, you have to have an imagination, dear. I know that's not your forte, but it's going to look lovely when it's all finished.'

'I certainly hope so.' I stepped gingerly over a hole in the floor and pointed at it. 'How did you break your hand? Falling down there?'

'No. Something far more exciting, I'll tell you later,' said Mum. 'Just leave your suitcase here – bring the strawberries and we'll have a drink.'

I brandished the bottle of wine. 'Your favorite.'

Mum pulled a face. 'Blue Nun? I only drank it

to please your father. I'd rather have a gin and tonic.'

'But you like Blue Nun,' I protested. 'You always have.'

'Nope. Couldn't stand the stuff,' Mum said cheerfully. 'These days I drink gin. Bombay Sapphire to be precise. William bought me a bottle as a housewarming present and I've become quite partial to it. Gin has such a *clean* taste, don't you think?'

'I suppose so,' I said. 'Is William the handyman?'

'No. He's the stable manager,' said Mum. 'Now, he'd make someone a good husband.'

'Possibly,' I said. 'But it won't be me.'

'You haven't met him yet. Don't be so quick to judge,' said Mum. 'He looks good for someone in his late fifties and I know how much you like your men *mature*.'

'I'm happy with David,' I said crossly.

The place stank of damp and decay. The wallpaper was left over from the seventies – a depressing brown, cream, and mustard hexagonal design. The linoleum was cracked and what scraps of carpet remained were stained and torn. The paintwork had a yellowing brownish tinge, hinting of the days when it was popular to smoke. Brown nylon curtains drooped from wires in the windows.

'No one has lived here for decades,' Mum enthused.

'Really? I would never have guessed.'

'This is the sitting room.' Mum opened a door on her right to reveal chaos.

Linens, tea cloths, and towels were piled on top

of the sofa, paintings leaned against the back of an armchair, and a large rolled-up rug had been propped in the corner. Moving boxes, all neatly labeled – GLASSWARE, BOOKS, SHOES, and TOWELS – were stacked everywhere. On top of a box marked FRANK – DOCUMENTS sat an orange Tupperware container.

'You haven't got very far with your unpacking,' I said.

Mum rolled her eyes. 'I *have* broken my hand, Katherine.'

'Please don't tell me those are Dad's ashes in that Tupperware?' I went on, knowing full well they were. 'At least keep him in your bedroom or something. Show some respect!'

'I'd rather keep Frank in here where I can keep an eye on his respect. At least this way I know where he is.'

Pointing to the box marked FRANK I said, 'Dad specifically wanted you to go through that box of documents, remember? He told you they were very important.'

'Give me a chance,' said Mum.

'He'd hate you living here. He loved the idea of us going into business together – didn't you, Dad?' I said to the Tupperware box. Turning to Mum I added, 'I bet he's watching you.'

Mum snatched a tea cloth from the sofa and, with surprising skill given that she could only use one hand, threw it over the Tupperware box. 'There, now he won't have to suffer.'

'I had no idea we had a hoopla champ in our midst.'

'You'd be surprised at what I can do.'

55

Mum shooed me out of the room. On our left was an oak-paneled latch door. 'That leads to the main carriageway and stables. I thought I'd leave it in its original state–'

'Uninhabitable, you mean?'

Mum scowled.

'So, are you just going to renovate the living quarters?' I said. 'How many bedrooms are there?'

'Two,' said Mum. 'The head groom and his family used to live here before the new stable block was built.'

Mum stepped around a bucket filled with water. 'I'll have to fix the roof, of course.'

I looked up to see a gaping hole in the ceiling revealing the room above and – I could swear – a patch of sky. 'Oh it's still light outside.'

'Actually, that's your bedroom up there,' said Mum. 'Imagine you're camping under the stars.'

'I've never liked camping.'

'I'm afraid you'll have to sort out the sheets and make up your own bed,' Mum went on. 'It's so infuriating not being able to do anything. The doctor said it would take at least six weeks before I can begin to use my hand again. I can't dress myself, put on makeup, do up buttons, zips. I can't even open a can of soup.'

'It's just as well I came then,' I said and meant it.

With every step deeper into the house my heart sank further. Central heating consisted of ancient storage heaters. It would be freezing in the winter. The place was falling down and Mum seemed oblivious. My head registered the thousands of pounds that were needed to get it remotely habitable but I was far more worried about Mum's mental state. Who, in their right mind would have acted so recklessly? Dad had been the Do-It-Yourself expert. Mum couldn't even change a lightbulb... And why, of all places, choose *here?*

'Looks like you've got rising damp,' I said pointing to a sinister stain in the corner of the skirting board. 'That's another expensive job.'

'Katherine!' Mum swung around, eyes ablaze. 'I know what I've let myself in for. I'm not an idiot.' She tapped her cast. 'This is what's holding me up and yes, your father would turn in his grave if he knew.'

'That would be a challenge considering he's been cremated.'

'*He* wanted to be cremated,' said Mum exasperated. 'Why are you being so difficult?'

'Dad wanted *me* to take care of you,' I protested. 'How can I do that when you've decided to live in squalor hundreds of miles away?'

Mum looked hurt and turned abruptly away. I felt a pang of remorse and put my arms around her but she elbowed me in the ribs. 'Be careful!' she snapped. 'Don't touch my hand. There are pins in it.'

We continued to the end of the hallway in a frosty silence and entered a large kitchen with a Victorian pine table in the center. 'Did you buy that?' I said, surprised. 'I thought you only liked IKEA.'

'No, it was already here,' said Mum.

I opened the refrigerator to put in the wine and found it well stocked.

'William,' said Mum, reading my mind. 'Malcolm the Meat comes on Mondays, Fred the Fish on Fridays and there's a daily milk service.'

'Really? I'm impressed.' And I was.

'I'm not completely cut off from civilization,' said Mum. 'Cropper – he's the butler up at the Hall – makes honey from the estate's very own hives. William brings it over.'

'William sounds like a godsend.'

'He is.'

Mum had put up white net curtains at the large picture window. I loathe net curtains but realized that constantly criticizing my mother was not going to help matters.

'The curtains look great. What are those?' I stepped closer to inspect half a dozen strips of paper that dangled from the ceiling and were covered in black dots. 'Flies!' I exclaimed. 'How disgusting!'

'But effective,' said Mum. 'I found a box of coils in the old tack room. They're coated with arsenic. We seem to be having an invasion of flies this summer.'

A huge oak dresser stretched the length of one wall. 'Nice dresser. Was that here, too?'

'I'm glad you approve of something.'

'It's nineteenth century. Quite valuable actually,' I said. 'And perfect for your china.'

'I know.' Mum had displayed her collection of royal commemoration plates, reproduction Buckingham Palace china, and Queen Elizabeth II Diamond Jubilee china on the shelves above the dresser. A framed wedding photograph of Prince William and Kate Middleton stood in the center. Mum had an obsession about the royal family – something Dad and I used to joke about.

'William told me that Princess Anne is a regular visitor up at the house,' said Mum. 'All these aristocratic families are connected, you know, especially when there are horses involved. His Royal Highness Prince Philip – that's the Duke of Edinburgh – is a personal friend of the dowager countess.'

'Would this dowager countess ride sidesaddle by any chance?'

'Yes. I've seen her out riding, but of course her sort wouldn't mix with the likes of us,' said Mum.

'What do you mean *her* sort?' I scoffed.

'The gentry.'

'That's silly, Mum,' I said. 'They're just like you and me.'

'No, Katherine, believe me, they are not,' said Mum. 'There are them ... and there are us.'

'I saw the little boy out riding,' I said. 'He looked pretty normal.'

'Normal?' said Mum. 'Who wears flying goggles on horseback? William told me they have a lot of problems with that child. He's a little light-fingered.'

'Light-*fingered?*' I laughed again at Mum's old-fashioned terms and then remembered that Harry had wasted no time in borrowing Jazzbo Jenkins, which was rather worrying.

'I wonder how old Lady Lavinia was when she had him?' said Mum. 'How old are you now? I lose track.'

'I'm absolutely starving. Shall I rustle up some scrambled eggs for supper?' I said, steering the subject away from my childbearing years. 'Let's go to the kitchen.'

'Why do women these days leave it so late to have children?' asked Mum. 'Don't they realize their own mothers don't live forever? I am so looking forward to being a–'

'Grandmother, so you keep telling me,' I said. 'Where do you keep the bread?'

'In the pantry.' Mum gestured to two doors, side by side, next to the oak dresser. I tried the door on the left and was startled to find it opened directly into a field. Equally startled was the small herd of Devonshire cows that took off at great speed, splashing through a large pool of muddy water and snorting with indignation.

I hastily closed the door. 'There are cows outside!'

'Yes. I know,' said Mum mildly. 'This is the country. Lovely, aren't they?'

The pantry was the walk-in kind with floor-to-ceiling shelves and a square butcher table set against a tall, narrow window that looked directly into a hedge laden with ripe blackberries. The small room was in desperate need of a coat of paint but it was clean and Mum had painstakingly lined every surface with adhesive paper in a cheerful red gingham pattern. Presumably this fiddly job was done before her accident.

The shelves were stacked with cans of soup and long-life cartons of food. Dad had always had a thing about being prepared for an invasion – even after the Berlin Wall came down. On the floor were at least a dozen one-gallon containers of water.

I retrieved the bread from a china bread crock, grabbed the Bombay Sapphire and set it down on the kitchen table. 'I'm glad to see you're still prepared for a nuclear attack,' I said. 'Why all that water? Can't you drink from the tap?'

'Oh yes,' said Mum. 'But the water is for emergencies.'

'In case there is a drought?'

'No. Because of that wretched, disgusting Eric Pugsley.'

Mum's tone suggested that now was not the time to mention I'd already met him and that he'd damaged her brand new MINI. 'I gather you don't like him?' I said tentatively.

'*Pugsley*,' she spat. 'He wanted this place, you know. He rents the two fields behind – Cromwell Meadows.'

'Cromwell, as in Oliver Cromwell?' I said, steering the subject away from Eric. 'Was there a battlefield here by any chance?'

'Oh yes,' said Mum. 'Honeychurch Hall used to be a Royalist stronghold during the English Civil War. Fascinating stuff. It's where Cromwell supposedly set up camp for the final attack which is exactly what *Pugsley* is doing to me – attacking.'

'But you did *buy* the Carriage House, didn't you?' I asked.

'In a sealed bid,' said Mum. 'Why?'

'It *does* belong to you. You've got the deeds?'

'Of course!' Mum was getting irritable. 'But *Pugsley* won't have it. Every night that odious man turns off the water supply to this house.'

'How?'

'The water valve is in his field,' said Mum. 'You must have seen the giant puddle when you looked out the back door.'

'No, I was too fascinated by the cows.'

'I can't switch the water on again because you need both hands to use the crowbar thingy to turn the valve.'

'Why would Eric bother to turn it off?'

'Because he's furious and is determined to make my life difficult and get me out.' Mum gestured at the oak dresser. 'Fetch the glasses, dear, otherwise I'll die of thirst.'

I did as she asked and unscrewed the lid from the gin bottle. Mum poured us both a huge measure that could have knocked out a horse. 'Tonic is in the fridge.'

On seeing my expression she said, 'You're not driving anywhere.'

I fetched the tonic water and grabbed a box of eggs, noting the color of the deep-brown shells. Spying a bowl of ripe tomatoes I inhaled the sweet scent. 'These are wonderful. I can even smell them.'

'All from the walled garden,' said Mum proudly. 'And you can definitely taste the difference from the supermarket – or to be more precise, the Patels' corner shop.'

'Did you confront Eric about the water situation?'

'Of course I did and of course he denied it. He even offered me money to move – but I told him to stuff it.'

A few minutes later I set two plates of scrambled eggs, tomatoes, and buttered toast on the table. 'I'll make something a bit more adventurous tomorrow.'

'As long as it's not that revolting chicken thing. The one with the grapes.' Mum picked up a fork and held it awkwardly in her left hand. 'You see! I can't do anything. Anything at *all*.' She threw her fork down on the table with a clatter.

'Let me,' I said, cutting up the toast into soldiers and halving the tomatoes. 'I'll get you a spoon and then you can tell me all about your accident.'

'Two weeks ago I was driving through Eric's field – before he put up that ridiculous gate banning me from using the tradesman's entrance–' Mum took a large sip of gin and gave a satisfying shiver. 'There is a sharp bend and a deep grassy ditch on one side and suddenly, he zooms out of nowhere on that huge tractor of his, hand hard on the horn and it startled me so much that I swung the wheel and plunged into the ditch. The steering wheel caught my hand and I heard a loud *snap*.'

'Oh Mum, that's terrible.'

'And he didn't even stop! He just breezed on by. No, I actually think he was laughing.'

'I can't believe–'

'He was *laughing*, I tell you.' Mum was getting heated and took another large swig of gin.

'How did you get to the hospital?'

'Fortunately, William came along in his Land Rover. He took me to the hospital and yes, my thumb was broken. *Broken!* Six weeks in a cast, then months of physical therapy.'

'Did your airbag go off?'

'I was only going five miles an hour–'

'And how did you get the MINI out of the ditch?'

'William. Without so much as a scratch – thank *heavens*,' said Mum. 'You should see his biceps. He may be the wrong end of fifty but he's very strong – then, *Pugsley* had the nerve to say it was my fault because I was trespassing on his land!'

'What about your black eye?' I said. 'How did you do that?'

'Pugsley.'

'He *hit* you?' I gasped.

'I fell down the drain in the dark on my way to the dustbins.'

'How can that be Eric's fault?'

'I'd put some planks of wood over the hole and he must have removed them,' Mum said. 'Deliberately.'

'Maybe you need a surveillance camera,' I said lightly.

'Exactly,' said Mum. 'The equipment should arrive tomorrow.'

'Actually, I was joking.'

'I'm not.'

'Is it worth living here with all the hassle, Mum?' I said. 'Put your emotions aside and be practical for a moment.'

'You sound just like your father.' Mum picked up a tomato with her fingers and popped it into her mouth.

I had a sudden thought. 'But if you'd already broken your hand, how did the MINI get stuck down that old farm track?'

'How do you know it's stuck?'

'Because, *Mother,* my Golf is parked right behind your MINI. I told you.'

'I thought I could get out that way.'

'You seriously thought you could drive in a cast?'

'I only needed one hand. The MINI is an automatic, you know,' said Mum. 'I had a hair appointment. Look at my roots! I'm completely gray but we'd had rain and my car has no traction in the mud. William said he'd help me pull it out. That reminds me, he still has my car keys. He said he'd do it today.'

An image of Eric pulling off the broken fender flashed through my mind. Perhaps Mum was right about him trying to get her to leave. I changed the subject. 'Is there a loo down here?'

'Yes, off the old tack room. Go through the latch door into the carriageway.' Mum reached for the bottle. 'I'll just pour myself another gin. I must say I'm feeling a lot better now you're here.'

'I think that's got something to do with the gin.'

I slipped into the old part of the building. A full moon shone through the central skylight that ran the length of an arch-braced roof, illuminating a world that belonged to another century.

Mum was right when she said that this part had not been touched for decades. At the far end stood a pair of twenty-foot-high arched double doors on iron runners. Tendrils of ivy had forced their way through bricks and rusting hinges. The floor was cobbled herringbone. At one time there would have been room for four horse-drawn carriages but now it stood empty.

All the original fixtures remained. A row of stalls stood on either side accessed through redbrick arches bearing the family crest of arms and motto. I stepped through one to find six stalls divided by wooden timber boards topped with iron railings and newel posts. Bite and hoof marks peppered the dividers.

Each stall had a triangular water trough in one

65

corner and an iron hayrack in the other. Above that was a small hatch accessing the hayloft. The cobbled floors still bore faint signs of habitation – dried dung that had crumbled into dust, wisps of straw black with age, and endless droppings from birds nesting in the eaves. Metal name plaques were attached to each stall door: FIDDLE-STICKS, CHINA CUP, TIN MAN, LADY, BRIAR PATCH, and MISTY. Horses from long ago that were now resting in equine heaven.

I closed my eyes and for a moment, could hear the chomp of hay, a whinny, the hustle and bustle of stable lads fetching feed and water. I could smell the leather harnesses and see the horses being groomed. A golden time when the rich were very rich and the servants – if they were lucky – had one afternoon off a month.

Another door opened into a small sitting room, where a pair of moth-eaten wingback armchairs sat beside a Victorian fireplace filled with empty cigarette packets and rubbish. Beyond that was the loo – a rectangular wood-clad box with a hinged lid. Above, the wood-clad cistern clung unsteadily to the wall. Suspended from that was a silver pull chain with a painted porcelain handle.

I gingerly lifted the lid and peered inside. The bowl was painted with horse heads and decorated with wildflowers. It almost seemed a crime to use it. However, my opinion changed rapidly afterward when I pulled the chain and the cladding from the cistern came crashing down onto the floor, narrowly missing my big toe.

I stalked back to the kitchen. 'You should have warned me about the loo.'

'Ah, there you are, dear,' said Mum. 'This is William.'

An enormous man in his late fifties was sitting at the kitchen table gently massaging Mum's bare arm just above her cast. His hands were the size of hams and Mum was certainly right about his biceps. They were so large that they almost seemed deformed.

'Hello. I'm Kat,' I said.

William looked up and smiled. 'Yes I know. I've heard a lot about you.'

I detected a faint northern accent. William was still handsome with piercing blue eyes and thinning blond hair. He must have been stunning in his youth like Robert Redford in his Sundance Kid days. 'Does that feel better, Iris?'

'Yes, thank you,' Mum said. 'William says he massages the horses' legs to get the circulation going.'

'That's right,' said William. 'It's an important step on the road to recovery.'

Mum pointed to the draining board. 'He brought some strawberries. *Chocolate* strawberries.'

An alarm bell went off in my head. Chocolate strawberries? He probably thought she was a merry widow. 'Well, I can massage Mum's arm now, William,' I said firmly. 'Thanks for stopping by.'

'I'm glad you're here.' William got to his feet. 'I've been worrying about you, haven't I, Iris?'

'Fussing, more like,' scolded Mum.

'You should see a doctor about those headaches of yours.'

'She's always had headaches,' I said. 'Ever since I was a teenager but she won't listen to me.'

'I'm fine.'

'Iris needs to be more careful here,' said William. 'This place is a death trap.'

I was beginning to warm to him. 'You see, Mum?' I said smugly. 'William doesn't think it's practical for you to be here, either. Nor is it safe. I practically broke my foot in the loo. The casing flew off.'

'I'll take a look tomorrow,' said William. 'It's already bruised Iris's foot once. I told her not to use that toilet but she's a stubborn old thing.'

'I'll have less of the *old*, thank you very much,' Mum grumbled.

'Anyway, I'd best be off.' William rewarded me with yet another dazzling smile and got to his feet. He had to be at least six foot three – David was tall, but William seemed gigantic. 'Maybe you can talk some sense into her, Kat. I know I can't.'

'Don't worry, I will.' Chocolate strawberries aside, perhaps I could enlist William's help to persuade Mum to return to London with me.

William headed for the back door. He pulled a set of car keys out of his pocket and put them down on the dresser. 'I moved your MINI into the yard by the way, Iris.' Turning to me he added, 'I would have moved your Golf – that *is* your car?'

'Yes, but don't worry,' I said. 'I can move it myself.'

'And I put the fender in the barn.'

Mum looked blank. 'Fender?'

My heart sank. 'Mum, I was going to explain but–'

'Naughty Iris,' William said with an indulgent chuckle. 'I told you that I could lift the MINI out' – he flexed his biceps – 'but you couldn't wait and had to ask Eric for help.'

'I don't understand,' said Mum.

'You'll need a new fender,' William went on. 'Eric is like a bull in a china shop.'

Mum turned to me with a shriek. 'Eric Pugsley! What possessed you to ask Eric Pugsley?'

'I didn't know you and he had had a falling out,' I protested.

'Oh dear,' said William. 'Have I put my foot in it?'

'Yes, you have,' I said.

'Don't worry. I'll get it sorted,' said William smoothly. 'I'll take your car into Dartmouth on Monday, Iris.'

'Thank you, William,' said Mum, shooting me a furious look.

'What time shall I come and get you for your hair appointment tomorrow?'

'I can take Mum,' I said. 'That's why I'm here.'

'In that case, I'll be off. Enjoy the strawberries, ladies,' said William. 'Kat, can I have a quick word?'

'Is it about me?' said Mum coyly.

'It's always about you, Mother.'

Once we reached the courtyard William turned to me. 'I wasn't joking about the place being a death trap.'

'Nor am I.'

'Does she have any other family members? Brothers? Sisters? Someone who can make her see sense?'

'Mum is an orphan.'

'An orphan?' said William. 'She never told me.'

'Mum's very private,' I said.

'Do you know why she decided to come and live here?' William seemed worried. 'I mean, why move from London? Does she know anyone in the area?'

I was touched by his concern. 'Your guess is as good as mine.'

'Well – perhaps you can persuade her,' said William. 'The winters can be pretty brutal.'

'I intend to.'

'I must get on,' he said. 'Edith will be waiting for me in the stable yard.'

'Is that the dowager countess?'

'She's incredible – still rides sidesaddle to hounds,' William enthused. 'Her bark is worse than her bite, but she's a good person. Sharp as a tack – whatever you may hear to the contrary.'

I waved William goodbye and returned to the kitchen.

'William certainly seems to have the hots for you,' I teased.

Mum didn't answer. She was busy scribbling on a block of Post-it Notes. I couldn't read very well upside down but I deciphered the word 'strawberry.'

'Hmm?' Mum continued scribbling.

'Did you hear what I said? I don't trust his motives.'

'What was that?' Mum bit her lip and frowned. 'Wait a moment.' And began scribbling again, tearing off each Post-it Note with gusto and sticking them under her poncho.

'Just as well you write left-handed,' I pointed out. 'Mum, seriously. This William–'

'He reminds me of Lurch,' she said suddenly. 'From the *Addams Family*, only friendlier. You know, I feel a headache coming on. I'm going to lie down.'

'Well, I'm tired,' I said, relieved that she didn't want to rant about Eric and the broken fender. 'Can I help you get ready for bed?'

'I don't need a nanny.'

'Oh God!' In all the excitement I'd forgotten my promise to Gayla. 'Speaking of nannies, I need to make a phone call.'

'Be my guest,' said Mum.

Retrieving the business card for Bumble-Bee Cars I dialed the number but just got voice mail. It would appear that the taxi company's operating hours were from 6 a.m. until 9 p.m. I didn't leave a message. 'They're closed. Can you believe it!'

'This isn't London, dear.'

'I hope Gayla made her train.'

'Gayla the nanny?' said Mum.

'I met her at the top of the drive waiting for a taxi. Apparently she left in disgrace.'

'Disgrace? Really?' said Mum. 'How do you know?'

I related the conversation I'd overheard in the general store earlier between Muriel and Vera, adding, 'Vera doesn't seem the housekeeper type.'

'I'm sure she had something to do with Gayla's dismissal,' said Mum. 'Vera is insanely jealous of any pretty girl who comes near her precious Eric.'

'*The* Eric?' I said surprised. 'She's married to Eric Pugsley?'

71

'Vera told me she thinks he is the most beautiful man she's ever seen.'

'With those eyebrows?' I laughed. 'Is she blind?'

'Yes, old beetle-brows,' Mum said. 'I half expect them to crawl off his face.'

'Mum!'

'You know what they say – beauty is in the eye of the beholder.' Mum paused for thought. 'Take you, for example. I don't know what you see in Dylan. Is it his money? His power?'

I retorted with a barb of my own. 'And I wonder what you see in staying in this dump? Is it for the remote chance of meeting royalty?' Mum winced and I felt horrible. 'Sorry, that was unkind. But honestly – even the nanny said you should move back to London.'

'How nice of you to discuss me with a stranger,' Mum said coldly. 'And a foreigner at that. Your father never trusted the Russians.'

'Actually, Gayla was very complimentary about you. But she said you were in great danger.'

'I am. From beetle-brows,' said Mum.

'She said – and I quote, "Rupert is a wicked man and should be stopped."'

'Are we going to bicker all evening?' Mum grumbled. 'I'm game if you are.'

'No,' I said wearily. 'Let's call a truce.'

'Good – because *Walk of Shame!* starts in five minutes,' said Mum. '*Do* watch it. It's hilarious.'

'No, thank you.' I sniffed. 'I don't want to see people get humiliated by Trudy Wynne, thank you very much.'

'Don't be so dramatic. It's all scripted.'

'It's *not* all scripted,' I exclaimed. 'Trudy goes

out of her way to dig up the dirt.'

'I hope you didn't quit *Fakes & Treasures* because of her.'

'Of course not,' I said hotly, hating Mum for touching a nerve. *Had I?*

'Your father would be *so* disappointed if he knew you packed it in because you'd let Trudy get to you.'

'I'm not packing it in because of Trudy Wynne,' I cried. 'And I don't want to talk about her. I've always wanted my own antique shop. At least *look* at some of the property brochures I've brought with me, Mum.'

'You are wasting your breath,' said Mum. 'I'm not moving anywhere.'

'Let's not argue,' I said.

'Who's arguing?'

I made a monumental effort to keep my temper, picked up my tote bag, and pulled out *Gypsy Temptress.* 'Here,' I said. 'A peace offering.'

'Oh!' Mum brightened. 'What did you think? Did you enjoy it?'

'You know I don't read that rubbish. It's for you.'

Mum opened her mouth but before she could say thank you, the puke-green phone mounted on the wall let out a series of chirrups. 'Who on earth is calling so late?' Mum snatched up the receiver. 'Yes?' she snapped. 'Oh, yes, this is Iris Stanford speaking.' Mum's expression changed from annoyance to disbelief. 'Could you repeat that please?' She listened again and then put the phone down, eyes wide with excitement.

'Did you win the lottery?' I asked.

'That was Cropper from the Hall,' Mum gushed.

'We're expected for coffee tomorrow morning at ten-thirty with the Earl of Grenville – that's Lord Honeychurch, they have all kinds of titles. Well I never! I *am* surprised. Fancy the gentry asking us for coffee!' Mum's face was pink. 'But what should I wear? Oh dear, I can't go looking like this!'

'What exactly did Cropper say?' I asked.

'Something about not using the tradesman's entrance.' Mum beamed. 'You see! We're even told to use the main drive!'

'I am sorry to dampen your excitement,' I said. 'The reason we are going to the Hall is to discuss the tradesman's entrance – and a few other things.'

'Why do we have to discuss the tradesman's entrance?' said Mum.

'I met Lady Lavinia this afternoon and told her that old beetle-brows had closed all access – meaning you couldn't drive through his field.'

'Oh.' Mum's face fell. 'Really Kat, I do wish you wouldn't interfere. I don't want to cause a fuss.'

'I thought you'd be pleased.'

'Well, I'm not. I'm embarrassed. They are the aristocracy and now I'll look common. You're just like your father. Always putting a wet blanket on everything.'

'That's not true, Mum. I'm worried for you, that's all.' I waved *Gypsy Temptress* at her. 'I do try, Mum. See?'

Mum regarded my gift with what seemed like disgust. She turned on her heel, wrenched open the kitchen door, and vanished.

I just couldn't win.

Chapter Five

I washed up the dishes and gave the work sur-
faces a thorough cleaning. Under the stone sink
was a very smelly pedal bin in dire need of
emptying. Obviously, William hadn't been put on
bin duty.

A sudden burst of birdsong erupted from a
round clock hanging above the pantry door.
According to the chaffinch, it was ten o'clock. I'd
bought that clock for Mum decades ago and Dad
had never liked it so it stayed in the box. I wondered if my parents had really been happy all those
years and yet I knew my father had idolized Mum.

Dad never exactly forbade her to do things, but
rather suggested it wasn't a good idea as in, 'Iris,
it's lovely but where would you put it?' When she
saw a dress she liked and wanted to buy it – Mum
had no money of her own – Dad would say, 'Of
course you can have it but would you wear it? You
know you hate going out.'

Perhaps I needed to change tactics and adopt
some of Dad's persuasion techniques.

A shaft of moonlight shone through a crack in
the net curtains. I pulled a panel aside and
looked out onto the cobbled yard. Mum's MINI
was parked in front of the barn. A figure entered
the courtyard from the direction of the woods
and stood in the shadows.

I was certain it was William and felt a twinge of

alarm. Was he going to turn out to be a peeping Tom? Switching off the kitchen light, I returned to the window and watched. He stood there for several minutes before creeping over to the dustbins.

Tying up the bag of rubbish from the pedal bin, I walked to the front door and out into the courtyard. Taking a circular route, I crept around the corner of the barn determined to confront him.

To my annoyance, William was busily scouring the contents of the dustbins with the help of a flashlight and a walking stick. Balls of yellow paper and food wrappers were scattered on the ground and there was an overwhelming stench of rotting garbage.

I'd had to deal with 'fans' rifling through my dustbins before hoping to find some gem to sell to Trudy Wynne and was furious.

'Looking for something?' I said and then stepped back in surprise. *'Eric?* Is that you? What are you doing?'

Eric slammed down the lid and spun around. Shielding my eyes from the glare I snapped, 'Turn that thing off.'

'Yes, what *are* you doing, Eric?' Vera materialized from thin air. 'Or should I say, what are you *both* doing?' Her voice was slurred and I suspected she'd been drinking.

'Oh, for heaven's sake, woman. Can't a man use a dustbin?' Eric said, exasperated. 'I was on my way to my office.'

'At this time of night?' Vera's voice was heavy with accusation.

'Yes,' said Eric. 'And don't start nagging.'

'You don't waste time, do you? That Russian tart only left this afternoon,' Vera shouted. 'What's wrong with you?'

'I know what's wrong with you,' Eric shouted back. 'You're bloody drunk, woman.'

Vera stepped toward me. Her breath reeked of alcohol. 'And you should keep your hands off other people's husbands,' she cried. 'You're on *Fakes & Treasures!* You're Rapunzel. I knew you were lying ... *Jazzbo.*'

'Excuse me,' I said coldly. 'I'd like to throw this lot out.'

Wordlessly, Eric took the rubbish bag from me, gallantly lifted the dustbin lid, and threw it in.

'Thank you,' I said. 'And please clear up this mess.'

'Keep away from my Eric,' said Vera. 'I'm warning you.'

'I'll try to restrain myself,' I muttered, as I squeezed past Vera and hurried back to the house thoroughly irritated. What an awful woman.

Picking up my overnight case from the hall, I headed upstairs, promptly tripped on a loose floorboard at the top of the stairs, and went flying headlong on the landing. Despite the crash and my cry of pain, Mum did not come out to investigate. She must have taken her headache straight to bed.

There were no prizes for guessing that the first door I opened was mine. Apart from the gaping hole in the floor behind the door exposing the hall below, Mum had recreated my 1980's teenage lair complete with my Laura Ashley curtains. She could easily have made this a guest room. I was touched.

My white-painted furniture was set out exactly as it used to be. The mattress on my single bed was thirty years old and always gave me a chronic backache, but as Dad had said, what was the point of buying a new once since they never had guests and I only slept over for family birthdays, Christmas, and Easter.

Boxes were stacked neatly in one corner labeled CHINA HORSES, BOOKS, RIDING STUFF, and PHOTOS – 1980–90's. A vintage iron steamer trunk filled with my dressing-up clothes stood under the window along with the blue suitcase full of old bears and soft toys. A part of me wondered why I still kept these things if I never had children to give them to.

Pushing that awful thought to the back of my mind, I went off in search of the linen cupboard.

The upstairs landing was a narrow L-shaped corridor with three more doors leading off – two on my right, and one on my left. Lit by one naked bulb, the décor looked a hundred times worse than downstairs. With no wallpaper to speak of, the lath and plaster were exposed and there were alarming clumps of fleshy mushroom-type growths that did not bode well.

I opened the next door. Flipping on the light I stared in confusion. It was my mother's bedroom but she was not asleep in her bed.

Again, the furniture was arranged exactly as it had been in Tooting. In the corner, an upholstered low stool stood before a kidney-shaped dressing table draped with lace. Mum's silver brushes were neatly laid out on the glass top along with perfume

78

bottles and a box of Kleenex tissues.

Familiar photographs in silver frames – Mum and Dad on their wedding day, me at age five on a pony, and one of the three of us taken on holiday in Scotland – were on the mantelpiece above the Victorian fireplace that now housed a hideous 1940's gas fire. But there was a new addition to the collection – a photograph I had never seen before.

Guessing it must have been taken in the early fifties, I recognized Mum – grinning from ear to ear, aged around nine or ten, standing between two boys in front of a boxing booth at a fairground. The boys were dressed in boxing attire and were hamming it up for the camera. I guessed they must be Alfred and Billy – part of Mum's past that I knew nothing about until today. A sudden wave of grief welled up as I looked at the matching night tables. The left had the clock, a glass of water, and a romance novel by Joan Johnston. The right table was bare. Dad had always slept on the right-hand side of the bed and now he was gone.

Forty-nine years was a long time to be married. Even if David and I married right this second it was unlikely we would live long enough to make it to thirty-five. I just couldn't imagine how Mum must feel and resolved to be nicer, more patient, and compassionate.

I went to find her and knocked on the next door, that turned out to be the bathroom. Mum wasn't there, either.

The bathroom was basic to say the least with hideous blue-and-pink-checked linoleum. An ancient three-bar electric wall heater was fixed askew above a long, deep china bath. Of course there was no shower so washing my hair would be a nightmare.

The sound of voices carrying on the night breeze drew me to the open window where a full moon and a gazillion stars – a sight I never saw in London – illuminated Eric and the man with the English setter standing outside a beaten-up old caravan in the field.

Gayla's name was spoken several times before the man with the dog patted Eric's shoulder and said, 'I won't forget this, I owe you,' before striding off out of view.

Vera emerged from inside the caravan – I guessed this was Eric's so-called office – and shouted, 'What did his lordship say? Why does he owe you?'

I couldn't hear Eric's answer but whatever he said made her cry. Vera grabbed the sleeve of his jacket. 'Please don't go, *please.*'

I quickly shut the bathroom window. The last thing I wanted was to listen to their marital squabbles and turned my attention to hunting for some bed linen.

I heard murmurings coming from the far end of the corridor where a fourth – and last – door stood closed. I'd assumed it was a cupboard.

'Mum?' I tried the handle. It was locked. 'Are you in there?' Abruptly, the murmuring stopped. I tapped again. 'Mum. Are you okay?'

There was the click of a key and Mum opened the door a crack. 'What is it? What do you want?'

I tried to sound casual but I was actually worried. 'I thought you'd gone to bed.'

'Well, I haven't.' She sounded annoyed. 'Did you find the sheets?'

'Not yet. What are you doing in the cupboard?' I said, trying to look over her shoulder.

'It's not a cupboard.'

I was struck by a ghastly thought. 'Is *William* in there?'

Mum's expression of horror was so comical that I laughed.

'Give me some credit, dear.'

'Well, I had to ask,' I said. 'I assume your headache is better now?'

'I'll help you find the bed linen,' she said. 'Go on ahead. Shoo! I'm right behind you.'

I turned away but heard another click and, out of the corner of my eye, saw her lock the door using a key attached to a pink ribbon that was hanging around her neck.

'Are you sure you haven't got a man stashed in there?' I asked.

Armed with clean sheets and a duvet, we returned to my bedroom and as I made up my bed Mum said, 'I suppose you heard Vera shouting outside.'

'I couldn't help it.'

Mum perched on the edge of my steamer trunk. 'I hear them all the time. They've already been divorced twice, you know.'

'From each other?'

'Oh yes. This is the third time around,' Mum said. 'Vera reminds me of Blanche in *A Streetcar Named Desire* – although beetle-brows is no Marlon Brando.'

'You can say that again.'

'Poor things,' said Mum. 'Passion is all very well but it can be so destructive.'

I gave a snort of derision. 'What do you know about passion?'

'A lot more than you think,' said Mum. 'And don't snort. It's so unattractive.'

'I caught Eric rifling through the dustbins this evening,' I said.

Mum looked up sharply. *'My* dustbins?'

'And Vera called me Rapunzel. She guessed who I am,' I said. 'She told me to keep my hands off other people's husbands.' I was struck by a horrible thought. 'Oh God, I hope she's not a *Star Stalkers* type.'

'Such is the price of fame, dear.'

I gave a heavy sigh. 'Oh Mum, will that wretched Trudy Wynne ever leave me alone?'

'You did steal her husband.'

'I didn't. I told you. They were already separated.'

'But not divorced.'

'It's complicated when children are involved.' I knew I was getting defensive.

'If he really loves you–'

'Mum, stop please–' Fortunately, my protests were drowned as my mobile phone rang. I recognized the caller ID. 'It's David.'

'Speak of the devil.' My mother stood up. 'I'll leave you to it.'

'Are you sure you don't want any help undressing?' I said as I hit answer.

'Hello, Dylan,' Mum called out in a voice that David couldn't help but hear. 'Ask him when he's getting a divorce.'

I kicked the door closed behind her.

'Your mother doesn't like me,' said David with a chuckle.

'She does, really she does,' I lied. 'I am so glad to talk to you. This whole situation is a complete nightmare.'

Quickly, I summarized the events of the day. 'She just can't live here. It's ridiculous.'

'Why not?' David said. 'It's her life.'

I was taken aback. 'It's hugely impractical and this building is falling down. It's not structurally safe,' I said. 'I thought you'd be on my side.'

'I'm just saying–'

'Dad specifically asked me to keep an eye on her,' I went on. 'How can I do that from London?'

'Judging by what you said about your father, I'm sure she's enjoying her newfound freedom,' said David. 'Believe me, after twenty years with Trudy I feel like I've been let out of prison.'

'I hate it when you bring that woman up,' I snapped.

'Sorry, I was making a point,' said David.

'Well ... don't.'

'Now that your mother is out of the picture, I assume you'll drop this ridiculous antique shop idea and–'

'I am not going back to *Fakes & Treasures*,' I said. 'I want my life back.'

'You're making a terrible mistake, Kat,' said David. 'You'll never earn the same kind of money running a shop.'

'It's not about the money.'

'It's *always* about the money,' said David. 'Trudy is going to cripple me with this divorce.

She wants everything. And I've got to put the kids through university. We need that income, Kat.'

'Isn't the main thing that we're going to be together?' There was a silence on the other end of the line.

'David?' I said. 'Are you still there?'

'Yes,' he said wearily. 'Look, I've got to go. There's a lot going on.'

'What's the matter?'

Another silence.

'I wasn't going to tell you but...' David paused. 'Trudy's father is terminally ill.'

'And what's that got to do with you?'

'God, Kat. I thought you of all people would understand,' said David. 'I was close to Hugh for heaven's sake. I'm not divorcing him, I'm divorcing his daughter.'

'You're making me feel terrible–'

'The hospice is somewhere between Totnes and Dartmouth. I'm driving down tomorrow. Why don't I come and see you and we can talk about what to do about your mother. Sound like a plan?'

'Okay,' I said. 'Yes. Look, I'm sorry. Of course you must see Hugh. You could stay here but–'

'And risk your mother's wrath?' said David. 'Don't worry. I'll find a local pub.'

We said our good-byes and I switched off my mobile. Talking about Trudy always unsettled me and much as I wanted to confide in Mum, I knew she'd have very little sympathy.

It was unbearably stuffy in this small room. I opened a window and climbing into bed, my thoughts turned to the squabbling couple. True,

Vera had recognized me but it was Eric who had been rifling through the dustbins. I wondered what on earth he had been looking for.

I was utterly exhausted and at a loss as to what to do about my mother. I could hardly let her stay here in this backwater alone.

I'd promised Dad that I would keep an eye on Mum. I'd hoped that helping me run the shop would have meant she'd meet new people – perhaps even a nice widower.

Somehow I had to find a way to make her change her mind.

Chapter Six

It took me ages to fall asleep. I wasn't used to the silence. Living so close to Putney Bridge tube station, I no longer heard the last train rumbling out or the first train screeching in. Yet here, in the middle of nowhere, the quiet seemed – loud – apart from the occasional burst of scrabbling claws overhead that I was convinced were rats.

David's insistence that I stick with *Fakes & Treasures* really bothered me. I wished I could make him understand that I wasn't like Trudy. I'd never sought fame and I hated it. I was still haunted by the most humiliating moment of my life known as 'The Big Sneeze' that continued to fly around the Internet on YouTube. Just thinking about it made me feel hot with embarrassment.

I must have drifted into dreamland because the

next thing I heard were voices under my window. According to my old pink alarm clock, it was almost eight-thirty in the morning. I scrambled out of bed and peered outside where Mum and William in Wellington boots, stood ankle deep in a pool of muddy water.

William – sleeves rolled up – was rotating a long iron rod that was stuck into the ground. Presumably this was the infamous water valve that Eric loved to tamper with.

'Thanks, William,' I heard Mum say. 'And thank you for making me a cup of tea. Katherine's never been an early morning person. It was impossible getting her out of bed when she was a teenager.'

It was true, I was not a morning person but even so I threw open the window and yelled, 'It was because I had glandular fever,' and slammed it shut, rather enjoying their startled expressions.

I had suffered quite badly – enough to fall behind in school, delay taking my A-levels, and in the end, I didn't bother to go to university. Instead, I started working for a French antique dealer and never looked back.

After getting washed and dressed, I met Mum coming up the stairs. 'You're a bit of a grumpy puss this morning.'

Ignoring that remark, I said, 'Shall I help you put on some clothes? I'm sure you don't want to wear your poncho to meet his lordship.'

'I've got nothing *to* wear,' moaned Mum. 'This is the extent of my entire wardrobe – pajamas and a poncho.'

'I've got an idea. But first, let's get you in the bath.'

I ran the water and Mum produced a plastic bag and some tape which I helped her slide over her cast. 'Now, don't get it wet.'

'I won't get it wet,' she snapped. 'I've managed to get myself in and out of the bath before you arrived, you know.'

'It's too early for naked flesh,' I said, pulling the poncho over her head. 'I promise I won't look.'

'I don't care. You can look all you like. We all get old.' Mum placed a block of Post-it Notes and a pen on the stool. 'In case I think of something.'

'Are you getting Alzheimer's? Should I be worried?'

'It's a bit cold in here,' said Mum. 'Can you turn on the electric heater?'

I pulled the cord, slightly anxious that it seemed to wobble a little off the wall. 'You can't use this. It'll fall into the bath and you'll get electrocuted. You'll just have to freeze.'

No sooner had I turned away, there was loud splash. The entire fixture fell into the bath.

Mum and I shared looks of horror. 'Oh my God,' I whispered.

'Well, that's another of my nine lives gone,' said Mum lightly but I could tell she was shaken. Her face was ashen. 'No harm done.'

'This time,' I said. 'Do you need a bodyguard?'

'Stop fussing.'

Leaving Mum in the bath I hunted through her wardrobe. Mum's clothes were all arranged by color and type. She was right. There was nothing in there that could accommodate a cast.

I returned to my own bedroom and opened the steamer trunk. The purple harem pantaloons and flowing top might do and she could wrap a scarf around her head. Not exactly a twinset and pearls to meet her so-called gentry but better than a poncho and pajamas.

Back in Mum's bedroom I was about to open the top drawer of her dressing table to pick out some undies when I saw the key, tied to a pink ribbon that she had worn around her neck. It was sitting in a Queen Elizabeth Diamond Jubilee coronation saucer. I knew it was wrong but I just had to know what was behind that locked door.

Slipping the key into my pocket I tapped on the bathroom door first. 'Just checking you haven't drowned in there.'

'No, still swimming laps,' Mum called out. 'Give me another ten minutes. Did you find something for me to wear?'

'Yes,' I said. 'You'll look very exotic.'

Even though I felt guilty, my curiosity got the better of me.

It was pitch black inside. I groped around for a light switch and flipped it on.

'Good grief.'

Set against one wall was our old dining room table on which stood Dad's Olivetti typewriter and various stacks of typewritten pages arranged in neat piles.

A gray metal filing cabinet five drawers high stood in one corner. In another was the standard lamp from the sitting room in Tooting, Dad's leather wingback chair, and a hexagonal table holding a book written by Elinor Glyn with a torn dust jacket and a few *Country Life* and *The Lady* magazines. But what really caught my attention was a vast corkboard that covered an entire wall.

Half of it was covered in photocopies of black-and-white photographs of Honeychurch Hall and the formal gardens in what must have been its heyday at the start of the twentieth century – the golden age of the English country house. Later colored photographs dated in the 1950s and early '60s showed the interior of a shell-lined grotto and the exterior of the Carriage House before it was abandoned for the new stable block.

Pinned in the top left-hand corner was a newspaper cutting dated six months ago. It showed Lady Edith riding sidesaddle on the same chestnut horse I'd seen yesterday. HRH Princess Anne was presenting her with a large silver cup. The caption below said:

DOWAGER COUNTESS LADY EDITH HONEYCHURCH: STILL A CHAMPION AT 84.

Mum had created a crude family tree that crept across the rest of the corkboard tracing the Honeychurchs back to the 1500s.

Post-it Notes were fixed to various family members with random information. Next to Edward Rupert b. 1835 – d. 1899 was CRIMEA/MUMMIFIED HAWK. Harold James b. 1840 – d. 1905 was EXPLORER/POLAR BEAR. Another family member perished on the *Titanic* and yet another ran a Turkish harem in London.

The family tree continued to the present day and ended with Rupert Honeychurch and his two wives – the first being Kelly Jones – then Lavinia, and finally, the current son and heir Harold Edward.

A few sheets of yellow paper lay facedown on the desk. Turning them over I skimmed the familiar handwriting.

Shelby the gamekeeper gently took her injured arm. His callused fingers, hardened by endless hours of cutting wood in the forest, fondled Lady Evelyn's naked skin. Little quivers of desire ran up and down her body. Slowly, her eyes met his. She found herself gazing into liquid pools of blatant lust.

Blushing, Lady Evelyn pleaded, 'Don't. Please, don't.' But her protestations were silenced as Shelby's full, sensual lips locked onto hers. He kissed her deeply. She felt dizzy, as if she were drowning in a whirlpool of desire.

'My brother will kill you if he ever finds out about us,' she panted.

'You want me,' whispered Shelby. 'I know you do. You've got to keep the circulation going.' Scribbled in red pen in the margin were the words, 'Awkward? Chocolate strawberries?'

A peculiar sensation washed over me as I inspected the neat piles of typewritten pages. Each bore the header STORM/FORBIDDEN (WORKING TITLE). A binder clip held more handwritten yellow pages marked with a Post-it, KAT TO TYPE but the word 'Kat' had been crossed out with red pen.

I was beginning to feel a little light-headed – especially when I realized that half the bookcase was filled with hardback copies of *Gypsy Temptress*. On the second shelf stood a crystal statuette of Cupid embossed with the name, KRYSTALLE

STORM and hanging on the wall behind the door was a gaudy gilt-framed pink certificate with a gold embossed heart – WINNER: KRYSTALLE STORM.

I couldn't get to the bathroom quick enough and barged straight in without knocking. Mum was standing there stark naked.

'Do you mind?' she squeaked as she grabbed a towel with one hand and clumsily clutched it to her damp bosom.

'*You're* Krystalle Storm, aren't you?' I cried.

'So what if I am?' Mum sounded defiant.

'I'm just...' I was speechless.

'How else could I afford to buy this?' she said, going on the attack. 'Did you seriously think I'd spend your father's money?'

'But ... but ... why didn't you tell me?'

'I tried to but you wouldn't have it. That's right. I tried. Many times. Just like I tried to tell you I do not want to live above a shop. Ever.'

My mother swept past me, dripping water from her plastic-encased cast. 'Excuse me. I have to get dressed.'

'Mum, wait!' I trailed after her to the bedroom. 'Did Dad know?'

'Of course not,' she snapped. 'Can you imagine what his friends and their stuck-up wives would say – let alone his dreary colleagues at the Inland Revenue? Well? Are you going to be difficult about this?'

'I'm just – well ... stunned. Gobsmacked. But impressed. I mean, how did you pull it off? How long have you been writing?'

'Years.' Mum picked up the purple harem outfit

91

off the bed and said, 'Oh yes, very Barbara Eden.'

'How did you do it?'

'I used to read romance books from the library and I thought, why not write one? It was a joke to begin with. I was lonely. You were at the riding stables–'

'Not all the time.'

'Well, you weren't exactly good company as a teenager, Kat,' she said. 'I remember one time you demanded that I *breathe* differently because you said the sound grated on your nerves.'

'Sorry.'

'Frank was always busy. I was bored, I suppose.'

'So that's what you were doing all those years in a dark room when you told me you had a migraine.'

'Sometimes I had a migraine.'

'But how did you get published?'

'I wrote a few short stories and sent them off to magazines. Then, I entered *Gypsy Temptress* into a competition run by Goldfinch Press. I won. I've been longing to tell *someone*.'

'Mum, I'm thrilled. Really I am.' And I was. I was proud of her.

I went to give her a hug but she yelped, 'Pins!'

'Just today, three people told me what a great book *Gypsy Temptress* is.' I told her about the woman at the motorway service station and of course, Vera and Muriel at the general store and post office. 'They're very excited that you are writing more. What *are* you writing exactly?'

'It's called erotic suspense.'

I had thought as much and groaned. 'Oh God, Mother.'

92

'Apparently Elinor Glyn – who used to visit Honeychurch Hall in what was known as the naughty nineties – was the first to write erotica.'

'I saw one of her books in your office.'

'Elinor Glyn was supposedly the original "It girl."'

'It meaning what?'

'You know, whether you have "It" or not. Sex appeal,' said Mum. 'Angelina Jolie does, poor Lavinia doesn't – nor do you, unfortunately, but you might if you tried harder.'

'Thanks, Mum, you've made my day.'

'I still think I've got it,' said Mum, studying the harem pantaloons.

I gestured to the family tree. 'If you're basing your erotic stories on the family here, you really should be careful.'

'No one recognizes themselves in a book,' said Mum dismissively. 'It's just a starting-off point, that's all. Besides, I'm setting *Forbidden* in Edwardian times.'

'And changing the names, I hope.'

'And that's where you come in,' Mum went on. 'I have to finish this manuscript in three weeks. I'm on a tight schedule. I'd already typed out the first one hundred and fifty pages before I broke my hand. But the rest is in longhand.'

'Don't you think typing up these racy pages might be bad for my health?' I said dryly. *'You've got to keep the circulation going?'*

'I thought that line a tad jarring,' said Mum.

'Is William supposed to be Shelby the gamekeeper in your new book?'

'No,' she said, a little too quickly. 'The real

Shelby – well ... never mind.'

'How could Dad not know about this?' I was still in shock. 'I mean, presumably you must have gotten paid by the publishers?'

Mum reddened and refused to meet my eye. 'It's complicated.'

'What do you mean?'

'I write under a pseudonym.'

'Krystalle Storm.'

'No,' said Mum. 'That's not what I meant. I submitted the manuscript under my maiden name.'

'Why?'

'Why? What do you mean, *why?* I didn't want your father to find out. It didn't occur to me that I'd actually make *money,*' said Mum, adding with a hint of pride, 'A *lot* of money.'

'Hence why you were able to buy the Carriage House.'

'For cash.'

Something didn't add up. Mum sat in front of the mirror at the dressing table and started rearranging her silver brushes.

'The publisher paid you in cash?' I said, puzzled. 'I didn't think they did that.'

'I didn't say they did,' said Mum.

'Well, how–?'

'Frankly, it's none of your business, Katherine.'

'Are you doing something illegal?' I demanded.

'Don't be ridiculous.'

I couldn't help but laugh. 'How ironic! And you, married to a tax inspector.'

'It's not funny,' said Mum crossly. 'I don't want to talk about it anymore.'

Silently she handed me her makeup bag. A few

minutes later I stepped back to admire my handiwork, pleased that I'd managed to tone down the livid bruise on Mum's jaw.

Mum got to her feet. She inspected her reflection in the mirror and gave a grunt of satisfaction. 'I made this costume, you know.'

'Aren't you pleased I kept it?'

'I've always wanted to live in the country again, Kat,' said Mum. 'I'm not a city person. I never have been.'

I realized Mum was serious. 'You really want to stay, don't you?'

She nodded. 'I know the place is falling down but I'm happy here.'

'A writer can write anywhere,' I pointed out. 'At least move closer to London. There are lots of leafy suburbs.'

'All my life I've had to please other people,' said Mum. 'Now it's my turn.'

'But what about Dad's dying wish?' I protested.

'Don't play that emotional card with me, Katherine,' Mum said coldly. 'My mind is made up and there is nothing you can say or do that will change it.'

'We'll see about that,' I muttered.

'Move down to Devon if you're that worried.'

'My life is in London.'

'And mine is here.' Mum glanced at the clock on the mantelpiece.

'We should start walking to the Hall,' I said wearily. 'We don't want to be late for his lordship.'

Chapter Seven

We stepped out into the bright sunshine of a beautiful summer morning.

Mum raised her hand and stopped. 'Wait.'

'Are you okay?' I said. 'Does your ankle hurt?'

'No, I told you it was just a sprain.' She inhaled deeply. 'Can't you smell it?'

I sniffed gingerly. 'What am I supposed to be smelling? Manure?'

'The fresh air, silly!' Mum inhaled deeply again. 'Wonderful, isn't it? Such a change from all the pollution in London.'

We walked on a few steps and Mum paused again. 'Listen. Can you hear it?'

'What?' I said irritably.

'The sound of birds singing.'

'We get birds in London.'

Suddenly, the ground began to vibrate. I clutched Mum's arm. An engine exploded into life with a heavy throb and chatter followed by an ear-splitting screech and deafening crunch of grating metal on metal. A vast cloud of oily black smoke mushroomed into the sky.

'What the hell is that?' I shouted.

Mum's expression was thunderous. Despite her limp, she practically propelled me out of the courtyard, wrenched open the latch-gate and pushed me into the muffled silence of the pine-woods.

'What on earth is it?' I said.

'The crusher.' Mum was trembling with rage. 'Pugsley is not supposed to use it on the weekends.'

My jaw dropped. *'Crusher?'*

'Please don't start.' Mum seemed close to tears. 'No, I didn't know about it when I bought the place.'

'Didn't know about what?'

She pointed to an overgrown footpath that ended abruptly at a wooden stile embedded in a thick hedge. 'Go down there and look. You'll see what I mean.'

I did as I was told. Horrified didn't begin to describe how I felt.

Dozens of beaten-up old cars – including an old hearse – a pyramid of tires, and discarded pieces of farm machinery were spread over the field beyond. There was a car-crusher machine – the source of the noise and pollution – a forklift truck, and a stack of pulverized cars. The whole monstrosity was encompassed by a muddy track that ran around the perimeter of the vast field.

None of this was visible from my bedroom window and Eric's caravan and red tractor could only be seen from the bathroom.

In a state of shock, I returned to Mum who was sitting on a log with a face as long as a wet week.

'It's a *scrap yard!*' I exclaimed.

'No, it's not called a scrap yard apparently.' Mum's voice dripped with sarcasm. 'They're called end-of-life vehicles.'

'End of life?' I snorted.

'I told you not to snort,' said Mum. 'And you

ask me why I don't think you've got "It"?'

'Whether I have sex appeal or not is hardly the issue here. Do you seriously want to live next door to a scrap yard?'

'I don't want to talk about it.'

'No wonder Eric had his eye on the Carriage House,' I said. 'He probably wants to expand his business and you put an end to his dreams.'

'Well hard bloody luck,' said Mum. 'I've got a plan. I wasn't married to a tax inspector for nothing, you know.'

'I can't wait to hear it.'

'Oh, don't worry. You will.'

Mum hobbled on ahead.

'Do you know where you're going?' I shouted, hurrying after her.

'Shortcut!' she yelled back.

The footpath through the pinewoods ended at a second latch-gate that opened into a potholed lane, bordered by thick laurel hedgerows.

'This used to be the service road to the rear of the Hall,' said Mum. 'In Victorian and Edwardian times, service roads were always screened from the main house so the guests wouldn't have to see all the activity that was going on behind the scenes.'

Fifty yards farther on stood a terrace of three stone cottages that backed onto a twelve-foot-high brick wall enclosure covered in ivy.

I gestured to the cottages. 'Are those the estate cottages?'

'Vera and Eric live in number one with the broken window. The Croppers – that's Seth the butler and Peggy the cook – in the middle with the window box of red geraniums–'

'Very pretty,' I said. 'And what about number three? It's all boarded up. Is that where Lady Evelyn's lusty gamekeeper used to live?'

'I have no idea.'

'I thought you knew everything and everyone,' I said. 'I love the family tree in your office. We should trace ours.'

'Whatever for?' Mum exclaimed. 'It's not very interesting.'

'It is!' I cried. 'I want to know more about your brothers, Alfred and Billy. I really missed out not knowing my grandparents.'

'Well, at the rate you're going, it looks like I'll be missing out on not knowing my grandchildren–'

'Touché,' I said. 'That reminds me, David will be visiting sometime over the weekend.'

Mum frowned. 'I'm just not ready for guests.'

'Don't worry, it's just for one night and he's offered to stay in the local pub.'

'It's a long way to come for one night,' said Mum.

'David is visiting … a sick relative.' Deftly changing the subject, I pointed to a tall wooden gate that stood between two granite pillars topped with hawks. The gate was bleached silver-gray with age and surrounded by a sea of ragwort and stinging nettles.

'What's behind there?' I asked.

Mum brightened. 'The walled garden,' she said and pushed the gate open. 'Come and see. Lady Evelyn and Shelby have a few secret trysts in here in my new book.'

I followed her inside.

'I love coming in here,' said Mum in a low voice.

'Why are you whispering?' I whispered.

'I don't know,' Mum whispered back. 'Why are you?'

'It's a whispering sort of place,' I whispered again and giggled. There was an inexplicable reverence here within the high walls – rather like being in church. 'Oh Mum – it's wonderful!'

Mum pointed to a sturdy-looking wooden bench. 'I sit over there for hours just thinking about my characters.'

Within the ivy-clad walls, wide borders were bounded by a perimeter path with two main central paths. One ran north to south, the other east to west, dividing the garden into four equal sections. A line of glasshouses stretched along one side. Behind them, hugging the boundary wall, were abandoned hothouse furnaces, potting sheds, tool rooms, and a henhouse. Despite the abject neglect and knee-high weeds, it was easy to imagine how achingly beautiful the garden would have been in its prime.

'They grew peaches in the middle glasshouse,' said Mum. 'Take a look.'

Inside stood rows of slatted benches, broken clay pots, and the remains of a solitary withered vine clinging to the red brickwork. Most of the glass panes were cracked or broken. A dozen or so hens were wandering around, scratching for grubs.

'These Victorian glasshouses are really valuable,' I said. 'People pay a fortune to have them these days.'

'The last glasshouse used to be an orangerie.

They were all heated, of course. What a job it must have been, carting the coal back and forth.'

'Yes,' I said.

'There used to be five gardeners here after the war,' Mum went on. 'Can you imagine them busily weeding, digging, sowing, washing, trimming, bunching, carrying the vegetables to the house?'

'And you'd be the one getting up before dawn to light the grate,' I reminded her.

Three ancient hand-drawn water barrows were parked in front of an abandoned trellis partially covered by a grapevine. 'There are grapes on here, Mum,' I said, taking a closer look.

'They used to make their own wine.'

In one corner, steps led down to a beehive-shaped building partially below ground.

'That's the icehouse,' Mum enthused. 'Gayla told me that Harry called it his secret underground bunker.'

'I think I'll try calling that taxi company again when we get back,' I said. 'Just to make sure they picked Gayla up.'

'I'm sure if something has happened we'll soon know about it.'

Only the far corner had been reclaimed from the wild. Runner beans flourished on three rows of pitched bamboo canes; cucumbers grew under glass frames; strawberries, under hoops, were covered with plastic; and there was a wire cage filled with raspberry canes. Against one wall, shoulder-high tomato plants staked in clay pots were bowing over with rich, red fruit

'Your father would have loved it here,' said Mum. 'He loved his allotment, didn't he?'

'Yes, he did, Mum.'

We were quiet for a few moments. Remembering. I tried to lighten the mood.

'Did you enjoy William's strawberries?' I said. 'I wonder if he actually melted the chocolate himself. Do you think he's the domestic type?'

'I threw them out.'

I laughed. 'Why?'

'I didn't know where his hands had been.'

'Were his eyes liquid pools filled with blatant lust or green with pound signs?'

'Very funny,' said Mum. 'I told you, I'm using William for research purposes. I just wanted to see what his fingers felt like on my skin so I could describe it.'

'And?'

'Rough. His hands were like a grater. Now I know what it feels like to be a piece of cheese.'

We returned to the service road and headed toward the Hall. Glimmers of sparkling white flashed in and out of the trees. I pointed to a cluster of whitewashed wooden beehives in a clearing.

'Remind me to give you some honey to take back to London,' said Mum.

The lane passed by the archway, that opened into a smart stable yard. 'Through here,' Mum said, leading the way. 'You'll like this.'

Built around a stone courtyard, three sides of the quadrant housed four loose boxes each with the fourth side being divided by a second archway topped with the dovecote and clock. Horses peered over green painted split-stable doors.

Mum was right. I felt instantly happy. 'How lovely!'

I walked straight up to a pretty chestnut mare peering over the half door and stroked her nose. Her name plaque said TINKERBELL. 'You're beautiful.' She nudged my hand for a treat. 'I should have brought a carrot or something.'

Mum said suddenly, 'I'm sorry we couldn't afford to buy you a horse. Your father wanted to.'

'He did?' I was surprised. 'He was always complaining about taking me to the stables.'

'He looked into it but living in London–' She shrugged. 'Where would you keep it? In a potting shed on the allotment?'

We cut through the yard and under the archway to find William, stripped to the waist, hosing down a big black horse tied to a rail in the paddock. William gave us a nod of acknowledgement.

'Good grief,' said Mum, turning pink and giving a wave. 'I've never seen him with his shirt off.'

'Good grief, indeed,' I echoed.

Despite his age, William's physique was hard and toned. He still sported a six-pack. I couldn't help thinking of David, who – years younger – had a potbelly and an aversion to any form of physical exercise.

'Wait a moment.' Mum pulled a Dictaphone out of the pocket of her harem pantaloons and hit the record button. *'Rippling muscles. Cherry-red sensual lips. Droplets of water like diamonds of morning dew.'*

'Long, tapered thighs encased in impossibly tight jeans,' I added.

Sensing an audience, William deliberately flexed his muscles and Mum and I started giggling like teenagers. We waved again and continued on our way.

Our trek finally brought us to the rear of the Hall. Here, it was easier to see the different architectural periods. A series of exposed wooden beams hinted at a Tudor beginning. It was as if the Hall kept being swallowed up by bigger and more fashionable additions as time went by.

'There is a secret tunnel somewhere,' said Mum. 'It's supposedly three hundred feet long, very narrow, very steep, and very dark.'

'How do you know?'

'It's in the local history books,' said Mum quickly. 'Oh, and the sunken garden is rumored to be haunted by a lady in a blue dress called Lady Frances. She was a Royalist. The ladies of Honeychurch Hall held out for a year whilst their men went off to fight Cromwell.' Mum thumped her chest. 'Can't you feel the history of the place? Can't you just feel it *here?*'

'Yes,' I said. 'I can.' And I could.

Extensive grounds stretched to the south in a confusion of neglected box hedges and ghosts of topiaried shapes. Spectacular formal gardens and overgrown flower borders rolled toward a shimmer of blue – the River Dart.

We followed a weed-infested gravel path through a wild rose garden, continued under a wire-hoop pergola consumed by purple-flowering clematis and fragrant honeysuckle, and reached the grand Palladian front entrance to the Hall.

I rang the doorbell – a rusted pull-down iron contraption – and waited.

'Perhaps it's not working,' I said.

'Do you think we should curtsey when we're introduced to the earl?'

'He's not royalty, Mum,' I said. 'He's just a normal person with a title.'

Mum looked worried. 'But we're not gentry, are we? Perhaps we should have gone around the back to the servant's entrance.'

'Didn't you meet him when you bought the Carriage House?'

'I told you I didn't. I went through a land agent called Laney.'

Suddenly, Mum turned away from the front door.

'Where are you going?' I demanded.

'I've changed my mind. What if the dowager countess is there?'

'If she is, then you can be formally introduced,' I said.

'No. No, I don't think so.'

I grabbed Mum's good arm. 'Relax, we're just going for coffee – not to the Tower of London.' I'd never seen her so nervous.

There was a rattle of chains and the sound of a key being turned in a lock. The door began to open.

'Here we go,' said Mum tightly. 'This is it.'

Chapter Eight

Cropper the butler was a dapper man in his late seventies with oiled, thinning gray hair and who reeked of mothballs. He was dressed in formal butler attire of starched collar, gray-striped

105

trousers, and tails.

'We're here to see Lord Honeychurch,' I said. 'This is my mother, Iris Stanford and I'm Katherine.'

'Good morning,' he said. 'Do come this way. His lordship is expecting you.'

We stepped into an inner front porch that bore a huge gilt mirror on one side beneath which stood a rarely seen nineteenth-century elephant-foot umbrella stand.

I pointed to the umbrella stand and whispered, 'Remember that game we used to play on long car journeys? *I went to the shop and I bought an elephant's foot umbrella stand.* None of my friends had ever heard of it. What was wrong with *I Spy?*'

'So you *did* have friends,' said Mum. 'You always said you didn't have any.'

Cropper motioned for us to follow him and we proceeded – at glacial speed – into a magnificent two-story galleried reception area. A huge crystal chandelier hung suspended between two domed-glass atriums. Shafts of morning sunlight illumin-ated patches of damp, cobwebs, and crumbling plasterwork.

The floor was a chessboard pattern of black-and-white marble. Full-bodied suits of armor were arranged randomly throughout the hall. Small gold nameplates identified the family portraits that lined the walls. On the right, below each oil painting stood a seventeenth-century Dutch walnut marquetry side chair inlaid with flowers, foliage, parrots, and urns. I knew at once that the furniture scattered throughout were valuable an-tiques – most likely handed down from generation to generation. The set of Dutch side chairs would fetch enough to repair the Carriage House roof alone.

Interspersed between the chairs were Victorian pedestal plant stands on top of which sat aspidistras that – on closer inspection – were plastic and coated in dust.

'I wonder how many staff work here,' said Mum, taking in her surroundings with nothing short of awe.

'Not enough to do all the dusting,' I murmured.

Cropper stopped – he may not be fast on his feet but his hearing was sharp. 'Just the three of us work at the Hall, madam.'

'Three!' said Mum aghast. 'The place is enormous.'

'Most of the house is closed off these days,' said Cropper. 'But when my father was butler here before the war, we had twelve live-in staff and five gardeners.'

'You've lived here all your life, Mr. Cropper?' I asked politely, hoping he didn't notice Mum barking into her Dictaphone, *Twelve servants.*

'I was born here,' said Mr. Cropper. 'So was my wife, Mrs. Cropper. Everyone in the area used to work on the estate whether it was in the house, the gardens, or on the land. At one time there were three large farms – all sold off now.'

'I met Vera Pugsley, the housekeeper, yesterday,' I said.

'Yes. Her mother was the housekeeper before her, and her *grandmother* was lady's maid to the dowager countess, Lady Edith.'

I looked at Mum to see if she'd recorded that snippet of information but she seemed preoccupied with an ornate portrait hanging over the vast marble fireplace. The nameplate said:

LADY EDITH HONEYCHURCH,
NOVEMBER 10, 1950.

'That's Lady Edith on her twenty-first birthday,' said Cropper.

'She was very beautiful,' I said.

Lady Edith was wearing a strapless sapphire-blue evening gown. She had dark blue eyes and pale skin – a classic English rose. Her brown hair was swept off her face in finger waves. Most striking was the exquisite seed pearl necklace with a delicate leaf motif and matching drop earrings.

Mum, stepped up to take a closer look. 'What unusual pearls.'

'They were presented to her ladyship on her coming-of-age birthday,' said Cropper. 'They have been in the family since Elizabeth I.'

'Seed pearls were often given to young women to symbolize purity and innocence,' I whispered. 'I'll tell you more about them later.'

Mum whipped out her Dictaphone, *Elizabeth I. Pearls. Purity.*

At the end of the gallery Cropper stopped in front of a closed paneled door and said, 'Please wait here a moment.' He slipped inside.

'I hope you're not going to use your Dictaphone in front of the earl,' I said.

'Did you notice the same pearl necklace was worn in all the female portraits?' said Mum.

'How fascinating. I must use that in my book.'

Cropper reappeared and stood aside to allow us to pass into the library where an English setter sprawled in front of the fireplace fast asleep.

'Mrs. Iris Stanford and Miss Katherine Stanford,' Cropper announced, 'The Earl Grenville, Lord Rupert Honeychurch–'

'Oh for heaven's sake, Cropper, just plain Rupert will do,' said Rupert. He pointed to the dog. 'And this is Oliver. He's deaf, I'm afraid.'

Rupert was a good-looking man in his early fifties, slightly balding with a trim military mustache. Dressed in beige cords and a yellow shirt under a green tweed jacket he seemed the epitome of an English country gentleman – far removed from the impatient driver I'd seen yesterday in the black Range Rover.

Mum had already dropped into a deep curtsey and, to both our embarrassment, had to lean on me to get up.

'What on earth happened to you, Iris – may I call you Iris?'

'Yes. Please do. I had a car accident, your lordship ... sir, I mean Mr. Rupert,' Mum said, flustered.

'What bad luck.' Turning to me he added, 'And this is the lovely Katherine? You look very familiar. Have we met before?'

'Yes. My car was blocking the entrance to the driveway last night.'

Rupert flushed. 'I'm sorry. I was in rather a hurry. You must think me frightfully rude.' With an ill-disguised leer he added, 'I'll just have to make it up to you, won't I?'

'I'm sure I'll survive,' I said dryly.

'Katherine is on the telly,' said Mum with a hint of pride. *'Fakes & Treasures.'*

Rupert snapped his fingers. 'You're Rapunzel! Rapunzel of "the Big Sneeze."'

'I warned her that dress was too tight,' said Mum. 'The press reported there were fifty buttons but there were actually only thirty-four,' said Mum. 'I know, because I sewed them all back on.'

'I'm sure Rupert has better things to do than talk about my buttons,' I said.

He winked at me and said, 'I doubt it.'

'Will you require some light refreshments m'lord?' said Cropper.

'Of course. I was forgetting my manners. Coffee? Tea? Sherry?'

Mum brightened. 'Sherry–'

'Coffee will be fine.' I answered for the both of us.

Cropper withdrew from the library.

'Do sit down.' Rupert led Mum toward the burgundy leather Chesterfield sofa. On the carpet lay an animal skin. 'Watch the tiger.'

'Oh goodness! It's real!' Mum cried.

'No, very much dead, I'm happy to say,' said Rupert. 'One of my ancestors was into big-game hunting.'

'No, I meant the tiger skin and Elinor Glyn,' said Mum. ' *"Would you like to sin: With Elinor Glyn: On a tiger skin? Or would your prefer: To err with her: On some other fur?"* How exciting. I believe she stayed at Honeychurch Hall a few times.'

'You know a little history about our house, I see,' said Rupert. 'Yes, Elinor Glyn often came here in the naughty nineties, as they were known. There were all sorts of wild parties.'

Mum shot me a look of triumph that said, *I told you so.* We sat down on the Chesterfield and Rupert took a cracked leather wingback chair.

The library was beautiful – a man's domain. The walls were papered with marbled pages from old books. The room smelled of cigars. One entire wall sported a mahogany floor-to-ceiling bookcase filled with leather-bound sets. I was itching to take a look and see if there were any first editions.

Heavy dark crimson brocade curtains framed the two casement windows that looked over the parkland toward the ornamental lake and white angel memorial that seemed jarring when viewed from the house.

A captain's chair stood behind a walnut partners desk. Oil paintings of animals – stags, dead pheasants, and shot rabbits – cluttered every empty wall space.

On top of a long mahogany dresser were display cases filled with carefully posed stuffed animals – a Victorian hobby that I never really liked or understood – badgers, foxes, ferrets, an owl, and various birds of prey. One glass case held a particularly gruesome bloodstained hawk.

Mum nudged me and whispered, 'You see that last case on there? It's the mummified hawk from the Crimea.'

'Well, what do you think about Sawmill Cottage?' Rupert said hopefully.

'Sawmill Cottage?' Mum frowned. 'What about Sawmill Cottage?'

111

'Didn't Lavinia mention it to you?'

'She mentioned it to me,' I said. 'But I thought you could tell us what is going on.'

'What *is* going on?' said Mum.

'I'm afraid there has been a terrible mistake,' said Rupert. 'My mother – Lady Edith – should never have put the Carriage House up for sale. She's eighty-four and suffers from early dementia. Dreadful business.'

'I don't understand,' said Mum, looking to me for an explanation but I was none the wiser. 'I've already bought the Carriage House.'

'Through a sealed bid, I believe,' said Rupert.

'Yes, and through an estate agent,' Mum said. 'It was advertised in *Country Life* magazine.'

'Ah, that would be Laney & Laney.' Rupert nodded gravely. 'I thought as much. Old man Laney will do anything my mother asks. The thing is ... it's vital that we keep the estate together. It's been in the Honeychurch family for six hundred years. It's my son Harry's legacy, you see.'

Mum's jaw dropped. 'You want me to sell it *back?*'

'No, nothing like that,' said Rupert quickly. 'We'd like you to have Sawmill Cottage instead, Iris. A simple switch.'

'A *switch?*' Mum cried.

'My mother isn't one of your tenants,' I said.

'Of course not,' said Rupert. 'But Sawmill Cottage has central heating, a lovely view of the village green, and a pretty garden. Given your mother's age and physical condition... Frankly, you've got yourself a bargain.'

'I don't want Sawmill Cottage,' said Mum

112

coldly. 'And there is nothing wrong with my physical condition. Eric Pugsley is responsible for all these injuries.'

Even though I wanted Mum to move, I didn't like Rupert's patronizing attitude. I had a sudden thought. 'Vera and Eric are under the impression that you promised the Carriage House to them. That's hardly keeping the estate together.'

Rupert stiffened. 'I have no idea why either of them would think that.'

'Eric Pugsley has been trying to force me to leave,' said Mum. 'He closed off the tradesman's entrance with razor wire and threatened to ... threatened to *shoot* me for trespassing—'

I regarded Mum with surprise and suspected that threat to be an exaggeration. 'What if my mother had needed an ambulance?'

'Exactly!' said Mum, eyes blazing. 'And every night Pugsley turns off the water valve so we don't have any water. And this morning, he was using that awful crushing machine. On a Saturday! It's harassment, I tell you.'

'Eric has a permit for the car crusher from the district council,' said Rupert mildly. 'And it sounds like the right-of-way was a simple misunderstanding that can soon be remedied. But as for the water valve...' Rupert shrugged. 'Since he does lease that field, you'll just have to reason with him.'

'Reason with Eric Pugsley?' Mum exclaimed.

I appealed to Rupert. 'He's your tenant. Can't *you* talk to him?'

'And whilst you're at it, ask him about those old cars? The field is full of scrap metal and tires...'

fumed Mum.

'Surely that's an environmental hazard,' I said.

'And a hearse!' Mum chimed in. 'Eric has parked it in full view of my window. If that's not a death threat, I don't know what is.'

'Don't be so dramatic, Mother,' I whispered.

'Eric's banger racing enterprise is very popular during the summer,' said Rupert.

'Banger racing?' Mum said faintly.

'And naturally he shares the profits with the estate.'

'You mean, with *you*,' I said.

'Yes, the first weekend of every month,' Rupert went on. 'Surely you knew about his business dealings when the property went up for sale, Iris?' When Mum didn't answer, Rupert added, 'That's why I really feel that Sawmill Cottage would be much nicer – and quieter. I'm just trying to be helpful.'

'What's this about Sawmill Cottage?'

'Mother!' Rupert jumped to his feet as Lady Edith, dressed in a midnight-blue riding habit swept into the room followed by a highly energetic Mr. Chips.

Mum and I jumped to our feet, too.

'I thought you were out riding!' said Rupert.

'You thought wrong,' said Lady Edith. 'Cropper informed me we had guests.'

The dowager countess seemed even smaller on foot but just as formidable. Although her face was heavily lined and she could benefit from a trip to the dentist, Lady Edith was still a beautiful woman.

Mum gave another awkward curtsey but Lady

Edith took no notice of us; however, Mr. Chips did and made continuous lunges at Mum's purple pantaloons, barking like a maniac.

'For goodness' sake, Mother,' said Rupert. 'Can't you control that dog?'

'Mr. Chips!' commanded Lady Edith. 'Here! Sit down. Now.' The Jack Russell obeyed instantly. Lady Edith regarded Mum and me with suspicion. 'Who are these people and why are they here?'

I stepped forward and offered my hand. 'I'm Katherine Stanford and this is my mother, who has just bought the Carriage House.'

Lady Edith broke into a yellow-toothed smile. 'Ah, yes. Good. I trust you will be happy there.'

'So there *isn't* a problem with the Carriage House after all?' I said. 'Rupert–'

'Of course there isn't,' said Rupert quickly.

Mum and I exchanged looks of confusion.

'What has my son been saying now?' Lady Edith demanded.

'A simple misunderstanding,' blustered Rupert. 'All sorted.'

'I suppose my son also told you that I was losing my mind and should be locked in a lunatic asylum?'

'Don't be ridiculous, Mother,' said Rupert.

'Have you offered our guests some refreshments, Rupert?'

'I asked Cropper to bring us some coffee,' said Rupert tightly. 'But don't feel you have to stay.'

'And miss more of your lies?' Lady Edith sat down primly on the edge of a wingback chair. Her back was so straight I wondered if she was wearing a corset, too.

There was an ugly silence.

'You've got a beautiful home,' said Mum suddenly. 'So much ... history. We were admiring the family portraits – especially the one of you wearing that beautiful necklace and earrings. We would love to see them, wouldn't we, Katherine?'

Lady Edith's eyes practically bugged out. 'I *beg* your pardon?'

'Perhaps another time,' I said hastily then whispered, 'Not now, Mum.'

'The seed pearls were stolen, unfortunately,' said Rupert, seemingly relieved to steer the subject into safer waters. 'Along with a few valuable paintings.'

'But wait,' said Mum, turning to me. 'You should get David on the case.' Mum beamed. 'Katherine's *fiancé* David Wynne flies all over the world recovering stolen art and antiques. I'm sure he could help.'

'How very interesting,' Lady Edith said. 'However, the police did all they could, thank you.'

'I think it's all a bit passé, now,' said Rupert. 'They were stolen years ago. Probably gone to America where everything seems to end up these days.'

'But perhaps your fiancé could look into my missing Meissen snuff boxes – in particular, the one with an elephant painted on the lid,' said Lady Edith suddenly. 'If, indeed, they *are* missing and not just squirreled away in my son's bedroom.'

Rupert bristled. 'I keep telling you to call the police if you're that worried.'

There was another awkward silence. Lady

Edith's gaze rested on Mum and me. I smiled politely.

'Rupert?' said Lady Edith. 'Who are these people and why are they here?'

I was momentarily taken aback. 'I'm–'

'You've already asked them, Mother,' said Rupert, shooting me a pained expression. 'Mrs. Stanford has just bought the Carriage House. Remember?'

'No. I do not remember,' said Lady Edith. 'But I trust you will be happy there.'

It was a relief when the library door opened and Cropper shuffled in with Vera. She was carrying a silver tray bearing bone china cups and saucers, a coffeepot, milk jug, and a bowl of sugar cubes with delicate silver tongs.

I hardly recognized her. Dressed in a plain black, long-sleeved dress and with her hair drawn severely up into a tight knot, Vera seemed like a different person. Gone were the leather trousers, plunging V-neck top, and Louboutin shoes. Instead she wore sensible pumps and no makeup.

'Vera, do see to our guests,' said Lady Edith.

Vera set the silver tray on the coffee table and poured each of us a cup as Cropper, with pain-staking slowness, passed them around.

Vera followed up by offering milk and sugar. When she got to me she gave a polite smile. 'Do you take sugar, madam?' There was no sign of the hysterical woman I'd met near the dustbins last night.

'No, thank you,' I said.

'And you, Mrs. Stanford?'

'Oh, there you are, Edith.' Lavinia entered the

library dressed in jodhpurs and an open-necked white shirt that looked in desperate need of a good ironing. Her hair was clamped under a thick hairnet. 'William had Tinkerbell tacked up for you ages ago. You know how she hates standing around.'

'I'm perfectly aware of Tinkerbell's temperament and – oh.' She stopped midsentence and frowned. Gesturing to Mum and me, she added, 'Who are these people, Rupert, and why are they here?'

Rupert rolled his eyes and stirred his coffee furiously.

'Mrs. Stanford has bought the Carriage House,' said Vera, surprisingly gently. 'And this is her daughter, Katherine. You might have seen her before because she's on television.'

'How lovely.' Lady Edith turned back to me and winked. And then I realized. She knew exactly what was going on. To her, it was all a big game.

'I'll take a cup, too, Cropper. I'm *parched.*' Lavinia took a seat opposite us. 'Did you tell them about Sawmill Cottage, Rupert?'

'Shut up!' hissed Rupert, gesturing to his mother.

'Sorry.' Lavinia reddened and then added with forced gaiety, 'Has anyone seen Harry? I've been looking for him all morning.'

'Surely he's with Nanny?' said Lady Edith.

'I'm afraid Gayla's gone, m'lady.' Vera leaned down and whispered into Ladyship's ear.

'Oh, that's just too bad,' said Lady Edith. 'I did like her.'

'We all liked her, Edith.' Lavinia gave a heavy sigh. 'But we can't have a thief in the house. For-

118

tunately Vera caught her red-handed.'

'Did she have the Meissen – the one with the elephant?' asked Lady Edith hopefully.

'No, it's still missing,' said Vera.

'I must say Gayla didn't seem the light-fingered type,' Lady Edith said.

'And what is the light-fingered *type*, Mother?' said Rupert.

'Your first wife. I know she took my pearls.'

'The pearls were stolen in the robbery as you know very well,' said Rupert.

'She had ideas above her station, didn't she, Vera?' Lady Edith went on.

'That's right, m'lady,' said Vera, pointedly looking at Lavinia.

'We shouldn't speak ill of the dead,' mumbled Lavinia.

'And we're reminded of the dead every day with that hideous stone angel. I don't know what you were thinking, Rupert,' said Lady Edith. 'What was her name? Kylie? Carly?'

'*Kelly,*' Rupert snapped.

Catching a spiteful gleam in Lady Edith's eye I realized it wasn't just my own mother who played the forgotten name card.

'Where *is* Harry?' said Lavinia desperately. 'He must have run off somewhere.'

'We'd love to meet him,' I said, and then wondered if Harry would let on that he and I had already met. The morning was rapidly turning into a farce.

'It's so tiresome getting him ready for boarding school,' said Lavinia. 'We have to drive *all* the way to Plymouth this afternoon to get to the *only* department store which stocks his school uniform and–'

'Never mind,' said Rupert. 'Soon you won't have to bother about him at all.'

Lavinia reddened again. 'That's not what I meant and you know it.'

'I'll go and look for Master Harry.' Vera excused herself.

'And what about tonight, Rupert?' Lavinia went on. 'We need to find a babysitter unless you can cancel your plans. Vera has the night off.'

'I am not canceling my plans,' said Rupert.

'Well, Edith and I can't cancel our plans, either,' said Lavinia. 'She's on the sidesaddle committee and this is the last meeting before next month's event.'

'Get William to drive her there,' said Rupert. 'I'm sure he'd love to do that. He'll do anything for Mother.'

Mum and I exchanged looks. It was as if we weren't sitting there at all. I wondered if this was how servants had felt back in the day – invisible.

Mum suddenly said, 'Kat is good with children. I'm sure she'd love to babysit Harry.'

'Mum!' I was horrified.

'That would be *frightfully* kind,' gushed Lavinia. 'Oh, there you are, Harry.' Harry, in flying helmet and goggles perched on top of his head, sauntered in with Vera.

'He said he was on one of his missions, m'lady,' said Vera indulgently. 'Top secret.'

'At ease, Squadron Leader Bigglesworth,' said Rupert. 'Come and meet our guests, Mrs. Stanford and her daughter, Katherine.'

Harry gave his father a snappy salute and greeted Mum and me with a formal, 'How do you do.' To my relief, he made no indication that we'd met the day before and neither did I.

'You shouldn't encourage him to play that silly game, Rupert,' said Lavinia.

'Give him a break, Lav. Let him enjoy his last few days of freedom.'

'And don't call me Lav. I'm not a public convenience – oh!'

The library door flew open and a lanky man in his mid thirties with a mop of curly brown hair strode in. He wore a vintage beige trench coat – an odd choice given the sunny weather – over light brown trousers and an open-neck khaki military shirt.

The newcomer seemed highly agitated. 'Sorry for the intrusion,' he said as Mr. Chips bounded toward him, yelping with excitement.

Cropper, who had been standing in the corner possibly having a nap, snapped to attention. Clearing this throat he said, 'Detective Inspector–'

'You can't just burst in like this, Shawn,' said Lavinia.

'It's Detective Inspector today,' he said. 'Police business.'

'On a *Saturday?* Why? Whatever's happened?' said Lavinia.

'I'm afraid I have some bad news.' Shawn paused as we all turned expectantly toward him. I felt as if Mum and I were part of an unfolding soap opera.

'It's about your nanny, Gayla Tarasova,' said Shawn. 'We received a phone call this morning from Nannies-Abroad. Gayla never caught the train last night.'

A twinge of foreboding swept over me.

Shawn took a deep breath and said, 'I'm afraid she's been reported as missing.'

Chapter Nine

'As you know, the first twenty-four hours are crucial.' Shawn helped himself to a cup of coffee but as he plopped in a cube of sugar, it fell to the floor. Surprisingly, Vera made no sound of protest – even when he vigorously ground the granules into the carpet with the heel of his shoe.

Disheveled didn't begin to describe Shawn's appearance. What looked suspiciously like dried egg had dribbled down the front of his shirt. Noticing mismatched socks and scuffed brown shoes, I suspected the police officer lived alone.

'Don't you think you're overreacting a bit, old chap,' said Rupert. 'Gayla only left last night. She might have stopped off to see a friend.'

Harry's face was creased with concern. 'What's happened to Gayla?'

'Nothing. He shouldn't be here.' Lavinia stood up and held out her hand to Harry. 'Come along–'

'Yes, but I'd rather you stayed, m'lady.' Shawn retrieved a moleskin notebook and pencil from inside his trench coat. 'Lady Edith, would you mind taking Harry from the room? I don't think you're under suspicion.'

'That's a pity,' Lady Edith said dryly. She rose to her feet. 'Come along, my pet.'

'Why is Gayla missing?' said Harry, in a querulous voice. 'Is she lost?'

'Let's go to the stables.' Lady Edith took Harry's hand and they left the library with Mr. Chips trotting along obediently behind them.

Lavinia turned on Shawn furiously. 'See what you've done? Harry's got a vivid enough imagination as it is.' She sat back down in a huff.

'Should we leave?' I said to Mum.

'No, I need you all to stay here – oh!' Shawn turned beetroot red. 'It's – you're – Rapunzel, I mean Ms. Stanford. Your hair...'

'Please call me Kat,' I said.

Shawn broke into a dimpled smile, revealing a chipped front tooth. *'Fakes & Treasures*. My favorite show.'

'Told you so,' muttered Vera.

'And this is Detective Inspector Shawn Cropper,' Rupert said wearily. 'And yes, he *is* related to our butler and cook.'

I glanced over at Cropper who appeared to have dozed off again, carefully wedged in the corner of the room with each elbow resting on a bookshelf.

'My grandparents,' said Shawn.

It certainly explained why everyone was on first-name terms.

'I've just bought the Carriage House,' Mum said.

'The *Carriage* House?' Shawn exclaimed. 'I thought Lady Edith swore she'd never break up the estate!'

123

'So did we.' Rupert checked his watch. 'Can we just get on with this, Shawn? Gayla did not catch her train. So what?'

'Obviously you've never had to deal with nannies, Shawn,' Lavinia put in.

'Some of us can't afford them, m'lady,' said Shawn.

'They're all alike,' Lavinia went on. 'Unreliable, flighty–'

'Gayla Tarasova is the daughter of a high-profile Russian industrialist,' said Shawn.

'He's a *what?*' said Rupert.

'She didn't mention it when I interviewed her.' Vera reddened.

'Her father was waiting for her at Paddington Station last night but she wasn't on the train. He phoned Nannies-Abroad and they immediately alerted the police.'

Lavinia seemed equally taken aback. 'Who is Nannies-Abroad? What's wrong with our regular agency?'

'I wanted to try somewhere new,' said Vera defensively.

'But don't we pay Knightsbridge Nannies a monthly retainer?' said Lavinia.

Vera looked down at her feet and didn't comment.

'How long had Gayla been working here, m'lady?' Shawn asked.

Lavinia shrugged. 'I don't know, about three months.'

'And why do you think she left after such a short time?'

'Perhaps you should ask Mrs. Stanford.'

Lavinia's cold gray eyes rested on my mother. 'Didn't she spend a lot of time with you?'

Mum looked startled. 'Not really. I've only lived here for three weeks.'

'According to Gayla, she visited you every day when Harry was off riding. I knew the little minx was up to something.' She shot Rupert a filthy look. 'And we all know what that was.'

'Don't look at me,' Rupert protested. 'You should ask Eric. He's the one who attracts the ladies not me.'

Vera opened her mouth to protest but seemed to change her mind.

'I've had two or three conversations with her, that's all, although...' Mum frowned. 'She mentioned a friend called Anna.'

'Anna?' Shawn scribbled in his pad. 'Any last name?'

'No, I got the impression they'd come to England together.'

'From Nannies-Abroad?' Shawn asked.

'I didn't think to ask.'

'Gayla always acted as if she was better than the rest of us,' Vera said. 'And she refused to do Harry's laundry or lift a finger in the kitchen – and then I caught her red-handed, helping herself to one of Lady Edith's snuff boxes.'

'And when was this?' said Shawn.

'Yesterday afternoon at around three o'clock. I found her on the landing opening one of the credenzas.'

'Doesn't Lady Edith keep her collections under lock and key?' said Shawn. 'At least she used to when I was a kid.'

'I know what I saw,' Vera declared.

'So you *saw* Gayla actually taking a snuff box *out* of the credenza?' said Shawn. 'She wasn't, shall we say – just admiring it?'

'I found another one under the pillow in her room. It was very valuable,' Vera said. 'Meissen. From her wild animal collection.'

'And obviously you told Lady Edith?' Shawn tapped his pencil on his chipped tooth.

'No. I put it back,' said Vera.

'We try to protect my mother from domestic issues for obvious reasons,' Rupert said. 'She gets easily distressed – especially about her wretched snuff boxes.'

'I see.' Shawn continued to make copious notes. 'And what did Gayla say when you confronted her about the snuff box under her pillow?'

'She denied it, of course.' Vera paused before adding in an apologetic voice, 'I'm afraid she blamed it on Harry, m'lady.'

'Outrageous!' Lavinia cried. 'There was no question that Gayla had to go. I gave her a week's pay and purchased a single railway ticket – at *frightful* expense, I may add – to Paddington railway station.'

'We're already checking the CCTV footage at Plymouth and Paddington Stations.'

'Perhaps Gayla missed her train,' I suggested. 'When I spoke to her she was waiting for a taxi to take her to the railway station.'

'You *spoke* to her?' Shawn dropped his pencil and had to stoop to pick it up. 'What time was this?'

'Around six-thirty,' I said.

126

'No one offered to give her a lift to the station?' said Shawn.

Lavinia flushed and muttered something about horses.

'Did she mention the name of the company?' Shawn asked me.

'Bumble-Bee Cars,' I said. 'I called them later that evening to make sure that Gayla had been picked up, but I just got the answering machine. Perhaps the taxi didn't show up after all. I feel terrible.'

Mum put her hand on my knee and gave it a sympathetic squeeze.

'Or it did – and the driver had something to do with it,' Mum declared. 'You should find out, Officer.'

'We will,' Shawn said gravely. 'Thank you.'

'I bet Gayla hitched a lift,' said Rupert suddenly.

'From Cavalier Lane?' Lavinia sneered. 'Don't be ridiculous. It's a back road. Only locals know the shortcut.'

'Did Gayla say anything else, Ms. Stanford – Kat?'

'Well...' I hesitated. 'She did mention that my mother could be in danger.'

'*Danger?*' said Lavinia. 'What an extraordinary thing to say.'

'I told you Eric Pugsley was out to get me,' said Mum.

'My Eric said that?' Vera exclaimed. 'He wouldn't hurt a fly.'

'Do you remember what Gayla was wearing?' Shawn went on.

'Jeans, white ruffled shirt, and a turquoise bandana,' I said. 'She had a suitcase on wheels.'

'A *suitcase?*' said Rupert sharply.

'Of course she'd have a suitcase,' Lavinia said. 'She was leaving.'

'Color?' said Shawn.

'Pink,' I said. 'Or more of a fuchsia pink – wouldn't you say, Rupert?'

'*You* saw her at the top of the drive, too?' Shawn exclaimed. 'Why on earth didn't you say so?'

'I didn't see her,' said Rupert quickly. 'I was in a bit of a hurry.'

'I was blocking the entrance with my car,' I said. 'By the time I'd moved it, Gayla had disappeared.'

'Where were you going, m'lord?' Shawn asked.

'Good question,' Lavinia put in. 'I'd love to know since you missed supper.'

Rupert reddened. 'I – I–'

'Some sheep escaped,' said Vera smoothly. 'I got a phone call from a passing motorist. It happens all the time.'

'Wasn't William around to help you?' Shawn asked.

'He visits my mother at Sunny Hill Lodge on Friday evenings,' said Vera. 'As you know, she's got Alzheimer's.'

Was there no end to William's saintly gifts?

'Does it matter?' Rupert snapped. 'I heard Vera on the phone and I offered to help.'

Lavinia gave a snort of derision. 'That's a first.'

'And what time did you get back?' said Shawn, pencil poised.

'Around nine, I suppose. I went to the Hare & Hounds for a quick snifter,' said Rupert. 'Bumped into Eric, as a matter of fact. You should go and talk to him.'

'We intend to,' said Shawn.

Chuffah-chuffah-chuffah-chuffah.

'What's that noise?' said Mum, head cocked. 'Surely that can't be a train.'

The chuffing sound grew louder, drowning out all further conversation as Shawn fumbled in his pocket and withdrew his iPhone. 'Actually, it's the Scarborough Spa Express from Wakefield Westgate to Ardsley Tunnel,' he shouted as the ringtone reached its crescendo with a loud *whoop, whoop, whoop!*

Shawn hit the answer button, barked, 'D. I. Cropper here,' and walked over to the window to take the call.

Mum turned to me, highly amused, and mouthed the words, *'Whoop, whoop?'*

'Shawn's always been fascinated by trains,' said Lavinia dryly.

Despite the seriousness of the situation, I fought the urge to giggle. It all seemed surreal. Gayla hadn't even been missing for twenty-four hours and here was the local plod – with dried egg on his shirt – convinced of foul play. I couldn't imagine the Metropolitan Police conducting such an investigation.

We waited in silence whilst Shawn finished his phone call behind one of the brocade curtains. When he rejoined us, his expression was grave. 'Bad news, I'm afraid. Gayla's suitcase has been found but there is no sign of her.'

My stomach gave a lurch and Mum grabbed my hand. Suddenly, it was no laughing matter.

129

Lavinia bit her lip. 'Oh dear, you don't really think something frightful has happened, do you?'

'Let's hope not,' said Shawn.

'Where did you find this suitcase?' demanded Rupert.

'In the hedge along the bridleway to Cavalier Copse,' said Shawn. 'Tom from Home Farm found it concealed in the undergrowth.'

'Why would she leave it there?' Lavinia cried. 'How odd.'

'Perhaps it was deliberate,' said Vera. 'She didn't want to go back to London to see her dad because she knew she was in trouble for thieving. Maybe she's crying wolf.'

'Yes, I think Vera's right.' Rupert nodded in agreement. 'Did you find anything of interest in the suitcase?'

Shawn regarded Rupert thoughtfully. 'Just the usual effects. Why?'

'What I mean is—' Rupert hesitated. 'How do we know for sure it was Gayla's suitcase?'

'Oh for heaven's sake,' cried Lavinia. 'The poor girl is obviously in some kind of trouble. This is your fault, Vera. You and your meddling.'

'Mine?' Vera's mouth dropped.

Lavinia suddenly stood up. 'This is all frightfully distressing but frankly, I'm not sure what more we can do.'

'Quite right, quite right,' Rupert said. 'I think we've done all we can to assist you, Shawn. Life goes on and all that.'

Clearly we were all being dismissed.

'Right then,' said Shawn. 'I suppose I know

where to find you.'

Lavinia moved toward the library door. 'And Katherine, six o'clock sharp. Staff always eats in the kitchen.'

Mum and I trooped out after her.

'Kat!' Shawn called out. 'A quick word, please.'

We waited for him to join us and yes, I was right. It was definitely dried egg on his lapel.

'If I seem overzealous it's because nothing ever happens here – not that I'm making light of Ms. Tarasova's disappearance, you understand.' Shawn smiled. 'You are grockles–'

'*Grockles?*' I said.

'Tourists – I mean outsiders. Sorry.' Shawn looked sheepish. 'You may notice things that are unusual that we take for granted. If either of you think of anything else Gayla may have said – however insignificant – please call me on this number.'

Shawn pressed a business card into my hand and looked intensely into my eyes. His were dark brown with a speckle of gold freckles in the iris. Perhaps it was the steamy passage I'd just finished typing up from Mum's *Forbidden* but a tiny frisson of je ne sais quoi passed between us.

I actually blushed.

'Oh! Inspector, there *is* something I'd like to talk to you about.' Mum lowered her voice and beckoned us over to the window. 'It's about Eric Pugsley.'

'You think he may have something to do with the nanny's disappearance?' Shawn retrieved his notebook from his pocket and flipped it open.

'I wouldn't be surprised,' said Mum. 'But actually, this is about me. I'd like to file a complaint.'

'Not *now*, Mother,' I said, exasperated. 'Inspector, I apologize for–'

'Eric Pugsley has launched a vendetta against me,' Mum declared.

'But does this have anything to do with Gayla?'

'No, it does not,' I said firmly.

'But it could,' said Mum.

Shawn looked puzzled. 'Go on.'

'Pugsley wants me out of the Carriage House. He's been deliberately turning off my water supply.' She waved her cast. 'He did this, you know!'

'Mother–'

'And this!' Mum pointed at her bruised face.

'He attacked you?' said Shawn, appalled. *'Eric? Eric Pugsley?'*

'My mother is exaggerating, Inspector.'

'Pugsley parked a hearse in full view of my window and if that's not a death threat, I don't know what is.'

'Well, these are very serious allegations,' said Shawn.

'So you see, Pugsley is capable of violence,' said Mum.

Shawn nodded gravely. 'If you'd like to come down to the police station on Monday morning, we can take a statement.'

'Thank you, Inspector,' said Mum triumphantly. 'At least someone believes me. My daughter felt I was being overdramatic.'

Shawn gave a polite smile.

'And of course, if Kat remembers anything about Gayla, I will make sure she calls you immediately.'

'Yes. Please do.'

Mum beamed. 'Good. We will see you first thing on Monday morning – if not before.'

Chapter Ten

'You're impossible, Mother,' I said as we set off for home.

'That policeman seems a pleasant man. Nice sensual lips. I saw him give you that look. And no wedding ring.'

'He's twelve years old and had egg on his shirt. Definitely not my type.'

'You're just used to going out with old fogies.'

'And what about his phone ringtone?' I said. 'A *train?*'

'But not any old train, dear,' said Mum. 'The Scarborough Spa Express. If he's passionate about steam trains he'll make a steamy bedfellow.' She chortled at her own joke.

I groaned.

She clicked on her Dictaphone. *'He pressed his business card into her hands. His dark eyes searched her face for any sign of encouragement. A faint blush spread across her porcelain cheeks–'*

'Ha-bloody-ha,' I said dryly. 'You are so hilarious.'

'She was afraid to look at him. Afraid he would see her desire and find her lustful and wanton–'

'How can you be so frivolous at a time like this!'

133

'Nothing's happened to that young nanny,' said Mum with scorn.

'How do you know?'

'I saw her and Rupert in the Greek garden one afternoon – all huddled together, whispering and laughing.'

'You think they were having an affair?' I said.

'I wasn't sure until Lavinia mentioned how well – apparently – I knew Gayla,' said Mum. 'I was obviously some kind of alibi.'

'Why didn't you say so?'

'In front of Lavinia?' said Mum. 'I wouldn't do that. Besides, I don't have concrete proof and it's obvious she's besotted with her husband.'

'Lavinia? Besotted? With Rupert?' I exclaimed. 'You must be blind. She can't stand him.'

'There is a thin line between love and hate, you know that,' said Mum. 'I notice these details.'

'So why didn't you tell Shawn all this when we were alone – instead of talking about Eric Pugsley?'

'It's a good excuse for *you* to call him later.' Mum grinned mischievously.

'Stay out of my love life, please,' I said. 'In fact, stop interfering. I mean it. Why on earth did you say I'd babysit tonight?'

'Sorry about that,' said Mum sheepishly. 'It just came out.'

'And why did you say that David was my fiancé?'

'You're too old to have a boyfriend,' said Mum. 'Anyway, David *should* be your fiancé by now. How long have you been together?'

Fortunately we'd reached the white angel memorial and it was the perfect time to change the subject. Stray rose petals scattered on the grass reminded me of Lavinia's tantrum last night.

Cut like a Rose in Full Bloom
Only Good Night, My Beloved, Not Farewell
Kelly
July 31, 1982 – August 26, 2005

I studied the dates. 'Twenty-three years old. She was young. They couldn't have been married for very long. I wonder how she died.'

'She was stung by a bee,' said Mum.

'A *bee?*'

'That's what Muriel told me at the post office,' Mum said. 'Apparently Lord Honeychurch's first wife was allergic to bees. According to Muriel, Lady Kelly started life as one of the servants below stairs—'

'And she married Rupert! What a scandal!' I said. 'I bet that didn't go down well with the dowager countess.'

'They were star-crossed lovers,' Mum said wistfully. 'He was tied by the duties of his class and what was demanded of him by his cold, heartless mother—'

'Who, I noticed, also has a knack of getting names wrong just like you – Kylie, Carly, Kelly – Dylan, David?'

'Surely you're not accusing *me* of being cold and heartless?' Mum cried. 'We mothers just want to protect our own, that's all.'

'So you say.' I turned my attention back to the memorial. 'Wasn't yesterday the twenty-sixth of August?'

'Clever you,' said Mum. 'So it was.'

'That would make it the anniversary of Kelly's death.'

'How interesting,' Mum said. 'How old is Harry?'

'Seven next week – oh!' I exclaimed. 'I see what you mean. Rupert didn't waste any time marrying Lavinia, did he?'

'The classic rebound,' said Mum. 'And I suspect his lordship still loves his first wife. That angel memorial statue sticks out like a sore thumb.'

'Poor Lavinia. It must be a constant reminder,' I said. 'How awful knowing that your husband is still in love with someone else.'

'Poor Rupert,' said Mum. 'Losing the love of his life forever. Either way, their marriage is doomed.'

'And then there's Harry,' I added. 'Packed off to boarding school.'

'At least we didn't do *that* to you,' said Mum.

Back at the Carriage House, three boxes sat on the doorstep. 'Oh, good. Parcels!' Mum gestured for me to deal with them. 'I've been waiting for the postman.'

I picked up the first box, and then the second. 'These two are for Vera,' I said. 'Shoes and – oh – goodness, one box is from Ann Summers.'

'Isn't that something to do with sexy lingerie?' said Mum with delight. 'Let's open it and look.'

'No, we're not opening Vera's parcel!'

'I wonder why they've been delivered here?'

'Because that's the address on the label,' I said.

'I bet she doesn't want Eric to find out what she's been buying.'

'The third box is for you. Something from a

company called We-See-You!'

Mum beamed. 'That'll be the surveillance equipment.'

'I thought you were joking.'

'Your bedroom overlooks the cow field,' said Mum. 'We'll get William to install it this afternoon.'

'You can't install a camera.'

'Why not? The government has them everywhere...' Mum trailed off. 'I hope I'm not wrong about Gayla. You hear about these quiet country villages harboring serial killers.'

'All the more reason for you to come back to London,' I said.

'I told you I'm going to catch Eric out,' said Mum, changing the subject. 'I'll have evidence to support my complaint – and that's just the beginning of the end for old beetle-brows.'

'Alright,' I said grudgingly. 'But let's leave William out of this. *I* will install the camera.'

Carrying the three boxes into the kitchen, I said, 'I'll ring Vera and tell her to come and pick these up.'

'Would you mind?' said Mum, already heading upstairs. 'I must write something down before I forget.'

'I'll bring up lunch and my laptop and we'll get cracking,' I said. 'Presumably you don't have the Internet here.'

Mum paused, 'Do I look as if I would?'

'It's the twenty-first century. I'd like to see your website. It'll give me an idea of what your books are all about.'

'I don't get involved in that side of things,' said

137

Mum quickly.

'But you must have a website.'

'Why are you asking, Katherine?' Mum sounded irritated. 'Does it matter?'

'No, it doesn't *matter*, I was just curious. You must get a ton of fan mail.'

'I told you, the publisher handles that,' said Mum. 'Are you making egg sandwiches?'

'Eggs again?'

'Just watch the mayonnaise. You always put too much in.'

I boiled some eggs and made the sandwiches, found some crisps, a couple of apples, a bar of Cadbury's milk chocolate, and put the lot on the tray.

I knocked on the door to Mum's office and stepped into the gloom. The room was lit by one naked lightbulb. Mum was perched on a three-legged stool in front of the corkboard adding Post-its Notes to the Honeychurch family tree.

'Why on earth don't you have the curtains open and let the sunlight in?'

I set the tray on the top of the filing cabinet and moved to the window.

'Don't!' shouted Mum, but it was too late.

'Good grief.' I stared at the full horror of Eric's scrap yard in the field beyond. An old hearse was parked next to a wide band of raw tree stumps that marked the boundary line. Some of the stumps had pieces of paper pinned to the bark. 'What happened there?'

'I used to look out on a beautiful bank of old trees,' said Mum, joining me at the window. 'And then one day I came home from the shops and

Eric had cut the lot down.'

'That's terrible,' I said. 'Why would he do such a thing? Judging by the size of the stumps, they must have been pretty mature trees. What are those pieces of paper?'

Mum gave a bitter laugh. 'Of course I reported Eric to the council. They are restraining orders to prevent him from cutting down any more trees.'

'It's a bit late for that!'

'He just got a small fine.'

'Oh, Mum,' I said. 'It's going to be awful here when the banger racing starts. If you're determined to stay in Little Dipperton are you sure you don't want to look at Sawmill Cottage?'

Mum shook her head. 'Why would Lady Edith allow banger racing here? Do you think she really is losing her marbles?'

'Rupert seems to think so.'

'Did you notice how she kept repeating herself?' asked Mum.

'Yes, but afterward she winked at me.'

'No!' Mum exclaimed. 'Are you *sure?*'

'Frankly, I think Lady Edith knows exactly what she's doing. I think she just enjoys tormenting her son – rather like you enjoy tormenting me.'

'I'm such a terrible mother,' said Mum. 'I am surprised you still talk to me at all.'

'Let's eat,' I said. 'I'd like to get started on the typing since we are going to the hairdresser this afternoon and, thanks to you, I'm going *baby-sitting* tonight.'

'You said Harry was adorable,' said Mum. 'Just watch your purse.'

'You really think he's a thief?' I asked.

'So William implied as much. How much is one of those snuff boxes worth?'

'It depends. I've known some to reach six figures at auction.'

'You should sell snuff boxes in your new shop.'

'*Our* new shop,' I said. 'Oh Mum, please come back to London. How can you be happy here with all the drama?'

'But it's all so exciting. Have you any idea how bored I used to be?' Mum picked up a sandwich, took one bite, and pulled a face. 'Mayonnaise.'

As we ate our lunch I studied the corkboard in more depth. Mum had written, 'Seed pearls Elizabeth I,' on a Post-it next to EDITH ROSE B. NOVEMBER 10, 1927.

'You were going to tell me about the pearls,' said Mum.

'The official name is parure,' I said. 'Very popular in Elizabethan times and then again, in the eighteenth and nineteenth centuries. They were handed down from mother to daughter. Along with the necklace and earrings we saw in the portrait, there was often a corsage, a tiara, bracelets, rings, and brooches. Obviously far more valuable as a suite though I suspect it's been split up by now. Pity.'

I pointed to another Post-it: EDWARD RUPERT B. 1870 TITANIC. 'Did you know that after the *Titanic* sank in 1912, Steiff made six hundred special mourning bears to commemorate the tragedy?' I said. 'One sold for eighty thousand pounds at Christie's.'

'Yes, I know,' said Mum. 'You were there.' She

reached down and picked up a copy of the *Daily Post* from a basket at the foot of her chair. 'William brings me the morning newspapers.' She opened it to Trudy Wynne's wretched *Star Stalkers* column and pointed to a photo of me emerging from a janitor's cupboard. Someone had Photoshopped my handbag and replaced it with a floor mop. The caption read NO MORE *FAKES & TREASURES?* RAPUNZEL SWAPS HER SPINNING WHEEL FOR CINDER-ELLA'S BROOM.

'What on earth were you doing in the janitor's cupboard?' said Mum.

'Avoiding Trudy Wynne,' I said wearily.

'Hell hath no fury, dear,' Mum reached over and patted my knee. 'Just think that she wouldn't be doing that if she didn't feel you were a threat.'

'Threat for what? He left her – and don't start that again. I'm going to get my laptop.'

Moments later I was sitting at Mum's desk. 'It's going to be hard coming into the middle of the book when I don't know what's going on.'

'Just jump right on in,' said Mum. 'All I need you to do is type it up.'

'I might have comments.'

'I don't want your comments.'

'How will I print out the pages?' I said. 'Is there somewhere in Dartmouth? A printing place I can use?'

'I have no idea.' Mum yawned. 'Now you know why I don't have a computer. With a typewriter, you just type, pull out the paper, and it's done.'

There was little point in arguing.

Mum settled into the wingback armchair. 'I'm

going to take a nap.'

I read the first sentence and cringed. *Odors of sweat and love mingled with the smells of damp wood and sun-warmed grass. Inflamed with desire, Shelby the gamekeeper wanted to ravish her here, out in the open in broad daylight.*

'Mother,' I said. 'This is so corny.' But she didn't answer. I glanced over to find her eyes closed, snoring gently.

I read on. *He kissed and licked her salty neck, unable to get enough of her, not wanting to ever let her go. Lady Evelyn lay still, floating on a river of passion.*

'Leave the old earl,' he demanded. 'Come away with me.'

'I love you but you know I can't,' she whispered. 'I love my brother. It would break his heart.'

'Are we destined to meet in secret forever?' he said angrily.

She began to cry. 'Don't torment me, you know my life is here. I could never leave the Hall.'

A horse whinnied close by and there was a shout. 'Evelyn! Where are you? Are you in the spinney?'

Lady Evelyn turned white. 'It's my brother! God help us.' She scrambled to her feet, her face ashen. 'Quick, get Jupiter. We can never meet again.'

Mum's love scenes were steamy and extremely graphic yet they had a compelling sensuality about them that made me hot and bothered. No wonder Mum didn't want Dad to know about this.

My thoughts drifted to David and our somewhat predictable sex life. When we first met we couldn't keep our hands off each other but not anymore.

Reading Lady Evelyn's adventures brought back those early days with David. Although I couldn't quite recall 'floating on a river of passion,' I vividly remembered a trip to New York City when we didn't leave our hotel room for five whole days. What had changed between us?

Mum awoke with a loud grunt. 'Goodness,' she said. 'What's the time?'

'Time to go to your hair appointment.'

'How are you getting on?'

'I think I need to take a cold shower,' I said. 'Seriously Mum, this is very hot stuff. I didn't know you had it in you.'

'Everyone was young once.'

As we shut the front door behind us and headed for the courtyard I said, 'By the way, you may want to do a word search on the phrase *peaked nipples*. I counted five in forty pages.'

'Pairs, I presume?' said Mum.

We took my Golf. I opened the corrugated iron gate and drove on through Eric's scrapyard. He was standing outside his caravan polishing the shiny red Massey Ferguson.

'I bet he's fiddling the books,' said Mum. 'Do you know how much those tractors cost?'

'No, but I suspect you do.'

'Tax evasion,' Mum declared. 'I'm sure of it. A nice hefty fine will take care of old beetle-brows.'

'Just be careful and remember that what goes around, comes around.'

'Tonight, we're setting up that surveillance camera,' said Mum. 'Pugsley won't know what's hit him.'

Chapter Eleven

We turned onto the narrow two-lane highway and joined a long stream of holiday traffic crawling toward Dartmouth.

'This is painful,' I said. 'We'll never get there in time.'

Finally we crested the brow of the hill where the magnificent building, home to the Britannia Royal Naval College, afforded a spectacular view of the fishing port below.

'Agatha Christie had a summer home called Greenway just up the river from here,' said Mum. 'I'm thinking of volunteering for the National Trust as a docent.'

'I think you should wait until you're looking better,' I said. 'You don't want to frighten the tourists.'

As we inched our way down the hill, colorful bunting was strung between the houses and shops and large banners pronounced it was Dartmouth Royal Regatta Week. The River Dart was full of all manner of sailing vessels and the entire town was heaving with activity.

Parked cars lined the narrow one-way streets. We passed three pay-and-display areas, but each one said PARKING LOT FULL. Pedestrians spilled off the pavements and walked in the road without a care.

'We'll never park,' I grumbled as yet another

wave of people ambled across in front of our car. I slammed my hand hard on the horn garnering more than a few glares. 'Oh, for heaven's sake! This is worse than London.'

'No wonder!' Mum tapped the dashboard. 'Where's our lucky mascot? Where's Jazzbo? Don't you always keep him up here?'

Mum's comment on Harry being light-fingered hit me afresh. I hesitated, wondering if it was worth the lecture about being careful whom I loaned my things to and decided it wasn't.

'I left Jazzbo at the house,' I lied. 'I thought he'd like to hang out with some of his old furry friends.'

'Oh well, we'll have to do without him. Turn right on Mayor's Avenue.'

'But won't that take us away from the town?'

'We're parking in Marks and Sparks.'

We passed the police station and then turned into Marks & Spencer. Apart from six disabled parking spots, it, too, was packed. 'I knew this would be a waste of time.'

'You have to trust me, dear.' Mum reached down into her handbag and brought out a blue disabled parking placard. 'There are some perks to frightening the tourists.'

As we got out, a dirty Ford Focus zoomed into the empty space beside us, only narrowly missing my open door. Vera jumped out. Dressed in a short skirt and wedge heels, she, too, produced a blue disabled parking placard from her handbag and fixed it onto her rearview mirror.

'Hmm, great minds think alike,' I said to Mum.

'But I *am* disabled–'

Vera slammed the door then spotted us. With a quick nod of acknowledgement, she walked off with an affected limp.

'And Vera is not,' said Mum.

I grabbed my tote bag and double-checked I'd brought my laptop. I made sure to stand close to Mum's injury as we fought our way upstream to the hair salon in Zion Place.

Tucked down a side street, nestled between the Old Curiosity Shop and an art gallery, the salon was called – unimaginatively – Snipxx.

We walked in to be greeted by a sullen girl in her early twenties sporting leggings and a nose ring. A name tag pinned to a plunging V-neck top said STACEY and was embellished with star stickers.

Vera was already seated at one of the washbasins that lined the rear wall with her eyes closed.

'God! I hope I won't get stuck next to her all afternoon,' groaned Mum. 'If she mentions Pugsley once I'll scream.'

Mum was hustled into the changing room. I told her I'd collect her in an hour and a half and left the salon.

I looked into the diamond-leaded window of the Old Curiosity Shop. Inside, a handful of browsers poked and prodded around but I sensed no one was really interested in buying, which was no surprise. A glance at the price tag for six beaded curtain tassels was double that of London.

There was French country furniture, rich velvet and brocade fabrics, copper bedpans, and glass showcases offering the usual vintage jewelry, cut crystal paperweights, and bone china. A Steiff bear made of white mohair caught my eye.

Behind the counter a petite woman in her early forties with a sleek black bob was perched on a stool leafing through a copy of *Paris Match*.

'Excuse me, I wondered if I could look at the Steiff bear in the glass cabinet,' I asked

'It's very expensive,' she said and continued to flip through her magazine.

I detected a strong French accent. 'Yes, I know. He's called Selby and was made around 1915.'

The woman looked up sharply. She frowned and then broke into a big smile. *'Mon dieu!* Kat Stanford! What a pleasure to meet you in my little shop. I'm Nicole Lassalle-Porter.'

We shook hands. 'Very nice to meet you, too.'

'You should have your own show in Dartmouth,' Nicole went on, 'So much fake stuff in these little shops – not my shop, you understand – and the tourists are so foolish, they buy everything.'

A few of the 'foolish tourists' turned around and glared. A woman dressed in tight shorts and wearing flip-flops took her husband's arm and left in a huff.

'Tant pis. Too bad.' Nicole shrugged. 'Come! Let us see Selby.' Picking up a fob of keys, she ducked under the counter and led the way to the glass display case.

'Tell me that the rumor is not true,' said Nicole. 'Tell me you are not leaving *Fakes & Treasures.*'

I hesitated. I'd grown used to guarding what I said to strangers for fear of it being misconstrued. 'Well–'

'No matter,' she went on breezily. 'I would hate to be in the public eye – and your paparazzi! They are *wolves.*'

'Yes, some of them can be.'

'And that Trudy Wynne is *mauvais* – a horrible woman,' Nicole exclaimed. 'No wonder her husband left her for you.'

'It wasn't quite like that,' I protested.

'David Wynne,' Nicole enthused. 'What is it like to be with such a fascinating man? He must have amazing stories to tell about his hunt for stolen treasures?'

'He does,' I said politely, glad when Nicole retrieved the Steiff bear from the cabinet and we could talk about something else. 'Oh – he's lovely.'

She handed him to me. Selby was adorable with a little clipped muzzle. I gently tilted him forward and to my delight, heard a low growl.

'Yes, he still growls,' said Nicole. 'For you, one thousand pounds.'

It was a fair price – he was worth at least two – but I still balked. 'Can you put him to one side?' I said. 'I need to think about it.'

'Come, let's have some tea. It's not often I have a chance to talk to someone who loves bears.'

'I can't stay today but perhaps another time. I have to find an Internet café and then meet my mother. She's just moved here.'

'Where does she live?'

'On the Honeychurch Hall estate,' I said. 'She's bought the Carriage House.'

'Very sad about Kelly, his first wife,' said Nicole. 'I knew her, you know. Sweet thing despite what you might hear otherwise.'

I didn't usually gossip – having been the subject of gossip myself – but I knew Mum would be intrigued. 'Such as?'

'Vera, the housekeeper – she's *crazy,* I tell you,' said Nicole. 'The two girls were born on the estate and grew up together the best of friends. When Kelly married Rupert, you can imagine the drama! Kelly said Vera was *livid* and refused to take orders from her. I think she was jealous.'

'I'm sure she was.'

'Kelly and Rupert were going to move to France,' Nicole went on. 'Then *pouf!* It all went up in a puff of smoke. I was giving Kelly French lessons. She was quite good.'

I was surprised. 'Lord Honeychurch was going to sell the Hall?'

'*Oui.* They were going to buy a vineyard in Provence.'

Obviously things had changed when he married Lavinia and had a male heir.

'Lady Edith was *furious* and tried to stop him,' said Nicole. 'Kelly was too low class for her ladyship.' She gave a snort of derision. 'You English and your aristocracy. There is no class system in France. Thank God for the guillotine.'

Now I was intrigued. 'But they got married all the same.'

'*Oui.* They eloped!'

I was quite certain Mum hadn't known about that juicy morsel.

'And when they eloped, Lady Edith disinherited Rupert on the spot!' Nicole said gleefully.

'What happened?' I asked.

'My husband, Luke, and I were there the night it happened,' said Nicole, clearly enjoying telling the story. 'It was during their annual New Year's Eve dinner party – Luke was at Stowe with

149

Rupert. Kelly worked under Mrs. Cropper in the kitchen. Rupert insisted on helping clear away the plates ... and the two of them ran off between the main course and pudding.'

'Good heavens!' I laughed. 'What a scandal!'

'We all sat there like lemons, waiting and waiting. Poor Lavinia was devastated. She and Rupert had been engaged for years, you know.'

'Lavinia – his *current* wife?' I said, surprised.

'But she got him in the end.'

'I heard Kelly was fatally stung by a bee,' I said.

'*Oui*. She was highly allergic,' said Nicole. 'Rupert told us it was the one day Kelly couldn't find her EpiPen. Of course, Lavinia went for help–'

'Lavinia was *there?*'Despite myself, I was riveted.

'She and Kelly were out riding together when it happened.'

'Were Lavinia and Kelly friends?' I was incredulous. I couldn't imagine ever being friends with my rival in love, Trudy Wynne.

'What do the young people call them now – frenemies?' Nicole lowered her voice. 'After all the fuss died down, Rupert went back to Lavinia and married her, little Harry was born, and Lady Edith forgave him.'

Much as I warmed toward Nicole, I suspected that if she gossiped about other people to someone she hardly knew she'd gossip about me, too.

'In France, Rupert would have kept his inheritance and taken Kelly as a mistress,' said Nicole. 'You English have it all wrong.'

'But at least we keep our heads!'

A nineteenth-century longcase grandfather clock chimed the half hour. 'I'm sorry Nicole, I must go,' I said, then had a sudden thought. 'Can you recommend a handyman?'

Nicole retrieved a number from her iPhone and jotted it down on the back of her business card. 'Use Tom – he's actually a cousin of Kelly's. So incestuous,' she said. 'He lives at Home Farm – it used to belong to the estate.'

The name rang a bell and then I remembered that Tom had discovered Gayla's abandoned suitcase. 'Did you ever meet Gayla, Harry's nanny?' I asked.

'No, but I did hear that nannies rarely stay there longer than a few months.'

'Is Harry that difficult?'

'No, but Rupert – *il a les yeux baladeurs*–'

'He has a wandering eye?'

'*Exactement!*' Nicole gave another smile. 'Do remember to let me know if you want the Steiff bear. Oh! And one more thing–' She fetched a clipboard from under the counter. 'The government want to put a high-speed train in the area. Everyone is up in arms. Do sign the petition.'

'Of course.' This time I added my real name to the very long list. 'I hope it helps.'

Nicole directed me to a nearby Internet café and copy center by the marina where crowds were gathering for an upcoming rowing competition just for the locals.

Four women dressed in black shorts and purple T-shirts emblazoned with a DART MARINA logo were passing around a silver hip flask.

'We're one short,' said a lively woman with violet eyes. She scanned the crowd. 'Volunteers, anyone? Come on, ladies! We always come in last so you're just ballast.'

Everyone hooted with laughter. She looked at me and raised a questioning eyebrow. I shook my head. 'Not this time. But thanks for the invitation.'

I heard someone mention *Fakes &Treasures*. A handful of mobiles and iPhones were brought out. I waved and smiled for the cameras and hurried away.

The Internet café – Buzz – was relatively deserted. To my delight, they also had a printer. I set myself up in the corner and got sorted. I checked my e-mails. I had two accounts – a personal one known only to a chosen few, and my 'fan' e-mail address.

I always had to brace myself when checking the latter. Many people wrote in and were extremely vocal about their opinions on what I wore, said, and did. Yet again, a viewer had sent me a YouTube of 'the Big Sneeze' thinking I couldn't have seen it, and yet again I couldn't help myself. I had to play it. The star counter informed me that it had been viewed 2,856,321 times. Lovely.

Someone told me that reliving a horrible experience over and over again gradually dulled the embarrassment but it didn't for me. There I was at the *Save a Child* charity event speaking earnestly in front of a gazillion would-be donors when suddenly, I had the overwhelming urge to sneeze.

My dress had been literally sewn onto me – the designer who had loaned the outfit had gotten my measurements all wrong. It was a massive wardrobe malfunction of epic proportions but as long as I moved slowly and didn't raise my arms, I was promised all would be well.

But then I sneezed. Every single button down the back of my dress flew across the dais. There was a scramble for souvenirs and for some time afterward, they were even for sale on eBay.

David had sent a short e-mail that said, *Arriving Sun late afternoon. Pls send address. David.'* There was no 'miss you,' 'looking forward to seeing you' or even a 'love, David.' Once again I suffered a pang of nostalgia for those early days when our e-mail exchanges were X-rated. I couldn't help wondering if Mum's stories about luscious women being ravished by smoldering, passionate men did more harm than good. Did they make women restless?

I responded to David and on impulse, asked if he had any information about a robbery at Honeychurch Hall in the 1990s – in particular, details of the rare Elizabethan parure.

On another impulse I Googled Krystalle Storm and a website flashed up. A striking woman with coiffed platinum hair stared back at me. She wore diamonds and a neat white shirt. On her lap was a caramel-colored Pekinese. The tag said KRYSTALLE WITH HER PEKE TRULY SCRUMPTIOUS. If this was my mother she'd been airbrushed beyond all recognition.

I Googled again, searching for a different Krystalle Storm but the same website came up. A sidebar confirmed my growing sense of alarm – *Gypsy Temptress* had sold over half a million copies worldwide.

I clicked the tab to Mum's biography. My jaw dropped as I learned that my father had been an international diplomat who had died in a tragic plane crash twenty years ago and that 'Krystalle Storm' split her time between her villa on the Amalfi Coast and her manor house in Devon.

A 'Contact the Author' tab sent me directly to Goldfinch Press, the publisher's website. A note said that the author was 'a recluse and rarely made public appearances.' However, Vera was right. They were running a contest. Readers were invited to send in their personal stories – with a 'star-crossed lovers' theme – and the winner would be rewarded with an all-expenses-paid romantic weekend for two to the Amalfi Coast including dinner with the author herself.

I stared at the screen for a full minute struggling to comprehend what Mum had done and the repercussions when – not if – she got found out. When Dad had specified that he wanted me to 'look after Mum' I thought he had meant her health ... not her sanity.

I dreaded having to confront her but I had no choice.

Back at Snipxx Mum looked very nice. Her hair was not the platinum shade in the website photograph but it was close. Vera was still there sitting at a nail station having a manicure and pedicure and leafing through a copy of *Cosmopolitan*.

'Thank God you're here,' whispered Mum. 'Vera did not stop talking once about her wretched husband.'

'Did she mention Gayla?' I asked.

'Of course not,' said Mum. 'I don't like Eric but he's definitely got his work cut out with her. She's obsessed with him.'

'Maybe it's the eyebrows.'

We made a quick stop at Marks & Spencer and loaded up with ready-made meals and quite a lot of snacks. It was hard to restrain myself.

'Don't you just love Marks and Sparks,' Mum said happily.

'Yes. Their food is so ... truly scrumptious.'

There was a long pause as it slowly dawned on my mother that I knew.

'Oh. You found out.' Mum looked sheepish. 'It's a good name for a Pekinese, isn't it? I got that from the film *Chitty Chitty Bang Bang*. Do you remember–?'

'Yes, I do.' I said coldly. 'A villa on the Amalfi Coast? A manor house in Devon? And – as for Dad ... an international diplomat?'

'A tax inspector sounded so dull.' Mum shrugged. 'I don't know what to say.'

'Nor do I.' I got into the car and slammed the door hard.

Mum slid in beside me and took a deep breath. 'I didn't want your father to find out,' she said. 'I couldn't do that to him especially after he retired and joined the Rotary Club. They were all so stuffy and straitlaced. It would have been humiliating for him. I wanted to protect him. That's all.'

Mum turned to me and to my surprise, her eyes filled with tears. 'I would never want to hurt him,' she went on. 'I didn't think *Gypsy Temptress* would sell. I didn't think anyone would find out.'

'It's the days of the Internet, Mum,' I said. 'Nothing is private anymore. Look at me? Everything is out there for people to pick over and laugh at. You'll just have to tell your publisher the truth.'

'No!' she said quickly. 'I couldn't do that. Besides, I *am* planning on buying Honeychurch Hall. Eventually.'

'What?' I squeaked.

'Yes, I am,' said Mum with a hint of defiance. 'The place could do with some TLC–'

'It could do with millions. Why is the Carriage House so important to you?' I was exasperated. 'Isn't there something equally as shabby closer to London?'

'You couldn't possibly understand.' Mum flipped down the sun visor and checked her reflection. 'I think Stacey did a good job with my hair.'

'She did,' I said. 'Although not quite as glamorous as the one on your website.'

Mum's face reddened. 'Alfred has a friend who does passports and that sort of thing.'

'Forgeries, you mean. Did you plagiarize another woman's photograph?'

'Of course not,' said Mum. 'It's me, made to look younger and then airbrushed to look older. Amazing what people can do these days.'

'So that just leaves the issue of the Pekinese,' I said dryly.

'I heard there were some puppies–'

'Mum!' I said sharply.

'Don't worry, it will all work out. Just you see.'

'Yes, but not necessarily for the best,' I said darkly.

Half an hour later we arrived back at the tradesman's entrance and Mum's good humor evaporated. 'Will you look at that?'

A fifteen-foot long banner straddled the gateway. Painted in red, it said:

BANGER RALLY. NEXT MEETING:
SEPTEMBER 2: 8 A.M. – 6 P.M.
LIVE MUSIC! HOT DOGS! TOMBOLA!

'That's next weekend,' I said with dismay.

'The sooner we get that surveillance camera set up, the better.'

Fortunately, installing We-See-You was surprisingly easy. The CCTV equipment turned out to be a simple camera positioned and angled using books on my bedroom windowsill.

I ran the cables back into Mum's office, connected them to the DVD, and turned on the television set. 'Excellent!' I said to myself as the cows grazing in the field below my bedroom window filled the screen.

'Eric had better watch out,' said Mum defiantly. 'No one messes with me.'

Chapter Twelve

'This is Master Harry's favorite,' said Mrs. Cropper, setting down two plates of shepherd's pie and peas on the kitchen table. It smelled delicious.

Harry threw a sketch pad to one side. It was covered in illegible squiggles. He was still wearing his white scarf but had pushed his goggles up on top of his flying helmet. A model Spitfire plane sat on a side plate next to him.

'A man has to eat,' he said, tucking in with his

157

fork. '*Especially* when we're going on a nighttime mission behind enemy lines. Let's hope that Flying Officer Jazzbo Jenkins is still alive.'

'A mission!' I said. 'How exciting.' Turning to Mrs. Cropper I added, 'Thank you for supper.'

'I like to keep with tradition,' said Mrs. Cropper briskly. 'Harry always eats his supper at six with the nanny–'

'I know what happened to Gayla,' said Harry, spearing a pea with relish. 'She was working for the Germans and now she's been captured by our chaps and taken to a secret location.'

Over the top of Harry's head, I met Mrs. Cropper's silent appeal to say nothing more. 'Now you be nice to Miss Katherine and don't give her any trouble.'

Mrs. Cropper returned to the table with two glasses of water. She was just a few years older than my mother, but plump with a florid complexion. Dressed in a pink striped pinafore over a plain white linen short-sleeved dress, she wore her gray hair tucked under a white mobcap and looked the epitome of a below-stairs cook.

Harry and I sat at one end of a huge kitchen table that had been scrubbed white through age and use. Half the room had been modernized in the early seventies with cheap built-in floor-to-ceiling cupboards made of plywood – but the rest of the furnishings clung to the 1920s.

One side of the kitchen held an old-fashioned huge iron range polished up with black lead. It was immense with ovens on each side and a steel fender polished to a silvery brightness.

A dresser stood opposite with great big cupboards on the lower half and five shelves on the upper half displaying perfectly arranged china. On top of the cupboards sat a soup tureen, vegetable dishes, and sauceboats – enough china for a small army of people, not the few that now lived at the Hall.

There was a stone sink and a wooden draining board with plate racks above. A counter held a battered toaster and an old color television set. An ancient refrigerator with rusting hinges stood in the corner covered in crayoned drawings of airplanes secured with Blu-Tack.

'We'll be fine, won't we Harry, or should I say Squadron Leader Bigglesworth?'

'Call me Biggles,' said Harry. 'You're Flying Officer Stanford. I'm afraid you're a man.'

Mrs. Cropper caught my eye and gave a nod of approval. 'Lady Edith's brother was a Spitfire pilot during World War II–'

'He was shot by a poacher, wasn't he, Mrs. Cropper,' said Harry cheerfully. 'There was lots of blood and everything.'

'That's enough, thank you, Master Harry,' said Mrs. Cropper. 'Where was I? Oh – yes, Lady Edith's father – the earl – flew Sopwith Camels in the Great War. The flying helmet and goggles belonged to him.'

'Harry is very lucky,' I said. 'They're collector's items.'

'The Hall is full of collections from all over the world,' said Mrs. Cropper proudly.

'My mother is very interested in the history of the house. She'd love to talk to you about it – if you wouldn't mind.'

'Honeychurch Hall was a military hospital during both World Wars,' Mrs. Cropper went on as she busied herself by the kitchen sink. 'Of course I was only a child during the second one. I still live in the cottage I was born in.'

'And Mr. Cropper?'

'He was born next door.'

'And I was born upstairs,' said Harry. 'Wasn't I, Mrs. Cropper?'

'That's right. You were a home birth. All the gentry were born at home. Vera's mother was also a midwife.'

'Does Vera's mother still live on the estate?' I asked.

'No, she's in the loony bin,' said Harry.

'Harry!' Mrs. Cropper exclaimed. 'We don't say loony bin.'

'Mummy does.'

'Unfortunately, Vera's mother suffers from Alzheimer's,' said Mrs. Cropper in a low voice. 'She lives at Sunny Hill Lodge. It's very pleasant.'

'It smells of wee and cabbages,' Harry chipped in.

'And your grandson, Shawn?' I asked politely.

'He said Gayla wasn't on the train,' Harry said. 'She's gone missing.'

'Only because she stopped to visit a friend,' I said quickly.

'And if you carry on listening to adult conversations,' Mrs. Cropper scolded, 'there will be no apple snow for pudding.'

'Sorry,' he said.

'Where was I?' Mrs. Cropper said again.

'Your grandson.'

160

'Our son, Robert – that's Shawn's father – didn't want to be in domestic service. He went into the police force and Shawn followed in his footsteps.'

'Who lived in the third cottage?' I asked.

'My brother was the gamekeeper there for a time.'

'Gamekeeper?' I said sharply, thinking of how Mum claimed she didn't know who had lived there when I questioned her this morning. 'What was your maiden name?'

'Stark, why?'

Mum's gamekeeper was called Shelby, close enough to Stark but not too obvious. 'I just wondered. And the cottages are still tied?'

'What are they tied to?' chipped in Harry.

'Tied cottages mean that they belong to the estate and if the family works on the estate, they can live there forever,' I said. 'Isn't that right, Mrs. Cropper?'

'As long as the estate isn't sold off.' Mrs. Cropper's expression darkened. 'I don't mind telling you that none of us are happy about the Carriage House being sold to an outsider. What will happen to us when Lady Edith dies and his lordship has his way?'

'Oh,' I said taken aback.

'What will happen to all of us? To Eric and Vera? William? This is our home.'

I didn't know what to say so I just mumbled, 'Gosh, I wonder.'

'People don't know their place anymore,' Mrs. Cropper plunged on. 'In the old days, you knew where you were. There was none of this American

161

dream nonsense – wanting to be something you're not. When you start marrying into the wrong class, that's when trouble begins.'

'Like Kelly. She was in the tart class, wasn't she, Mrs. Cropper?' said Harry. 'Do you think she was stung by killer bees because tarts taste yummy?'

'What's this nonsense about killer bees?' Lavinia swept in. 'Really, Mrs. Cropper, I've told you before not to put ideas into Harry's head.'

'No, m'lady,' said Mrs. Cropper.

Lavinia touched the string of pearls at her neck and fiddled with a strand of long blond hair that had escaped from a tortoiseshell comb. Tonight she'd given up her usual style of jodhpurs for a navy pleated skirt and neat white ruffled blouse.

'I was telling Mrs. Cropper that my mother is interested in the history of the house and all its dark secrets,' I said.

'Why? Whatever for?' Lavinia fiddled with her pearls again. She seemed nervous. 'We don't have any dark secrets.'

'Oh, I don't know about that, m'lady.' Vera slipped into the kitchen. She had switched her drab black housekeeper uniform to a flimsy black shift and donned another pair of mind-bogglingly expensive leopard-print Christian Louboutin sky-high heels. Her face was heavily made up and her flinty eyes bore the telltale signs of having already imbibed an aperitif – or three.

Puzzled, Lavinia turned to Mrs. Cropper. 'I thought it was Vera's night off.'

'She's here for a bit of Dutch courage,' said Mrs. Cropper. 'I'll get you a snifter, dear.'

Mrs. Cropper vanished through one of the three doors along the rear wall. Lavinia regarded Vera with obvious dislike. 'Don't let Lady Edith see you dressed like that.'

'If we don't have apple snow soon,' Harry cried, 'I'm going to die of starvation.'

'Are you coming or not?' shouted Lady Edith, who had entered the kitchen. Mr. Chips steamed in after her, dashing around the table in circles and then, just as suddenly, steamed out again.

The dowager countess had also given up her usual riding attire for a deep purple skirt and duster jacket. Her gray hair lay in neat pin curls that were clamped to her head.

'Granny!' cried Harry. 'We've got apple snow for pudding.'

'How lovely, my pet.'

Mrs. Cropper reappeared clutching a silver hip flask but on spotting Lady Edith, she slipped it into the pocket of her pinafore. Vera had disappeared. Once again I felt as if I was involved in a farce with actors coming in and out of various doors.

'Good evening, m'lady,' said Mrs. Cropper. 'Did you need me to leave you a light snack for later?'

'No, we're eating at Shipley Abbey,' said Lady Edith. 'Although I'm quite certain the food will be filthy. Come along, Lavinia, it must be a good hour's drive across Dartmoor and at this time of night, the place will be crawling with wretched tourists. Oh–' she said on noticing me. 'You found a new nanny. What's your name, gel?'

'It's Katherine Stanford, Edith,' said Lavinia, shooting me an apologetic smile. 'From the Carriage House. You met her this morning, remember?'

'No, I've never seen her before,' said Lady Edith.

I caught a worried look between Mrs. Cropper and Lavinia. Perhaps she really *was* losing her marbles.

'Is William going with you tonight, your ladyship?' Mrs. Cropper asked.

'He's keeping an eye on Jupiter,' said Lady Edith. 'She's restless and keeps kicking at her stomach again.'

'Sounds like colic,' I suggested. 'I was horse mad as a teenager.'

'If you want to ride out with us, we're always short-handed,' said Lady Edith.

'I'd love to!'

'Is that wise?' said Lavinia. 'These horses are frightfully valuable.'

Lady Edith ignored her. 'Talk to William tomorrow. He'll sort you out.' She kissed the top of Harry's head and swept out, shouting, 'I'll be waiting in the car. Hurry up.'

Lavinia went to kiss Harry, too, but he cringed. 'Ugh. Don't do that, Mother. I'm on duty.'

'Bedtime is nine o'clock,' said Lavinia. 'We won't be home until at least midnight. Do you want to stay the night, Katherine? Harry gets a little skittish.'

'No, thanks,' I said. 'Mum's still not very mobile with her broken hand.'

'Shall I wait up or come back later?' said Mrs. Cropper.

'What about his lordship?'

'No need for that,' said Lavinia. 'I have no idea

164

what time Rupert will be home.'

The moment Lavinia had left the room, Vera emerged from her hiding place that turned out to be a small cupboard filled with brooms and cleaning supplies.

'Have you got it, Auntie Peg?' said Vera.

'Auntie Peg?' I said. 'So, you two are related as well?'

'Vera is my brother's granddaughter,' said Mrs. Cropper.

'Your brother Shelby – I mean, Stark the game-keeper?' It was hard keeping all these relationships straight. Mum needed to draw a below-stairs family tree. That's where the real intrigue seemed to be.

Mrs. Cropper retrieved the hip flask from her pocket and handed it to her. 'And don't go drinking too much. You're already three sheets to the wind.'

Vera opened a small leather clutch bag that bore the logo CHANEL. For someone who worked as a housekeeper she seemed to be making good money. 'How much do I owe you?'

'Don't be silly,' said Mrs. Cropper.

Vera gave her great-aunt an impulsive hug. 'Do I look all right?'

'I hope Eric's taking you somewhere special in those new clothes. They must have cost a pretty packet.'

'He likes me in new clothes,' said Vera defensively. 'He said he booked a table in that new restaurant out on the Plymouth road called Crumb.'

'It doesn't sound fancy to me,' said Mrs. Cropper.

'It was featured in last week's *Walk of Shame!* *Celebrity Family Secrets Revealed.*' Vera turned to me. 'I love that show. Maybe you should be on it.'

Changing the subject, I just said, 'I hope you have fun tonight.'

'Yes, have fun!' echoed Harry.

'Thanks.' Vera smiled. It transformed her entire face. She actually looked pretty. 'Men, eh? Can't live with them, can't live without them.'

She tottered out of the kitchen on her Christian Louboutins. 'One of these days she'll fall off those shoes and break her neck,' Mrs. Cropper muttered.

After polishing off two helpings of apple snow each, Harry and I left the table. 'Can I help with the washing up?'

'No,' said Mrs. Cropper. 'You've got your job and I've got mine. Now you behave yourself, Master Harry, and do what Miss Katherine tells you.'

'Come on,' said Harry, pulling the goggles down over his eyes. 'This way. Let's go and break into the castle and rescue our man Jazzbo Jenkins.'

'You know where you are not allowed to go – do be careful Miss Katherine, the service wing was bombed during the war and the floors just aren't safe.'

'I'll watch out for him.' Pausing at the door, I said, 'What was in the hip flask?'

'Cherry brandy with a touch of magic,' said Mrs. Cropper with a wink.

'It has a secret ingredient, doesn't it?' said Harry.

'That's right. Let's just say it could give you a bit of a buzz.'

I paused again, wondering if I should give some to David. 'Does it work?'

'Oh yes,' she said. 'Every time.'

Chapter Thirteen

Harry and I left the kitchen and entered a low-ceilinged, flagstoned passage. High on the wall was a long row of service bells with indicators. It was a gloomy place, lit only by a yellowing light-bulb.

'Hold tight, Stanford! I'm putting her down in the field,' said Harry, running through a series of mimed gestures indicating that our imaginary airplane had made a bumpy landing. 'Rightey-oh. We've just broken into the dungeon. Let's check the cells.'

Half a dozen doors or so lined the corridor. Each bearing a wooden plaque that indicated the purpose behind each. There were an assortment of larders including dry, fish, meat, and dairy, and a lamp room. Most were locked – the doorjambs thick with grime and cobwebs. Only the wine cellar, gun room, and a stillroom bore signs of use.

'It doesn't look as if Jazzbo is down here, sir,' I said.

'Shh! There are Germans everywhere. Follow me.'

'Where are we going?'

'Bad news,' Harry whispered. 'Our man could be up in the tower.'

At the end of the corridor were two glass-paneled doors. One led to the outside courtyard, the other to a narrow staircase.

The back stone stairs wound up to the attics with walls painted a dull green. Harry stopped on the small landing next to another wooden door. 'We've just scaled up an outside wall under heavy enemy fire,' he whispered. 'Now we're about to scramble over the parapet. Ready?'

We stepped into the galleried landing that over-looked the great hall. Light spilled from the domed atriums above. A threadbare carpet bore several imprints of heavy furniture that had probably been sold off. A handful of picture lights illuminated empty squares. Two beautiful walnut display credenzas contained a collection of porcelain snuff boxes – Lady Edith's cherished collections. There had to be at least twenty in each cabinet and worth a small fortune.

Harry grabbed my hand. 'Come on, Stanford, there's no time to lose.'

He opened the first door off the landing and pulled me inside. It was a man's bedroom and I suspected it was Rupert's.

'I don't think we should be in here,' I said.

'We can't leave any stone unturned,' said Harry earnestly. 'You take one side, I'll take the other. Von Stalhein could have our chap locked up in a secret chamber.'

The room was heavily beamed and with ex-quisite linenfold paneling – obviously part of the original house. It was decorated in dark autumnal colors with seventeenth century oak furniture and more oil paintings of stags, dogs, and pheasants.

There was a vast wood-framed bed, armoire, and two sets of chests of drawers. The fireplace had an overmantel of carved wood bearing the Honeychurch coat of arms.

Harry began opening drawers and peering into corners. 'Check the desk for clues, Stanford!' said Harry. 'That's an order!'

An oak bureau stood between two casement windows that overlooked the park and the white angel memorial. Maybe Rupert really was still in love with his first wife and when I spied a wood-framed photograph of a couple on his desk, it certainly seemed so. Rupert stood with his arm around a young dark-haired woman who was dressed in a low, plunging neckline. Frankly, she did look a little on the tarty side.

There was also a brochure marked *Sunny Hill Lodge Residential Home for the Elderly.* A note was stapled to the cover from P. Pelham-Burns, Esq. saying, 'With compliments. Looking forward to meeting the dowager countess.'

I began to feel seriously uncomfortable. 'Harry, we *really* shouldn't be in here.'

I turned to find my charge dragging a blue telescoping mailing tube out from under the bed. 'It's a map of the dungeons!' he said excitedly. He tipped it upside down and shook it hard but nothing slid out.

Harry's face fell. 'It's gone.'

'The Germans must have stolen it,' I said.

'But it was here yesterday. Gayla found it.' Harry scowled. 'I wanted to show it to you.'

'Never mind. Let's put this back.' I took the tube from him and glanced at the shipping label.

It was addressed to H & P Developments of 14A The Passage, Dartmouth. The return address was from a company in Bristol called PlayScapes Planning. Kneeling down, I rolled the tube under the bed.

'I know!' said Harry. 'Maybe the map is in Fräulein von Stalhein's room?'

'No more bedrooms,' I said but he had already vanished through a connecting door. The fact that Lavinia and Rupert did not sleep together was not lost on me.

Lavinia's bedroom was chaotic. There was a saddle on the back of an armchair, *Horse & Hound* magazines stacked on the floor, and a walnut dressing table with a set of silver brushes, old-fashioned glass perfume bottles, and used tissues.

Clothing was heaped in piles on the carpet and the bed was unmade. On Lavinia's night table, next to a framed photograph of a much younger Rupert dressed in polo playing attire was – to my extreme surprise – Mum's book, *Gypsy Temptress*. It lay open, spine facing up. Perhaps Lavinia wasn't as cold-blooded as she seemed, after all.

Harry gave a heavy sigh. 'What the dickens happened here, Stanford? This must have been quite a show. Von Stalhein must have been tipped off and moved our man elsewhere.'

'No more bedrooms, Harry,' I said again. 'They're private. You wouldn't like it if someone went through your things.'

Harry's shoulders slumped. 'But Jazzbo could be in danger.'

'No more tonight,' I said firmly. 'Back to base, Squadron Leader Bigglesworth. We'll continue our search tomorrow.'

'Base' proved to be Harry's bedroom – a light and sunny room with a high ceiling, two casement windows, and a view of the walled garden.

The furniture was mainly pine – a narrow bed, freestanding wardrobe, and a chest of drawers upon which stood a tray with two glasses of milk and a plate of homemade biscuits. There was a pine blanket chest and matching bookcase filled with comic books and volumes of adventure stories.

In the corner was an ancient navy school trunk with old leather straps. The name RUPERT E. HONEYCHURCH had been scratched out and HARRY E. HONEYCHURCH written in black marker pen above it.

There was no television or computer – just a selection of board games including an antique chessboard, backgammon, cribbage, *Monopoly*, and *Scrabble*. I wondered how Harry would adjust to being around 'normal' kids who grew up saturated with modern technology.

And yet it was the model airplanes from both World Wars suspended from the ceiling that took my breath away. No wonder Harry created a world of make-believe. How could he avoid it?

A workstation stretched the length of one wall holding pots of paint, brushes, glue, and scissors. Underneath it was a stool.

'Did you make these models yourself?' I enthused. 'You must have a lot of patience.'

'Gayla tried,' said Harry, changing into his pajamas. 'But she got red paint everywhere! William tried, too, but his hands are gigantic because he's the strongest man in the world.'

'So I hear.' William went up a notch in my estimation. 'What about your father?'

'He's always busy but he said he was going to take me to the RAF Museum in London for my birthday.'

'You'll love it. You'll see real planes there – just like these models.'

Harry beamed with excitement. 'The Sopwith Camels and the Tiger Moths were built by Great-Uncle Rupert. This used to be his bedroom.' Harry gestured to a black-and-white framed portrait of a handsome pilot in flying suit and goggles. 'I see him sometimes.'

'What do you mean?'

'He likes to stand in the corner – oh!' Harry laughed with delight. 'He's there right now. Hello, Great-Uncle Rupert!'

I spun around but of course there was no one there. 'I can't see anything.'

Harry laughed again. 'He's right there! He's giving you a salute.'

'Well, say hello to Great-Uncle Rupert from me,' I said, happy to play along. 'Are there any other ghosts here?'

Harry grew serious. 'The lady in blue with the funny big dress.'

'Lady Frances?' I said. 'Is she in one of the portraits downstairs wearing the pearl necklace?'

Harry nodded. 'Shall I tell you what happened to her?'

'No, thank you. I'm sure it was horrible.'

'She was drowned by Cromwell's men in the pond near the grotto,' said Harry with relish.

'They held her under the water until her eyes bulged out and her head exploded–'

'Okay Harry, that's enough now,' I said. 'Not something we want to think about before you go to sleep. Bed please.'

Harry clambered into bed. 'Can I have a story?'

'Of course. Who usually reads you a story?'

'Father sometimes, Gayla used to – and William. He makes it funny.'

'You like William?'

'Yes. He's nice.'

I sat on the end of his bed and we drank our milk and ate all the biscuits.

'Who plays chess?' I asked.

'Father, when he's not too busy,' said Harry. 'Gayla used to play but she never let me win. She wouldn't let Father win, either.'

'They played together?' I said, recalling Nicole, the antique dealer's comment about Rupert's wandering eye.

'Yes, every night.'

'Let's have that story,' I said.

Children's adventure classics lined the shelves– *The Famous Five* by Enid Blyton, *Treasure Island* by Robert Louis Stevenson, *The Hobbit* by J. R. R. Tolkien, and of course, volumes of W. E. Johns and *Biggles*. My eye caught *Polar, The Titanic Bear* by Daisy Corning Stone Spedden.

'What about this one?' I said.

Harry pulled a face. 'It's about a boring old bear.'

'I thought you liked bears,' I said. 'Do you know the story?'

'No.'

173

I sat back on the edge of the bed and opened the book. 'It's about a very brave bear who belonged to a little boy who survived the sinking of the *Titanic*–'

'I know about the *Titanic*. My great-great-grandfather died on the *Titanic*.'

'The little boy in the story would have been the same age as you.'

'Wait–' Harry flipped back the duvet and leapt out of bed. He lifted the lid of the pine blanket chest and dragged out a black bear.

As I took in the bear's red-rimmed eyes, my stomach turned right over.

'Let me see,' I said, hardly daring to believe that this could be one of the rare *Titanic* mourning bears. The relatives of those who perished had purchased most of them. It *was* possible.

'Granny says he's named Edward after her grandfather,' said Harry. 'He's not very handsome, is he?'

'That's because he's a hundred years old.'

'As old as Granny?'

'Probably not as old as Granny.' My mind was whirling with excitement. 'Do you know if your grandmother has any other old toys?'

Harry shrugged again. 'I think Father has a train set somewhere but he won't let me play with it.'

To discover a private collection was a dream for any antique dealer and I made a mental note to talk to the dowager countess.

'All right.' Harry sighed. 'Let's read about the stupid bear.'

Fifteen minutes later I closed the book. 'Did you like the story?'

174

'It was sad,' said Harry. 'The little boy dies anyway. And what happened to the bear?'

'That will remain one of life's mysteries.' I stood up and went over to the window, surprised that it was nine o'clock and still light outside.

'Don't make it dark,' said Harry. 'I don't like it.'

I pulled the curtains closed but left a six-inch gap and switched on a night-light near the door.

Harry wriggled down into bed. 'Will it be dark in my dormitory at boarding school?'

'Let's hope not,' I said.

'You are going to be in Gayla's room, aren't you?'

'Yes, of course.' I propped the bear against his lamp on the bedside table. 'Since Jazzbo Jenkins is still in enemy hands, Edward bear will keep watch tonight. We don't want you kidnapped by Von Stalhein.'

I kissed the top of Harry's head, opened another connecting door, and stepped into the nanny's room.

It was furnished with a 1940's satinwood bedroom ensemble – a single bed, vanity, and dresser. Regarded as 'cheap' furniture before the war, a complete set now could fetch a high price at auction – although the mattress left a lot to be desired. I sat down and practically sank to the floor. Vera had not changed the duvet and sheets yet. They still bore traces of Gayla's musky perfume. Draped over a wooden Victorian towel rail were two thin pink towels.

On the matching satinwood side table was a small color television. A comfy armchair sat next to a Victorian fireplace that now housed a hideous three-bar electric fire. I turned the television on and discovered it had just four channels.

Gayla would have been lonely living here in the middle of nowhere. It must have been rather bleak. The Honeychurch clan didn't seem exactly warm and welcoming and I thought it likely that Vera would regard the young girl as a rival rather than a friend. Would she even frame her for theft?

Since Shawn had been concerned with Gayla's safety, I was surprised that her bedroom had not been searched yet.

A rattan wastepaper basket was filled with discarded magazines – and surprise – a copy of *Gypsy Temptress*. But what intrigued me most was a small bamboo novelty box containing an assortment of random objects – a mechanical pencil, a box of matches from Gino's Italian restaurant in Plymouth, a blue coat-check ticket, a single dead red rose, and most revealing of all, a lipstick kiss imprint on the corner of a crumpled white linen handkerchief with the initials R.E.H.

They were the discarded trophies of an infatuated young woman and the only reason I knew was that I, too, had been that young woman. Not with David, but with another man long ago. Gayla had called Rupert 'wicked' and I suspected it was because she felt she had been led on and then unceremoniously dumped.

Knowing full well that Vera would clean this room, Gayla must have deliberately left these items to be discovered and hoped to cause trouble. I wasn't sure if this was good or bad – proof that she was okay or evidence of something more sinister.

I wondered if Lavinia would divorce Rupert for this indiscretion but guessed it was probably one of many. Rupert had leered at me, too.

With time to kill, I settled into the armchair and flicked through *Gypsy Temptress*.

She knew she would miss the wind in her hair, the feel of bare earth on her feet and the sounds of birds singing their evening song. She'd miss the warmth of a nighttime campfire and drifting to sleep beneath a canopy of stars. Would she be happy giving all this up for him? Would her kin ever forgive her? 'I love you,' he whispered as he nuzzled her neck, sending quivers of delight down, down and into her innermost secret place...

'Good grief, Mother,' I muttered. 'Innermost secret *place?*'

Turning to the back cover I learned that the year was 1910 and it would appear that Lily's family ran a traveling boxing emporium and it was rumored that they were really racketeers. An undercover agent who worked for the king was sent to investigate. Naturally he fell in love with Lily and naturally the consequences were fatal hence the birth of the Star-Crossed Lovers Series.

I read for a good hour or more. There was a lot of quivering going on in *Gypsy Temptress* but again, to my surprise, it was well written and I found myself completely hooked. It was only the scream of a fox outside that snapped me back to the present. I had no idea what the time was, having left my iPhone in my tote bag in the kitchen. I checked on Harry who was fast asleep, and hurried downstairs to fetch it.

The empty corridors were dark and ominous. Half the light bulbs had burned out. I made my way toward the galleried landing and tried to forget Harry's Great-Uncle Rupert and Lady Frances in the blue dress. I had never believed in ghosts. It was Mum who claimed she could read palms and tell fortunes in the tea leaves although Dad and I never put her to the test. The house was creepy though and I was glad to reach the relative familiarity of the grand staircase and descend to the main hall.

Shafts of moonlight spilled through the domed atriums casting eerie shadows over the suits of armor. There were doors everywhere and I couldn't remember which one was the kitchen.

I tried the first on the left, flipped the light switch, and gave a squeak of surprise. Guarding the entrance was a life-sized stuffed rearing polar bear poised to attack.

The room housed a small museum filled with a varied collection of antiquities and artifacts, presumably accumulated by the explorers of the family. There were African relics, rare ostrich and osprey eggs, maritime ship models, and scrimshaw. Butterflies and insects were displayed in glass cases. Arranged around the room were unusual curios including a nineteenth-century Polyphon music box, armadillo handbag, and a stuffed giraffe head. David would have a field day in here.

Returning to the hall the next door revealed a downstairs loo that was far more elaborately painted than the one in the Carriage House.

Framed 'loyalty' portraits and photographs hung on each wall starting from the 1880s and spanning eighty-odd years. There were formal tableaus of the family and staff in uniform through the decades. Another set of photographs showed Bushman's Traveling Boxing Emporium set up in the parkland in front of the Hall. There was something oddly familiar about these that I couldn't quite put my finger on.

In each of the annual photographs the same group of disheveled-looking children and youths flexed their muscles and posed for the camera.

Just ten minutes ago I'd been reading about a traveling boxing emporium in *Gypsy Temptress*. I hadn't even heard of them up until an hour ago and yet my mother obviously had.

'I told you I destroyed them!' Someone was standing right outside the bathroom door. I froze – in a complete dilemma as to whether to reveal my presence.

'I didn't ask you to destroy them, Eric.' I recognized Rupert's clipped voice immediately. 'I told you to give them back to me.'

'I – I – couldn't. Vera turned up–'

'Vera! What the hell was she doing there?' Rupert's voice had gone up at least ten decibels.

'You know how jealous she gets. She saw my car parked by the gate and stopped.'

'She saw you with *Gayla?*'

'Don't worry,' said Eric. 'I calmed her down.'

'Vera will tell Mother, you bloody fool,' shouted Rupert. 'I can't trust you to do anything right.'

'It's not my fault her ladyship sold the Carriage House,' Eric exclaimed. 'I've tried to get rid of that Stanford woman but she's stubborn.'

Anger surged in my chest. Mum had been right all along about Eric's intentions but I'd had no idea that Rupert was involved, too.

'The Stanford woman doesn't matter any-more,' said Rupert.

'You mean, she agreed to move into Sawmill Cottage, after all?' Eric said hopefully.

'It's not about Sawmill Cottage, you idiot!' Rupert yelled. 'If Mother finds out the truth you can forget all about our agreement. It's over.'

'What about our investors?' Eric asked. 'What about Baker?'

'I told you to wait but you wouldn't listen.'

'I'll have to tell him something.' Eric sounded worried. 'What if he asks for the money back?'

'Not my problem.'

'You bastard!'

'Get your hands off me–' There were sounds of a scuffle followed by a thunderous crash of metal, as if a dozen drum sets had been thrown into a hollow bunker. 'Out! Out!' yelled Rupert.

The voices receded and I heard a door slam hard, leaving me shaken and more than a little anxious. The fact that Eric had spoken to Gayla and that Rupert was upset about it confirmed my suspicions that they were all somehow involved in her disappearance.

But I wasn't sure what to do.

Should I tell Shawn? But what if he and Rupert were really the best of friends? Everyone here was so interconnected.

I counted to fifty before checking the coast was clear and emerged cautiously from the bathroom. The hall was deserted. I'd been right about the armor. It was scattered across the black-and-white marble floor in a gazillion pieces. Cropper certainly had his work cut out for him in the morning.

I found the kitchen easily but promptly bumped straight into Rupert. 'Katherine!'

'Sorry. You're back! Hello,' I stammered. 'I didn't hear you come in because I was upstairs. Just got here actually to–' I gestured to the tote bag I'd left on the kitchen chair. 'Just ran down to grab that. Harry is sleeping soundly by the way.'

But Rupert didn't seem bothered by my garbled explanation. He looked tired and drawn and just gave a brief nod. 'Thank you. You may go now.'

'I'll just pop back upstairs,' I said. 'I left my book and of course I'll check on Harry again.'

'Thank you. I will be up shortly.'

I set off, aware that Rupert must have decided to escort me after all. In fact, he followed so closely behind that I started to feel a little freaked out. When I reached the landing, I felt his cool breath on my neck and spun around. 'Rupert–' I gasped in confusion.

Rupert was nowhere to be seen. I was completely alone.

A cold rush of air passed on by. Every nerve ending tingled and the hair on the back of my neck literally stood up.

'Rupert?' I called out again and hurried to look over the gallery banister into the hall below. It was empty.

Dad used to say we should fear the living, not the dead but I was thoroughly spooked. I ran to the nanny's room and grabbed *Gypsy Temptress*. Took a peek at Harry – who was snuggled up to Edward bear – and ran.

No wonder Harry was afraid of the dark. If I'd just encountered his Great-Uncle Rupert I didn't like it one bit.

The evening's revelations had left me unsettled. Now, more than ever, I was determined to take my mother away from here – by force, if necessary.

Chapter Fourteen

I walked quickly through the pinewoods, anxious to get back to the safety of the Carriage House.

Reaching the latch-gate, I slammed into Vera coming from the opposite direction.

She was hysterical, taking in great gulps of air and sobbing her heart out. The light from the full moon shone down on a face, blotchy with tears and streaked with mascara. Her dress was plastered in mud and she carried her leopard print Louboutin shoes in one hand.

My stomach turned over. Judging from what I'd overheard at the Hall, Eric and Vera must have just gotten into a fight. 'Good God, are you hurt?' I asked.

Vera shook her head. 'Where is he? Where's my Eric?' Her voice was slurred. She was clearly drunk.

'He was at the Hall with Rupert,' I said.

Vera poked my chest with her finger. 'You're after him now, aren't you?' she said. 'Just like that Russian tart.'

'Don't be ridiculous. Calm down.' Then I remembered. 'Weren't you and Eric supposed to have a romantic dinner date tonight?'

'Eric didn't show up.' Vera dissolved into another crying jag. 'I sat there in that bloody expensive restaurant like a bloody idiot for an hour with everyone staring at me.'

She sank onto a tree stump and flung her Louboutins to the ground. Her despair was so heartbreaking I actually felt sorry for her.

'Perhaps you went to the wrong restaurant?' I suggested.

'I'm not that stupid.'

'Or got the wrong day? I've done that myself before,' I said. 'Did you check that Eric made a reservation?'

'Yes – no, wait, I didn't,' said Vera, wiping her nose on the back of her hand. 'I just walked in and sat down at a corner table. He's always late.'

'Why don't we call the restaurant – it's probably still open.'

'I don't have the number.'

'It was Crumb, wasn't it?'

Vera nodded. 'Bloody stupid name for a restaurant.'

I brought out my iPhone, Googled the number, and called them. 'They said the reservation is for tomorrow night.'

'Oh, God,' she wailed. 'I'm such a fool.'

'All sorted,' I said. 'You see? And Eric need never know what happened.'

'I've ruined everything. Oh, God. Everything.'

If this was what passion looked like, I wasn't interested. 'Of course you haven't.'

'Eric will kill me,' Vera said in a small voice. 'Once he sees his precious tractor, he'll kill me.'

'Tractor? Why? Whatever have you done?'

'I'll go home and get my Wellies,' said Vera. 'Yes – that's what I'll do. And William. He'll help me find the keys, I know he will.' She grabbed my hand and squeezed it hard. 'Please don't tell anyone about this.' And she fled before I could say another word.

Back at the Carriage House I discovered that Mum had locked me out. I hammered on the front door for what seemed like ages.

Finally, the letterbox flew open and Mum hissed, 'Kat, is that you?'

'Of course it's me,' I snapped. 'I've been standing outside for hours.'

'Are you alone?'

'No, I've got the local cricket team with me ready to have hot sex on your kitchen table.'

The letterbox flapped shut and Mum opened the door. 'Did you see Vera?'

'Yes. She was in a terrible state. Why? Was she here?'

I followed Mum into the kitchen. She was walking a little unsteadily. 'You have no idea what I've gone through this evening,' Mum said. 'I just couldn't get rid of her.'

'It looks as if you both had a few too many gin and tonics.' Pointing to the two boxes in the hall I added, 'She didn't pick up her parcels.'

'Vera gets her parcels delivered here so that Eric won't find out how much money she spends.'

'Maybe you have more in common with Vera than you think,' I said dryly.

'What a mess it all is.'

'Mum, it really *is* a mess,' I said, wondering if now was a good time to tell her what I'd overheard at the Hall. 'We need to talk.'

'Apparently Eric stood her up,' said Mum.

'No, Vera got the wrong night.'

'Oh no! The *wrong* night?' Mum started to laugh. 'I don't believe it.'

'What's so funny? She's devastated.'

'Come into my office and see.'

Mum headed straight for the DVD and hit the rewind button. 'This surveillance equipment was a jolly good idea,' she chuckled. 'Watch this. Pity it's only in black-and-white.'

Mum hit play. The field outside my bedroom window filled the screen showing the cows peacefully dozing in the bottom right-hand corner.

Then, suddenly Vera – driving Eric's brand new tractor – entered the frame. She began to career around in circles, scattering the cows in all directions. Each time Vera zoomed passed the camera we got a clear view of her face. She looked manic.

I looked over at my mother who was laughing so hard that absolutely no sound came out of her mouth, at all.

'Those poor cows!' I began to laugh, too. 'Vera said something about Eric's tractor.'

'Yes. Yes.' Mum gasped for breath. 'But just wait until you see what happens next!'

The tractor came around again but this time it suddenly stopped dead. Vera shot out of the driver's seat and landed face-first in the mud. It was as if some divine power had hit the brakes. Then, to my amazement, the vehicle gave a violent jolt and pitched sideways, reared up, stayed vertical for a brief moment, and then began to sink.

'It's a bog!' I shouted.

Tears ran down my mother's face. 'No—' she gasped. 'It's a sink – sink – sinkhole. Oh my heavens.' She wiped her eyes with the sleeve of her poncho.

And then the tractor stopped.

'Unfortunately it hits the bottom.' Mum sounded disappointed. 'Now watch.'

Vera picked herself up off the ground and started leaping around the edge of the hole. She was shouting but since there was no sound, it was as if she were acting in a silent movie.

'Didn't you hear anything at all?' I asked.

Mum, still sniggering, said, 'Not really. I was working.'

'And you didn't go out and help?'

'What could I have done with one arm?' Mum gestured to the screen. 'Watch this bit. See what she does next.'

Vera removed her Louboutins and clambered back onto the seat. She wrenched the keys out of the ignition but promptly dropped them. Judging by her horrified expression, they must have fallen into the hole.

'I wouldn't want to be Vera tomorrow morning,' I said.

'Frankly, I don't care about Vera,' Mum said defiantly. There was no hint of amusement now. 'She's poison.'

'Mum!'

'She came over here all upset asking if I'd seen Eric,' said Mum. 'I gave her a drink to try and calm her down and do you know what?'

'What?'

'She asked me point-blank for a loan.'

'A loan? Whatever for?'

'The nerve! She was in my kitchen for hours. Told me all about Eric being fed up with her credit card debts and that the reason they had separated this time was because of her money spending habits–'

'Those Louboutins cost about six hundred pounds a pair,' I put in. 'But why ask you for a loan?'

'Vera is under the impression that I must be able to afford it because I bought this place – and then–' Mum took a deep breath. 'She said that the newspapers were always paying good money for celebrity sightings and unless I gave her a thousand pounds–'

'But that's blackmail,' I said, appalled. 'I hope you're not going to pay it.'

Mum went very quiet.

'You're not, are you?'

'This isn't just about you,' said Mum. 'What if Vera finds out about me – you know...?'

'The Italian villa?' I said. 'The manor house in Devon? Dad's tragic accident and a Pekinese called Truly Scrumptious?'

'No need to be nasty.'

'How could she find out?' I noticed Mum's wastepaper basket was filled with balled-up yellow paper covered in her handwriting. 'You *do* shred all that, don't you?'

'I recycle,' said Mum defensively. 'Devon is obsessed with recycling.'

'Recycling is not the same as shredding,' I scolded and then remembered Eric. Just before Vera had turned up on Friday night, he'd been rifling through Mum's dustbins. I distinctly recalled seeing balled-up yellow paper – the kind Mum used for drafting her stories. What's more, I'd left Eric and Vera there together. Who knew what they might have found?

'You don't write the name Krystalle Storm down anywhere, do you?' I asked.

Mum bit her lip and nodded. 'Vera is a huge fan of mine. *Huge*. At the hairdresser's this afternoon, she was talking to her stylist about Krystalle Storm. Apparently Vera knows all the answers to the questions to the contest. She's already through to the semi-finals! And don't you *dare* say I told you so.'

'I don't need to, do I?' I looked at my watch. It was nearly eleven-thirty. 'There's nothing we can do about it tonight, Mum.'

'How much money should I give her to keep quiet?'

'You're not giving her money.'

Mum got to her feet. 'I'm going to call her.'

'It's too late! She was drunk and you've had more than a couple yourself. Leave it, Mum.'

But my mother didn't appear to be listening. 'I'll never sleep. I'm too worried. Vera could ruin me.'

'Why don't I make you a hot chocolate?'

'I don't want a hot chocolate,' Mum snapped. 'Just leave me be. I'm going to lie down. I feel a headache coming on.'

'Let's talk about this in the morning,' I said. 'Did you write any new pages for me to type up?'

'I left them in your bedroom.'

Leaving Mum with her predictable 'headache,'

I grabbed my laptop and climbed into bed with the next installment of Lady Evelyn's road to ruin.

Diagonal shafts of sunlight sliced through the panes of the glasshouse where luscious figs, ripe for the picking hung heavily on the vine. It was midday and Shelby was late. Lady Evelyn began to pace up and down, anxious that her note had been intercepted by one of the servants. The walled garden was too close to the Hall. It was a foolish idea to meet here even though her husband and brother were away. She wasn't sure about the young girl either. Shelby had said Irene could be trusted but the child was of gypsy blood. Then, suddenly, Shelby was there, his manly presence filled the doorframe and he looked so beautiful that she thought she would die from love. Shelby took her in his arms and their bodies fused together

'I love you,' she whispered. 'Never let me go.'

He pushed her against the brick wall, his rough hands burrowing beneath her petticoats. Lady Evelyn was wild with desire but the sound of footsteps and the cry of a young voice shattered their afternoon delight.

It was the gypsy girl. 'If you please, m'lady.'

Mortified, the lovers broke apart, ever conscious of their flushed faces and clothing in disarray. The young gypsy girl stood there, with bright, curious eyes. 'Their lordships are but two miles from here – out on the old coach road.'

'Thank you, Irene,' said Lady Evelyn.

Shelby smiled. 'I told you the gypsy would earn her sovereign.'

I sat back deep in thought. First the *Gypsy Temptress* and now, in this new book, gypsies again. What was my mother's fascination with gypsies and traveling boxing emporiums?

I don't remember what time I actually shut down my laptop, but during the early hours of the morning I was disturbed by voices coming from under my window. It sounded like Vera had enlisted William's help after all.

I made a quick visit to the bathroom. A strip of light shone under Mum's door. Knocking gently, I said, 'Mum? Are you awake?'

But there was no response. Believing she must have fallen asleep with the light on, I slowly opened the door intending to turn it off. Mum's bed was empty.

I padded along to her office. It was locked. I rattled the handle. 'Are you in there?' I demanded but there was no reply. I checked all the rooms downstairs but there was no sign of her. I tried to stem a tide of worry.

Surely my mother wouldn't do anything rash like confront Vera. But no, I reassured myself – just moments earlier I could have sworn I'd heard Vera outside. Yet still I couldn't shake off a feeling of unease.

Much as I tried to stay awake to await Mum's return, the events of the day had exhausted me. I'd just have to deal with her first thing tomorrow.

Chapter Fifteen

I opened my curtains the next morning to leaden gray skies. Out in the field the tractor's chassis looked as if it was partially wedged in a wide gutter. Its giant rear wheels were buried up to the axle in mud – a stark reminder of Vera's irrational outburst last night.

Downstairs, I heard male voices and found William and – to my surprise – Eric sitting at the kitchen table. Up close his bushy eyebrows seemed a law unto themselves with stray hairs curling upward like insect feelers. Eric sported a black eye and a livid weal on his chin not unlike the imprint of a medieval spur from his altercation with several suits of armor.

'I was just commiserating with Eric over his tractor,' said Mum with what I *knew* to be complete insincerity. 'Very sad. He said they'll have to borrow a crane to get it out and that the chassis might be damaged beyond repair.'

'As I told Iris,' Eric said, 'it's not the tractor I care about, it's Vera.'

Mum rolled her eyes.

Eric turned to me. 'Iris told me you saw her last night.'

'Why? What's wrong?'

'Vera's missing. Apparently,' said Mum. 'Maybe she's run off with Gayla.'

Eric turned white. 'Why would she run off with

191

Gayla? What do you mean?'

'Because it's obvious that you both had a fight,' Mum said bluntly. 'And by the looks of things, Vera won.'

Eric didn't answer.

'I passed Vera on the footpath in the pinewoods last night,' I said. 'She told me she was on her way to see you, William.'

'Me?' William looked startled. 'I was in the lower meadow with Jupiter all night.'

'That's weird, I thought I heard you and Vera talking outside my window in the early hours. You woke me up.'

'Not me,' said William. 'Jupiter had colic. I had to call the vet. As I said to Eric, her car's missing. I reckon Vera's gone to stay with a friend.'

'Vera doesn't have any friends,' said Eric.

'That doesn't surprise me,' Mum muttered.

'Vera's never stayed out all night,' said Eric.

'How would you know?' said Mum. 'Yesterday at the hairdresser's Vera told me you'd moved out and were living above the pub.'

'Yeah, well–' Eric shrugged.

'Maybe she's finally had enough of you and decided to leave for good.'

'Mum!' I said sharply. 'Can't you see he's worried?'

Eric held up his hand. 'Okay, all right, I know we haven't seen eye to eye, Iris–'

'That's a bit of understatement.' Mum waved her cast at him. 'You did this. You shouldn't have run me into the ditch with your wretched tractor. You must have seen me coming down the track?'

'I'm sorry. I've got a bit of a temper, like, and

192

well – maybe we can start again.'

'I know you've been moving those planks of wood in the courtyard,' Mum went on. 'I could have fallen and broken my neck and what's more, you've been turning off my water supply. Go on. Admit it.'

Eric took a sip of tea and then said, 'Okay. I admit it.'

'What!' Mum's eyes widened in surprise. 'You really do.'

Eric shrugged. 'Sorry. It was just a joke.'

'A *joke?*' Mum squeaked.

I opened my mouth to protest that I'd heard otherwise but William intervened. 'That's not really important at the moment, is it?' he said soothingly. 'Let's go over Vera's movements. Kat, you saw Vera last. Did she say anything out of the ordinary?'

'She told me she was scared of Eric because of what she'd done to his tractor,' I said.

'Bloody silly cow got the date wrong and over-reacted,' said Eric.

'How do you know she got the date wrong?' I asked.

'I told him.' Mum got up and took the half-drunk tea out of Eric's hands. 'But we can't do anything about it now, can we? Some of us are busy today. Good-bye.'

'Thanks for the tea,' Eric said as Mum ushered him and William out the back door and into the cow field.

'Mum, that was so rude.'

'I thought it was just William but he had Eric with him. I couldn't look at those eyebrows for another second. I kept thinking that at any moment they'd leap off his face and attack me.'

'Perhaps Vera likes the way they tickle her, but joking apart,' I said, 'Eric does seem worried.'

'If you want my opinion, he and Vera had a fight and she bolted. She'd already gone by the time I got there last night.'

'Gone? Oh, Mum!' I said, exasperated. 'You promised you wouldn't go to her cottage. We had an agreement.'

'You agreed, I didn't.' Mum was defiant. 'I thought I'd take over her parcels. Save her a journey.'

Vera's parcels were still in the corner. 'If you're going to lie, at least think it through.'

'Let's have boiled eggs for breakfast – and not too hard.'

'You're impossible.'

'How did it go last night?' Mum asked.

'I started reading *Gypsy Temptress*,' I said. 'I found a copy in Gayla's bedroom. And Lavinia had a copy, too.'

'That doesn't surprise me,' said Mum. 'Lavinia is probably the most passionate of them all only she's too uptight to let go.'

'Well, I doubt if she gets the chance,' I said. 'She and Rupert don't sleep together. And I think you were right about Rupert having an affair.'

As we tucked into boiled eggs and toast, I filled Mum in on Gayla's little trophy box.

Mum smashed her empty eggshell into a pulp. 'Silly little fool.'

'I had a long chat with Mrs. Cropper, too. The servants – for want of a better word – are all related. Vera is Mrs. Cropper's great-niece. Mrs. Cropper's brother was Walter Stark who worked as the gamekeeper here. That wouldn't happen to be the Shelby character in your book, would it?'

'No. Why would I do that?' said Mum quickly. 'Oh! Speaking of lovers, that reminds me, your future husband called for you.'

'David? Why didn't he ring my mobile?'

'Not *him*. That nice policeman.'

'Shawn, with the egg on his shirt?'

Mum handed me a Post-it. 'He had a question about what Gayla was wearing on Friday. Call his mobile. I'm going up to write. Having beetle-brows here has completely wasted my morning.'

Shawn picked up on the seventh or eighth ring. I wondered if he waited for the entire steam train medley to play before answering.

'It's Kat Stanford,' I said.

'Hello. Wait a moment–' There was a piercing scream in the background followed by a crash of breaking china. 'Sorry. Where were we?'

'Is everything okay?'

'Fine, fine – hold on.' There was a long pause and then the sound of heavy breathing. 'I'm in the cupboard now,' said Shawn. 'Couldn't speak in the kitchen. Too noisy. It's Sunday morning.'

'Yes. It is Sunday morning,' I said. 'You had a question about Gayla's clothing?'

'Can you describe it again, please?'

'Jeans, a white long-sleeved ruffled shirt, and a turquoise bandana.'

'Are you certain it was turquoise?' Shawn asked.

'Positive. Why?'

'Wait a minute–'

195

I waited at least three, until a muffled cry sounded in the background followed by a loud bang. Shawn came back on the line. 'Sorry about that.'

'Are you sure everything is okay?'

'No,' said Shawn. 'I'm afraid we found a turquoise bandana in Cavalier Copse.'

My stomach turned over. 'You think it belongs to *Gayla?*'

'Would you be able to identify it?'

'Yes – I – I – think so.'

'We found traces of – oh. Sorry. Good-bye.' Shawn abruptly broke the connection.

'Hello?' I said. 'Shawn?' I hit the redial button but frustratingly enough it went straight to voice mail. What an extraordinary conversation. He couldn't just leave me *dangling* after asking me to identify the bandana and ... traces of *what?*

I retrieved Shawn's business card from my tote bag and rang the police station. The answering machine told me to call back between nine and five, Monday to Friday because of 'limited staffing' and for a 'real emergency' to call 9-9-9.

Exasperated, I rang the Hall.

'You could try the cottage,' said Cropper. 'Shawn often stops in Sunday mornings.'

I darted upstairs – tripping again on the top step – tapped on Mum's door, and went to open it but it was locked. 'Go away,' she shouted. 'I'm on a roll.'

'Aren't you interested in what Shawn had to say about Gayla?'

'No.'

'They've found her bandana.'

196

'Good.'

'I'm going to see Mrs. Cropper.'

'Parcels – and put on a coat. It's going to rain.'

Grabbing Vera's boxes I set off through the woods. A quick glimpse into the stableyard showed two stable doors wide open and a scattering of straw across the hard standing. Just by the walled garden I heard my name being called from a bank of beech trees.

Harry, wearing his Biggles attire of goggles and white scarf, sat astride a wide branch, just feet off the ground. Bouncing up and down he shouted, 'My plane has been hit by turbulence. Whoa! I'm struggling with the controls!'

'You can hold her, Biggles.' Laughing, I joined him. 'Are you flying all by yourself?'

'No.' Harry carried on bouncing. 'Mummy's gone inside to see Vera.'

'Oh good, so Vera is home.' All that fuss for nothing, I thought. 'Have you seen Shawn the police officer here today?'

Harry shook his head, then, gesturing to the parcels in my hands, he said, 'What are you carrying, Stanford? Military supplies?'

'Something like that, sir,' I said.

'Can we carry on with our mission to rescue Flying Officer Jazzbo Jenkins from the Germans? Please! You promised!'

'I'll just deliver these and – providing your mother says yes – we can.'

I pushed open the door to Vera's cottage, stepped into a small front room, and called out, 'Anyone home? Vera? Lavinia? It's Kat.'

There was no reply – just the sound of a clock

197

ticking on the mantelpiece.

With a low-beamed ceiling and partially drawn curtains, the room felt gloomy and claustrophobic. A dark blue sofa and armchair were in front of a wood-burner stove. Pushed against the wall stood a dining room table and four wooden chairs with matching blue cushion pads.

On the table was Vera's Chanel handbag – the one she was carrying last night – along with three shoeboxes – Jimmy Choo, Prada, and Gucci – that lay open with their lids off. The shoes inside were still wrapped in tissue paper.

I set my boxes down next to a Mont Blanc rollerball pen and hardback notebook labeled MY LOVELY SHOES.

Vera had expensive tastes. There were no prizes for guessing where she spent her money and why Vera had asked Mum for a loan.

At the back of the room in the left-hand corner was an alcove containing a computer workstation and next to that, a wooden latch door that led to a narrow staircase. I called out again. 'Vera? Lavinia?'

And again, I was met with silence.

I tried the kitchen. It, too, had low beams and a tiny diamond-pane window with a flagstone floor. Another glass-paned door led to a walled courtyard outside.

The kitchen was untidy with dirty dishes piled up in the sink. On the draining board were the leopard print Louboutin shoes that Vera had been wearing last night, still encrusted with mud. A dirty frying pan stood on top of the cooker along with a half-drunk glass of wine. On the worktop stood a butter dish, loaf of bread, and an empty wine bottle. Last night's supper – not this morning's breakfast. I felt a stirring of unease.

The back door was ajar. I stepped into the yard and discovered an old potting shed with a slate roof that presumably used to be the former wash-room and toilet.

Lavinia emerged and gave a cry of surprise. 'Katherine! Goodness. You startled me.'

She was dressed in riding gear and hairnet but her usual pale complexion sported a distinct pink flush. 'Thank you for babysitting last night. Harry's spoken of nothing else. You read him a story,' she gabbled on. 'Very kind. Lovely day.'

'Yes it is and Harry's a lovely boy,' I said. 'Is Vera with you?'

'Why?'

'Some parcels of hers were delivered to the Carriage House.'

'Just leave them inside. Lovely day, isn't it?' she said again and cast a nervous look over her shoulder at the potting shed door.

'I left them in the cottage,' I said. 'Is Vera out there?'

'Not at the moment, no.' Lavinia's face flushed deeper. 'Off we jolly well go, then. After you.' She gestured for me to walk ahead but I stood my ground.

'Did you notice if Vera's bed was slept in?' I asked.

'Me?' Lavinia sounded horrified. 'Why would I?'

'Eric seems to think she has gone missing.'

'All this on-again, off-again.' Lavinia shuddered with distaste. 'Really. It's all so frightfully *common*.

Marriage is marriage and frankly, my people just get on with it and don't make such a fuss. Excuse me. Must crack on.'

She slipped past me and went back inside the cottage. Curious, I walked over to the potting shed and pushed open the door. It contained the usual useless implements – cracked terracotta pots, empty jam jars, an old rake minus a few teeth, pieces of wood with bent nails – and a chest freezer. My stomach gave a lurch and for some farcical reason, I imagined Vera – or even Gayla, lying in there, dead. I know I was being ridiculous but even so, my throat went dry when I lifted up the lid. It was filled with frozen meats, boxes of sausage rolls, and ice cream.

Feeling somewhat silly, I returned to the cottage and met Lavinia waiting for me outside the front door. 'Harry said you promised to play with him–'

'Not play! Finish our mission!' Harry exclaimed, bouncing furiously on the beech branch.

'Do you mind awfully?'

'I'd be happy to,' I said. 'Should we lock the cottage?'

'Oh, no one does that sort of thing here,' said Lavinia airily. 'It's not London, you know.'

Harry clambered of the branch and trotted over to join us. 'Are you ready, Flying Officer Stanford?'

'Oh, don't bother Katherine with your silly games, Harry.'

'It's not a game, is it, Biggles?' I said. 'We've got to finish our mission. What time would you like him back?'

'That would help I must say,' said Lavinia, brightening. 'Got a young horse I'm bringing on who could really do with some schooling. Noon? Good.'

Lavinia strode off and Harry gave a jump of delight. 'Guess what,' he said. 'I've got good news and bad news.'

'What's the good news?'

'Flying Officer Jazzbo Jenkins has been spotted in the Black Forest.'

'And the bad news?'

Harry gave a heavy sigh. 'He's behind enemy lines.'

'Oh no!' I cried. 'Then what are we waiting for?'

'Climb in, Stanford.' Harry pretended to step into the cockpit of his imaginary aircraft and I followed suit. 'We're in a Mosquito two-seater and you are my observer.'

'Aye, aye, Captain.'

'We're not in a ship, Stanford! This is a plane! Tally ho! Let's go!'

We trotted tandem style across an overgrown lawn stricken with weeds and entered a grassy avenue of topiaried shapes that had long lost their original form. Passing under a stone archway we jogged through a wire-framed tunnel heavy with wisteria and honeysuckle and on into a series of color-themed gardens – white, red, yellow, and purple. The latter was spectacular and filled with lavender bushes, lilac trees, and patches of irises and delphiniums.

'We're nearly there,' said Harry, breaking my thoughts.

'Good, I was getting so tired I thought my

wings might fall off.'

Harry made all kinds of impressive noises, simulated the landing gear coming down, put the engines into a very noisy reverse thrust before coming to a halt.

We had stopped at the end of the formal gardens where a ha-ha – a deep grass-filled ditch with a wall on the inside just below ground level – formed the official boundary to the estate. Beyond stood acres of waving corn. To our right was a thick pine forest. We took the path on the left – another avenue of weed-strewn cobbles lined with the oldest chestnut trees I'd ever seen.

At the end was a towering yew hedge with a man-made arched entrance cut into the hedge itself.

Harry said in a low voice, 'We've reached the Black Forest. We're going in on foot.'

'Yes, sir,' I whispered back and pretended to clamber out of our plane.

'And keep low,' said Harry. 'There's an enemy pillbox up on the ridge.'

We passed through the yew hedge and into a sunken garden overgrown with stinging nettles, thistles, and bracken. Thousands of tiny shells and colored glass were embedded in the low stone walls and pathways that ran in every direction.

Rounding a corner, Harry threw himself to the floor. 'Lions!' he shouted.

'I thought you said we were in the Black Forest!'

'We are!' Harry cried. 'They're German lions. Get down, Stanford.'

There was, indeed, a pair of stone lions that were just visible in the bracken.

Harry jumped to his feet and ran on. We came upon a garden where lichen-covered stone benches were set in secluded nooks and chipped statues of Greek gods and mythical creatures graced hidden alcoves. A statue of Neptune stood in the dry bowl of a stone fountain opposite a miniature Parthenon.

Harry seemed to have disappeared.

'Where are you?' I shouted, feeling a twinge of alarm. It was deathly quiet.

'Ta-dah!' Harry jumped out from behind the Parthenon holding a mouse. 'Here is Jazzbo Jenkins! Safely returned from the enemy!'

'Mission accomplished,' I said but then took a closer look. It wasn't Jazzbo Jenkins at all.

It was a Merrythought mouse, very similar to Jazzbo with the same velveteen face and body, string whiskers, and thin rope tail but it wasn't mine. This mouse was also dressed in a hand-knitted cardigan but it was red – Jazzbo's was blue. What's more, this little chap wore a dozen or so souvenir badges commemorating British seaside piers – Blackpool Pier, Brighton Pier, Paignton Pier, Worthing Pier – half of which had been demolished decades ago.

When my mother gave Jazzbo to me, I knew there were other Merrythought 'Jerry' mice out in the world. They weren't in the same league as Steiff but even so, they were collectors' items and still highly sought after.

I regarded Harry with suspicion. 'This is not Jazzbo Jenkins, Harry.'

'Yes it is,' said Harry defiantly.

'Take off your goggles and answer me truth-fully. I'm not angry. I just want to know.'

'It *is* Jazzbo Jenkins! It i*s!*' Harry shouted and promptly ran off again.

'Harry!' I cried. 'Come back here!' I set off after him but he darted down a path and then another and finally, vanished.

I was out of breath – and lost. I wasn't worried about Harry who clearly, knew where he was going, but I was jolly worried about me. The place was a multilevel maze of tiny pathways overgrown with shrubs. I had visions of being lost in here forever.

I took yet another path and pushed my way through straggling laurel hushes and came across a high Devon hedge bank covered with ground ivy. At the foot, the vegetation had been dis-turbed, revealing a gap with a narrow flight of steps. Covered in black moss and glistening with damp, they descended to an arched wooden door that was embedded in the bank itself. Very Hobbit-like, I thought.

The sun emerged from behind a cloud just as the wind picked up and rustled through the trees. I got a distinct sense that I was being watched. My skin began to prickle, just as it had last night at the Hall. I thought of the infamous Lady Frances or 'blue lady,' rumored to haunt this place and shivered.

Another gust of wind, stronger than the last, sent branches chattering and a shaft of sunlight repeatedly bounced off a metallic object on the bank above. Morse code.

'Biggles,' I called out. 'I know you're up there.' I scrambled up the bank but there was no sign of Harry. The Morse code signals continued to flash in the undergrowth a few yards farther along. 'This isn't funny, Harry,' I said as nettles stung my naked ankles.

And then I realized what was catching the sunlight. A metal snuff box.

It was, in fact, an eighteenth-century Meissen porcelain snuff box inlaid with silver and gold. On the lid was a delicate painting of an elephant. I guessed this was the one missing from Lady Edith's collection.

I felt disappointed. Harry must have stolen it, after all – or had he? Perhaps Gayla had gotten away with pocketing a few but that didn't explain why the snuff box had been abandoned in such an unusual location.

From my vantage point I could see down into a gloomy stairwell below. At the base, dead leaves and pulp had been scraped aside.

Someone was down there.

I paused at the top of the steps for a moment.

'Harry? I know where you are.'

But there was no answer.

I was gripped by a feeling of such foreboding it was making me dizzy. Slipping the snuff box into one pocket of my coat and the mouse into the other, I slowly descended the steps.

At the bottom I saw I was right. A diagonal wedge of mulch had been pushed away from the base of the door. I seized the iron ring handle, pulled the door toward me, and stepped into the cool interior.

'Is anyone there?' I called out.

Speckled light from a blue glass porthole above cast an eerie glow on a circular chamber. The walls were lined with cockles, whelks, oyster shells, mussels, and mosaics of blue and green glass. Two narrow passages led off into the darkness.

It was then that I saw a naked foot with painted toenails at the mouth of the left-hand passage. One navy polka-dot Wellington boot lay on its side.

My heart thundered in my chest. I edged farther in, holding the wall for support. 'Gayla?' I whispered. 'It's Kat. Are you okay?'

A sudden sunbeam sent a shaft of blue light down the passage.

To my horror, there, face up on the floor was Vera still dressed in her Saturday night finery.

I didn't need to feel for her pulse. I already knew.

Vera was dead.

Chapter Sixteen

'Sit down and drink this.' William took a silver hip flask off the shelf and steered me over to the tattered armchair in the corner of the tack room. 'It's Mrs. Cropper's cherry brandy.'

I sat down allowing William to throw a light-weight turnout sheet around my shoulders. It smelled of horse and was extremely comforting. William gallantly withdrew a clean handkerchief from his pocket, wiped the top of the flask, and said, 'I don't have germs.'

I took a deep draft and felt a rush of fire sear my throat and warm my belly. It definitely gave me a buzz.

'I just can't believe Eric finally snapped,' said William. 'He seemed so upset this morning but he *did* look as if he'd been in a fight. Vera must have fought back hard.'

I nodded bleakly but was unable to speak. I couldn't stop thinking about her.

Vera had been lying on the floor with her eyes closed and her hands clasped over her chest as if in prayer. Apart from a deep purple indent on her right temple, there was nothing to show she'd been – dare I say – murdered. If anything, she looked peaceful.

I kept replaying the moment of sheer horror when I touched Vera's skin and realized she was dead. What a blessing it had been to stumble upon the latch-gate tucked around the side of the hedge bank. It opened directly onto the service road that ran parallel to the Hall and stableyard.

Panic-stricken, I'd found William mucking out a loose box. He took one look at my face and shouted, 'Edith? Oh my God, what's happened? Is she dead?'

When I told him that I'd found Vera in the grotto he refused to believe that she'd been – I still struggled to think the word, let alone say it – murdered.

Within minutes William had called Little Dipperton's police station but it was closed on Sundays. Another call to Shawn's mobile assured us he'd be fifteen minutes. There was no sign of Eric and William's repeated phone calls to his mobile went straight to voicemail.

'That's a guilty sign if ever there was one,' said William grimly. 'Edith is going to be devastated. She was very fond of Vera.' He groaned, 'I'll have to break the news to Joan – that's Vera's mother.'

'You're a kind person, William,' I said.

'She's got Alzheimer's,' said William. 'Such a cruel disease. Perhaps it's a mercy that she'll not really understand.'

I took another nip of cherry brandy and felt the fire again.

'That stuff helps, doesn't it?' said William.

'I'm feeling a bit hot.' I threw off the sheet and removed my jacket. The toy mouse fell out of the pocket and onto the floor. I bent down to pick it up.

'Where did you find that?' William said sharply.

'Harry gave it to me.'

'Harry shouldn't take what isn't his,' said William. 'It belongs to Lady Edith. Here, let me have it.'

'Do you mind if I hold onto it for a day or so?' I said.

'I really think I should slip it back before Edith notices.' William reached for the toy but, childishly, I held the mouse close to my chest.

'I have one very similar to this,' I said. 'Mine also wears a hand-knitted cardigan but no badges of seaside piers. I want to compare them.'

'How extraordinary,' William said.

I frowned. 'I wonder where Lady Edith found hers.'

'At an auction, perhaps?'

Somehow I couldn't imagine Lady Edith bidding on a toy mouse.

'Isn't that where you must have gotten yours?' William went on. 'At an auction?'

'My mother gave mine to me–'

'*Iris* gave it to you?' William seemed shocked. 'Did she say where she got it?'

'Mum has always said she couldn't remember, but this is just too much of a coincidence,' I said. 'I think I'll ask her ladyship.'

'No!' William cried. 'I mean – not a good idea. I don't want to get Harry into trouble.'

Fortunately, all further conversation was cut short by a wailing police siren bringing me back abruptly to the horror of the morning – Vera's death.

William's expression turned thunderous. 'Bloody idiots!' he screamed, bounding out of the tack room. 'Turn the bloody thing off!' he shouted. 'The horses! Goddamit!'

Pulling my jacket back on, I hurried after him just as an old panda car with orange-and-yellow stripes turned into the yard and came to a screeching halt.

Tinkerbell, Lady Edith's favorite horse, was frantic. Eyes rolling with fear, she kept hurling herself at the stable door with such force I feared it would break. William attempted to comfort her but it was only when Shawn cut the engine that the siren stopped and Tinkerbell quieted down.

Shawn got out of the car followed by two uniformed police officers – a man with an enormous potbelly and heavy Captain Pugwash beard and a pretty redhead, her beauty only marred by a dark smudge of hair on her upper lip.

William hurried over and got right in Shawn's face and for a moment I thought he was going to take a swing at him. 'You moron!' he exclaimed.

'Whoa, steady on.' Shawn stepped back hastily. 'Faulty siren.'

'We couldn't turn it off, mate,' Captain Pugwash put in. 'Calm down now.'

Muttering more obscenities, William turned on his heel and disappeared inside Tinkerbell's box.

Shawn looked even more disheveled than usual, having thrown his beige trench coat over faded denim jeans and a T-shirt.

He reached out and squeezed my shoulder. 'Are you all right?' I nodded and then, quite unexpectedly, my eyes stung with tears.

Shawn produced a very grubby handkerchief that smelled strongly of bananas and gave it to me.

'I thought at first it was Gayla and then–'

'Well, it was Vera,' the redhead said briskly. 'And frankly, I'm not surprised. Everyone knew she and Eric fought like cats and dogs.'

'Thank you for your opinion, Roxy, but let's not condemn Eric quite yet,' Shawn said firmly. 'Allow me to introduce WPC Roxy Cairns and DC Clive Banks.'

I murmured a hello.

'I suppose the place will be crawling with the media now,' Roxy went on.

'Of course we'll try our best to keep it out of the papers,' said Shawn.

'The papers?' I said, confused.

'Celebrity finds dead body in grotto,' said Roxy.

'It's not every day we have a TV star in Little Dipperton.'

'No need to make things worse, Roxy,' said Clive. 'You're looking a bit peaky, luv. You're in shock. You should lie down.'

'I need to tell my mother,' I said.

'Of course, of course,' said Shawn. 'Why don't you escort Kat home, Clive? There'll be plenty of time for questions later and we can get the gist of what happened from William.'

Clive and I headed for the path through the pinewoods.

'What's it like to be a celebrity, then?' he asked.

'Difficult,' I said and hoped that answered his question.

'Must be nice to have all that money,' Clive persisted. 'Move to the countryside and push up the house prices for the locals. Did you know that ninety percent of second-home owners don't even live in their second homes?'

'Well, this is my mother's only home,' I said curtly. 'And I live in London.'

'After you.' Clive jumped forward and opened the latch-gate into the woods. A brace of pheasants powered out of the bushes screeching with indignation.

I picked up the pace, relieved that we had to walk in single file. It was astonishing that my celebrity status seemed to be more interesting to Clive than poor Vera's demise.

'That's right,' said Clive, trotting behind me. 'Aren't you shacked up with that famous art investigator bloke? What's his name? Glynn? Wynne?'

'It's David Wynne.' Fortunately Clive couldn't

see my expression of annoyance. I loathed personal questions.

'Shawn Googled you,' Clive went on. 'Old Wynne's not divorced though, is he?'

I didn't answer but walked even faster. 'I've seen his wife on the telly, too,' Clive called out. 'She's hot.'

Still I didn't answer.

'We could have used David Wynne's services twenty years ago when there was a big robbery here.'

I stopped and waited for Clive to join me. 'You know something about the robbery?'

'I was fourteen at the time. Caused a lot of excitement but Shawn's dad – he was the local plod back then – never caught the buggers.'

'Did you live at the Hall, too?' The place was beginning to sound like a commune.

'Born here. My dad was one of the gardeners,' said Clive. 'Eric, Shawn, Vera, and I, we all went to the same school. Vera was neurotic even then. She and Eric were always off-and-on but I never thought he'd do it – and in the grotto, too. She hated it there. Refused to go anywhere near the sunken garden because of the blue lady.'

'I've heard it's haunted.'

'You don't believe me?' said Clive. 'Gospel truth. Vera knew that. Why would she go there? Doesn't make any sense. Just goes to show you never really know someone.'

I thought of my mother and all her secrets. 'Yes, you're so right about that.'

Thankfully, we walked the rest of the way in silence.

'Thank you for escorting me, Clive,' I said as we arrived at the Carriage House.

'Mind if I look inside?' said Clive. 'Haven't been here since I was a lad. We used to have a den up in the hayloft. I'd like to see what's been done to the place.'

'Nothing has been done,' I said sweetly. 'I suspect it's the same as it was when you were a lad.'

He thrust out his jaw. 'I'd still like to look. I suppose she'll rip it all out. Destroy the soul of the place.'

I couldn't be bothered to argue and opened the front door. 'Good-bye,' I said then paused, listening to a *thump-thump-thump* and a muffled cry for help.

'What's that noise?' said Clive sharply.

My stomach flipped over. 'It's my mother.'

'Stay where you are!' Clive produced a black telescopic baton as if from thin air and yelled, 'Police!'

'Help!' Mum cried again, followed by more thumping that appeared to be coming in the direction of the kitchen.

I shoved Clive aside, flung open the kitchen door, and gasped. A purple harem pantaloon leg was dangling through a hole in the ceiling.

'Oh God! Stay there, Mum.'

'I'm hardly going for a run,' came the response.

'Stay here,' said Clive. 'If she falls through ... just catch her.'

Clive thundered up the stairs.

'Mind the top step,' I yelled but it was too late. There was a crash and cry of pain.

213

I raced after him but surprisingly – for such a large man – he was up on his feet and already standing over Mum by the time I reached her bedroom.

My mother had partially fallen through the floorboards. Because of her broken hand, she'd taken the weight onto her right shoulder, causing her face to be squashed against the wall. Her left leg was bent back at an unnatural angle that had fortunately stopped her from plunging into the kitchen below.

Mum gave Clive a winning smile. 'I see the cavalry has arrived.'

'At your service, ma'am. Allow me.' Putting his hands under Mum's arms, he lifted her effortlessly up and onto the bed where she lay exhausted on her back like a stranded fish.

'I thought you'd never come,' she panted.

Mum's harem pantaloons had ripped on the jagged edges of the floorboards. Blood oozed through the fabric.

'Are you hurt?' I asked.

'She needs to see a doctor and get a tetanus injection,' said Clive.

'I don't want a tetanus injection. There's TCP in the bathroom cabinet,' said Mum.

'Your poor face,' I said. Mum's cheek bore pressure marks from the crumbling plasterwork. 'You look as if you have a severe case of acne.' But Mum didn't laugh. 'I'll get the TCP,' I said. When I returned from the bathroom she was sitting on the edge of the bed with a blanket around her shoulders. Her face was white. 'Has she gone into shock?' I asked.

'I told her about Vera.' Clive was standing with his back to the window. A series of unintelligible squawks and crackles emanated from his shoulder mike.

'I can't believe it – no, I *can* believe it,' said Mum. 'It's usually the spouse in situations like this. I remember how upset Vera was when she came to see me. Eric killed her. Oh God! I knew he was unstable. That could have been me lying there on a cold stone floor in a cave.'

Clive's shoulder mike blurted out a police code that was clearly important. 'Got to go. SOCA and old Fluffy has arrived.'

'Fluffy?' I said.

'English bloodhound,' said Clive. 'She's been brought out of retirement.'

Mum looked up sharply. 'Why do you need forensics and a tracker dog? I thought you said Eric was guilty.'

Clive paused at the bedroom door. I noted a tear on the knee of his trousers where he'd taken a tumble up the stairs. 'I like to think so but the boss goes by the book.'

I rolled both pantaloons up to the top of Mum's thighs. The cuts were nasty and the knee that had stopped her complete fall was badly bruised.

'This might sting.'

Mum winced as I dabbed the TCP on her raw flesh. She gave another whimper as I helped her down the stairs and sat her on a kitchen chair at the table.

'Tea?' I suggested.

I removed my jacket and was about to put the

215

mouse and snuff box on the dresser when Mum exclaimed, 'Oh my God! Where did you find that?'

'I found the snuff box outside in the under-growth.'

'No, not *that.*' Mum sounded irritated. 'Ella Fitzgerald.'

'*Who?*'

Mum picked up the mouse and examined it from all quarters. 'This is Ella Fitzgerald.'

'Harry gave it to me. He tried to pass Ella Fitzgerald off as Jazzbo Jenkins.'

'But no, it doesn't make sense.' Mum shook her head. 'Billy is dead.'

'Ella. Billy. Are you going to tell me what's going on or do I have to force it out of you with more TCP?'

'Forget the tea. Get the gin and tonic and I think you should have a large one, too.'

'I already drank some of Mrs. Cropper's medicinal cherry brandy, thanks.'

'Trust me,' said Mum bleakly. 'You'll need it.'

Mum didn't say another word until I sat down with our drinks. She seemed nervous and her hands were trembling.

'Well?' I demanded.

She took a long draft and gave a satisfying shiver. 'I knew the Honeychurch Hall estate before,' she said. 'A long time ago.'

'I thought as much. You seem to know a lot for someone who has only been here three weeks. Did you come to Devon with Dad on holiday?'

'Sort of.' Mum took a deep breath 'Katherine–'

'You only call me Katherine when you're either

annoyed or it's something serious.'

'This *is* serious.' Mum reached for my hand and squeezed it.

'Okay, I'm getting worried now.'

'There's nothing to worry about,' said Mum. 'I used to stay here as a girl with my family.'

'You told me you lived in an orphanage!'

'I did for a time but then I was adopted by Aunt June and Uncle Ron – not my real relatives, obviously because I didn't have any. They ran Bushman's Traveling Boxing Emporium–'

'The one you mentioned in *Gypsy Temptress?*'

'You read it?' Mum brightened. 'When I was a girl I lived in a horse-drawn caravan, sleeping under the stars. I loved it. It was so romantic.'

'Oh no,' I groaned. 'Don't tell me, you're a gypsy.'

'Not exactly a gypsy but–'

'*The* Bushman's Traveling Boxing Emporium?' I exclaimed. 'I saw the photographs in the downstairs loo at the Hall. You came here, didn't you?'

'I just told you I did. Every summer.' Mum went on in a dreamy voice. 'Billy and I used to sleep in the hayloft. It was such an adventure.'

'Billy your stepbrother.'

'I *told* you about Billy and Alfred. They were boxers, you know.'

'Stay here!' I demanded. 'I will be right back.' I raced upstairs to Mum's bedroom and snatched the framed photograph of Mum and the boys off the mantelpiece.

Thrusting the photograph under Mum's nose I said, 'This is you with Billy and Alfred, isn't it?'

'Yes.' Mum smiled. 'They were happy days.'

Mum took another draft of gin. 'Lady Edith gave Billy and me a mouse each. Mine – Jazzbo Jenkins – had a blue cardigan and Ella Fitzgerald's was red.'

'What about Alfred? Didn't he get one?' I asked.

'Her ladyship didn't like Alfred,' Mum said dismissively. 'Every time the boxing emporium set up camp by the seaside, Billy bought a souvenir badge.'

'I still can't believe you are actually talking about *the* Lady Edith.' It was hard to picture the fierce old woman as someone who collected velveteen mice and knitted tiny cardigans.

'You should have seen Lady Edith in her youth,' said Mum. 'She was so beautiful. We idolized her. Everyone was in love with her. Men fell over themselves just to walk in her shadow. She was always so nice and didn't treat us like scum – not like her brother.'

'Don't tell me, let me guess,' I said. 'The World War Two pilot who was shot in a poaching accident?'

'I don't know anything about that,' Mum said, rather too quickly. 'It was all so long ago.'

'Why on earth didn't you tell Lady Edith that you've been here before?' I demanded. 'I'm surprised she didn't recognize you.'

'The last time I came here was in 1959,' said Mum. 'That was – goodness – over fifty years ago and let's face it, I don't look my normal self.'

'You can say that again,' I said. 'Billy must have come back before he had his aneurism. Why else would Ella whosit be here?'

'I was thinking the same thing.' Mum frowned.

218

'Ella Fitzgerald was Billy's lucky mascot in the boxing ring. He'd never part with her.'

'You parted with Jazzbo.'

'That's different. I gave him to you,' said Mum. 'Where *is* Jazzbo anyway?'

'Tell me more about Billy.'

'Aunt June and Uncle Ron were convinced that Billy was Lady Edith's love child.'

'No! Honestly Mum, you have such a vivid imagination. No wait–' I laughed. 'Don't tell me – the father was the gamekeeper?'

'Yes,' said Mum with a haughty sniff. 'Why else would Lady Edith spend so much time with us? She bought gifts, clothes, and toys. Took us on walking adventures in the park. Played the elephant umbrella stand game–'

'Go on,' I said.

'After your father died, I tracked Alfred to – well, Wormwood Scrubs actually,' said Mum.

'Wormwood Scrubs, the *prison?*'

'Alfred told me that Billy died on Blackpool Pier,' said Mum. 'He was there with him.'

'You should definitely tell Lady Edith,' I said. 'If Billy was her love child, she should be told what happened to him.'

'No,' Mum exclaimed. 'It's none of my business and it's definitely none of yours.'

'You are so infuriating,' I cried. 'Then why buy this place if you weren't intending to tell Lady Edith?'

'I have my reasons,' said Mum stiffly. 'Don't get all hot and bothered. It's got nothing to do with you.'

'I *am* getting hot and bothered. Why can't you

ever be honest?' I realized I was angry – very angry indeed. 'First you admit that you spent my entire childhood pretending to be ill but really writing pornography–'

'Erotic suspense–'

'And then you make up this Krystalle Storm character who lives in Italy with her Pomeranian–'

'Pekinese.'

'And now – fanfare of trumpets – it turns out you *did* have a family after all! What did Dad think about all this or are you going to lie about how you met him as well?'

'I told you I met him on Brighton Pier,' said Mum. 'That part was true.'

'But he wasn't rescuing you from a flock of seagulls, was he?'

'I made that bit up.'

'*Just* that bit?'

'Your father was working for the tax office at the time. He was sent to investigate a suspected ticket receipt scam at our boxing emporium.'

'A scam,' I snorted. 'Oh lovely. Criminals!'

'Of *course* we were fiddling the books!' said Mum with a mischievous grin. 'I liked Frank and then we fell in love and–' She shrugged. 'You know the rest.'

'Was I born out of wedlock or did you definitely elope?'

'Frank and I eloped,' said Mum. 'After that, Aunt June and Uncle Ron never spoke to me again. They felt betrayed. And of course, Frank's father wasn't too happy. He was a vicar and died before you were born – in case you wondered.'

'You are unbelievable!' I sputtered. 'You wrote about it. *You're* the gypsy temptress! It's your story! *"He was a man of the cloth. She – an outcast from her kin."'*

'They do say to write about what you know,' said Mum sheepishly.

'Don't you *dare* write about me!' I cried.

'Not even if I make Trudy a lunatic?'

A knock on the door put an end to our conversation that was just as well.

'That must be Dylan,' said Mum. 'For the first time I'm grateful for his timing.'

'Stay right there,' I said. 'I'm not finished with you yet.'

Chapter Seventeen

'Thank God you've arrived!' I said.

David stood in the doorway dressed in navy slacks, blazer, and muddy Florsheim shoes. With his black, wavy hair streaked with silver at the temples, he looked every inch the powerful, sophisticated businessman that I loved.

I threw myself into his arms and kissed him full on the lips.

'Steady on,' he exclaimed, turning pink. 'Isn't your mother here?'

'I've missed you and I've had a horrible day.'

'I've missed you, too,' said David. 'This is a quick stop to say hello.' He took my hand and gave it a squeeze. 'We can meet up later.'

'How is your father-in-law feeling?'

'Not good, I'm afraid. I left Trudy and the kids in Dartmouth. We'll stay there tonight at the Dart Marina Hotel. The town is a zoo.'

'You're *all* staying in Dartmouth?' I said, unable to hide my jealousy and disappointment. 'I thought they were going to stay near the hospice and you would try the local pub.'

'Kat, please,' said David. 'It's just for one night. I'll share with Sam.' He ruffled my hair. 'Come on, don't be silly. Trudy knows I'm seeing you this evening.'

I wasn't sure if this was supposed to make me feel better. The shock of discovering Vera dead coupled with Mum's stupefying revelations and the mysterious business with Gayla had left me very wobbly. 'I really need you, David.'

'And Trudy needs me more. You must understand what she's going through, after all.'

Of course I understood but frankly, I found it hard to believe that Trudy had parents. I'd always felt she'd been beamed down from another planet.

'Alright,' I said with a sigh. 'Mum's in the kitchen. Follow me.'

I threw open the kitchen door and ushered him in.

'Iris!' beamed David. 'Good God. What happened to you?'

'I am truly a miracle to behold,' said Mum.

'Mum had a car accident, fell into a manhole, fractured her foot in the downstairs loo when the cistern fell off the wall, plunged through the floorboards, narrowly escaped electrocution – shall I go on?' I said.

222

'And it's all Eric Pugsley's fault.'

David raised a quizzical eyebrow.

'Eric is the man I told you about on Friday,' I told him.

'Ah yes,' said David. 'The bloke with the scrap-yard.'

'That's right,' said Mum. 'And he's just murdered his wife.'

'What?' David exclaimed.

'We don't know that, Mother,' I said.

'But it's true,' said Mum. 'Kat found Vera's body in the grotto this morning. Just before lunch.'

David's jaw dropped. 'What?' he said again.

'Yes, I did,' I said. 'I found her. It was horrible.'

'Why the hell didn't you tell me?'

'I'm telling you now!'

'She's telling you now,' Mum echoed. 'Would you like a cup of tea? We're on gin.'

David turned to me. 'Is she joking?'

'No, we're definitely on gin.' Mum raised her glass. 'Cheers!'

'It's true. It happened – actually, no one knows when it happened. Can we talk about something else please?' I marched over to the kettle, checked there was enough water inside, and flipped the switch. 'And honestly, I'm fine.'

The three of us waited in silence for the kettle to boil. I watched Mum, who kept on staring at David, who stared politely back.

'Good grief, is that a Meissen?' David walked over to the dresser. He picked up the snuff box and examined it closely. 'Very nice. The painting of the elephant is exceptionally fine. Is this yours, Iris?' Gesturing to the dresser shelves he added,

'No, of course not, you collect coronation china.' David didn't even try to mask his distaste. 'Not that there's anything wrong with collecting coronation china.'

There was another awful silence.

'The snuffbox belongs to Lady Edith,' I said, desperate to fill the silence. 'She has quite a valuable collection so I'm told.'

'Really?' David cocked his head. 'How interesting. Very interesting.' He put down the snuffbox and picked up the mouse. 'How is Jazzbo these days?'

'That's not Jazzbo Jenkins,' Mum and I chorused.

David jumped. 'Sorry,' he said and dropped the toy back onto the table.

'Don't do that,' we chorused again, shared a look, and laughed.

'Ah, what an interesting photograph,' said David, peering at the picture of Mum and her stepbrothers. 'Surely that isn't *you*, is it, Iris?'

'No.' Mum seized the photograph and put it back on the dresser.

David started opening and closing drawers, closely watched by my mother who mouthed the words *'nosey parker.'*

He wandered over to the pantry and looked inside. 'Lots of space here, Iris. Good heavens. All those long-life meals and gallons of water – are you preparing for an invasion?'

'I'm being invaded right this second,' said Mum sweetly.

David opened the back door and gave a start of alarm. 'Cows!'

'This is the country,' Mum declared. 'They live here.'

I joined him, whispering, 'I am so sorry about my mother.'

'She hates me.' David pointed to the partially submerged tractor in the field. 'What happened there?'

'It fell into an old tunnel.'

William was circling the submerged tractor with a long stick. Every few moments he'd poke the chassis.

David sniggered. 'He's not going to get that thing out in a hurry.'

'You might be surprised,' I said. 'Apparently he used to be the strongest man in the world.'

'Is that the bloke who was supposed to have murdered his wife?'

'No, that's William,' I said. 'He's the stable manager here.'

William spied us and strolled over. 'Afternoon!'

'Ask William in,' Mum called out. 'Then we can have a party.'

William poked his head in 'I can't stay long. Rupert is on his way. He's going to help me get Eric's tractor out.'

'Where *is* Eric?' Mum asked.

'Helping police with enquiries.'

'I bet he is,' she said.

William stepped onto the back doormat and removed his muddy Wellington boots and padded inside. He wore clean, white socks. I thought of Vera's lone polka-dot Wellington boot and her painted toenails.

'They've actually arrested Eric?' I asked.

'No. From what I've heard he's denying everything,' said William. 'Says he's got a firm alibi at the Hare & Hounds.'

'Of course he'd say that!' Mum said with scorn. 'But who else would have done it?'

William shrugged. 'We'll soon know. The police seem to think it could be connected with that poor girl – Gayla.'

'Do you think there *is* a connection?' I asked, surprised.

'Who's Gayla?' said David.

'She was the nanny,' I said. 'Unfortunately, she's gone missing.'

'Goodness, it's never dull around here.' David offered his hand. 'I'm David.' The two men introduced themselves.

'Grab yourself a mug – or a glass – from the dresser, William,' said Mum.

'Just tea, please. Are you feeling better, Kat?' said William. 'I was worried about you.'

David threw a protective arm around my shoulders. 'She's fine.'

'We're all in shock,' said Mum.

William padded over to the dresser. There was a crash as Mum's photograph fell onto the flagstone floor.

'Oh, what an idiot I am,' William cried. 'Sorry. I think it's broken.'

'Be careful of the glass,' said David. 'Dustpan and brush?'

I retrieved both from under the kitchen sink and handed them to David who stooped down to clear it up.

William removed the photograph from the

broken frame. 'Good heavens. Is that *you*, Iris?'

'No,' said Mum, snatching it from his grasp.

'Boxing, eh? Looks like one of those old emporiums at the fair,' said William with a nervous laugh. 'Where was it taken?'

'I have no idea,' Mum lied. 'It was here when I moved in.'

'Did you know that a boxing emporium used come here every summer?' said William.

'Really?' said Mum, feigning innocence. 'Well, I'll be blowed. Fancy that.'

'Let me.' William went to take the dustpan and brush from David but David held on tightly.

'I've got it.' David deftly swept up the pieces. 'Could have been worse,' he went on. 'Thank God it wasn't one of your coronation specials, Iris.'

William gave a cry of surprise. 'Or this – thank God!' He picked up the snuff box. 'It's Lady Edith's! She's been looking for it for weeks. Who found it?'

'Kat,' said Mum.

'*You* found it?' said William, turning to me. 'Where exactly–?'

'How many snuff boxes does the countess have, William?' said David.

'Quite a collection. About thirty or forty,' said William. 'I've never really counted. Where did you say you found it, Kat?'

'Are they all of this caliber?' David demanded.

William looked confused. 'This what?'

'Caliber. *Quality?*'

'I don't know,' said William, turning to me again. 'Lady Edith will want to know where–?'

'About twenty years ago, there was a robbery

here,' David broke in. 'I'm sure you remember it well.'

Mum and I exchanged looks of surprise as David seemed to give William the third degree.

'Actually, no,' said William. 'I am probably the only person who did not grow up on the estate – wait – can you hear that noise?' He strode to the back door and flung it open. I could make out the sound of a diesel engine.

'Rupert has brought the old Land Rover,' said William, exasperated. 'We'll never pull the tractor out with that.'

'Perhaps David can help?' Mum suggested.

William regarded David and his Florsheim shoes keenly. 'We could do with an extra pair of hands – someone who can stand in the tunnel. The water's not deep. We'll kit you up in a pair of Wellies. What's your size?'

David blanched. 'I'm not sure–'

'David would love to, wouldn't you, David,' said Mum.

'Don't make him, Iris,' William teased. 'He's a city boy. Doesn't want to get his hands dirty.'

'I'm afraid I'm due back in Totnes,' said David with a sniff.

'I thought you were staying in Dartmouth?' I said.

'I'll be off, thanks for the tea.' William pulled on his boots and slipped the snuff box into his pocket. 'I'll return this. Her ladyship is going to be happy.'

The moment William had gone, Mum said, 'What's happening in Totnes, David?'

'My father-in-law is in a hospice.'

'Oh, your *father-in-law*,' said Mum pointedly.

228

'I'm sorry to hear that.'

David gave an apologetic smile. 'My wife and I are separated but I was always close to Hugh. It's been a very difficult time.'

'*Separated,* you say.' Mum poured herself *another* large gin and tonic. 'I suspect you're waiting until he dies before you can move forward with the divorce.'

'Mother!' I said, appalled.

I knew it was a wicked thing to think but at this precise moment I completely understood what drove people to commit murder.

'Don't worry, Kat.' David gave Mum a dazzling smile. 'Your mother is only concerned for your welfare. She thinks I'm leading you up the garden path.'

'And are you?' Mum asked.

'What a question, Iris.'

I grabbed the biscuit tin off the counter and removed the lid. 'Chocolate digestive, anyone?'

'Lovely.' David took a biscuit. 'Tell me what you've been doing with yourself, sweetheart?'

'The usual,' I said with forced gaiety. 'Cleaning, washing, cooking, typing–'

'Helping look after the little boy at the house,' Mum chipped in.

'His name is Harry,' I said. 'He wears these goggles and is obsessed with Biggles.'

'My son Sam loves Biggles adventure stories, too.'

'Harry has a collection of model airplanes in his bedroom that used to belong to his grandfather and great-uncle. They were fighter pilots in both World Wars. Actually–' I paused, 'Harry says he's seen his Great-Uncle Rupert's ghost and last night, I had this really weird feeling he was there, too.'

David patted my hand indulgently. 'You are funny, Kat.'

'No, I really did. You believe in ghosts, Mum, don't you?'

But my mother seemed lost in thought. 'How old are your children, David?'

'Sam is fifteen and Chloe is seventeen,' said David.

'Oh, you have *two*. How lovely.'

I already knew what was coming and tried to kick Mum under the table but missed. 'More tea, David?' I said desperately.

'Well, that'll be quite a big gap then, won't it,' Mum said.

'Gap?' said David.

'When you have more little bundles of joy.'

I jumped up and grabbed David's arm. 'Don't you think you should be going?'

'Yes,' said David gratefully and got to his feet. 'Thanks for the–' but I'd already hurried him out of the kitchen and into the hallway.

'I am so sorry about my mother,' I said. 'She's not herself today. She's very upset about Vera. We both are.'

'No. Iris is always like that with me,' said David. 'But I really do try.'

'I know.'

'Nothing can be as bad as the first time I met your father.'

'God, that was awful, wasn't it?' I said. 'All those questions about your honorable intentions.

But you soon won him over with your charm.'

Quite unexpectedly, I was hit by a wave of sadness.

David put his arm around my shoulder and gave me a hug. 'I know you miss him. And your mother must miss him, too, but she does seem happy here.'

'Mum has been acting as if she's been let out of jail.'

'Well, Frank was pretty oppressive.'

'No he wasn't.' It was perfectly alright for me to criticize my father but I couldn't bear anyone else to. 'Dad was just old fashioned and believed that a woman's place should be in the kitchen.'

'So, allow Iris to do what she wants now,' said David. 'She obviously wants to stay here.'

'I'm not having this conversation again.'

'Rick really wants you to come back to *Fakes & Treasures*. He's begging you. He said to name your price.'

'I told you I'm finished with the show. I've got too much on my mind right now.' I felt my temper growing. 'I found a dead woman today for heaven's sake.'

'I know, I know,' said David soothingly. 'Let's talk about it another time, okay?'

We stepped into the courtyard where a silver-gray Porsche SUV was parked next to the barn. It had a personalized number plate – WYN 1 – and looked brand new.

I was taken aback. 'Oh! You've bought a new car. I thought we couldn't afford it.'

'It's just a car,' said David. 'Please let's not argue, Kat. I have enough of that with Trudy.' David hugged me again. 'I'll pick you up at seven.'

Thoroughly irritated, I tramped back to the Carriage House. Mum was waiting by the front door. 'It looks like David's bought himself a new car.'

'Were you eavesdropping?'

Mum looked hurt but didn't deny it. 'I came to tell you that nice policeman Shawn just called,' she said. 'He wants you to go to Vera's cottage right now to answer some questions. Shall I come with you?'

'No, thanks,' I said stiffly. 'I think you've done enough damage for one day.'

'Me?' Mum exclaimed. 'I don't know what you're talking about.'

'It's obvious you can't stand David,' I said. 'And what was all that about the photograph? Why did you lie?'

Mum bristled. 'It's none of anyone's business,' she snapped. 'I'm sick of people judging me.'

'You mean me,' I exclaimed.

'Yes, you!' Mum shot back. 'I told you not to come.'

'You asked for my help!'

'I don't need it and I don't need you.'

I opened my mouth to protest but realized there was little point. Instead, I turned away.

'Where are you going?' Mum demanded.

'To see that ridiculous policeman,' I said wearily. 'And perhaps by the time I come back you might be ready to apologize.'

Chapter Eighteen

An old black Fiat 500 was parked behind Shawn's police car outside Honeychurch Cottages.

Vera's front door was ajar. I stepped into the front room to find a balding man in white overalls and latex gloves dusting for fingerprints.

'Hello,' I said. 'I'm looking for Detective Inspector Cropper.'

'Stay there. This is a crime scene,' he replied without bothering to look up.

'And my fingerprints will be on those boxes,' I said. 'I was here yesterday. I'm Kat Stanford.'

'Rapunzel!' he exclaimed. 'Well, well, well. Shawn said we had a celebrity in our midst. I'm Dick, by the way.'

As always I gave a polite smile. 'Shawn wanted to see me.'

'Upstairs.' Dick nodded over to the open latch door in the corner. 'Don't touch anything!'

Shawn and Roxy were in the first room on the right that appeared to be a storage area. Three of the walls had been lined with custom-made honeycombed squares, each containing a shoebox. Stuck to the outside of each one was a photograph of the shoes inside. Vera had been very organized.

'How many pairs of shoes do you reckon, Roxy?' said Shawn.

'One hundred ninety five. Do you want to bet?'

'I say two-fifty. Winner buys the first round at

the Hare & Hounds.'

Roxy examined the sole of a Jimmy Choo peep-toe pump. 'We're the same size.' She slipped off her brogues and stepped up into the shoes, holding onto Shawn for balance. 'Blimey. How can anyone walk in these things? I've gained five inches! Here, you try.'

'Don't be daft.'

I tapped on the door and in a loud voice said, 'Sorry to interrupt. Dick sent me up here.'

Shawn turned pink. 'Hello. Goodness. Hello! Come on in!'

'Goodness indeed,' I said. 'That's a lot of shoes.'

'Most of them haven't been worn,' said Roxy, stepping down from the shoe. 'All designer. I was telling Shawn some of them fetch around a hundred quid a pair.'

'Try six hundred for the Louboutins,' I said. 'I wonder how she could afford them.'

'Lou-what?' Shawn said.

'They always have red soles,' Roxy declared. 'Personally, I think they're a bit tarty.'

'Vera was wearing a pair of leopard print Louboutins on Saturday night,' I said. 'When I found her she was wearing Wellington boots.'

'One Wellington boot,' Roxy said firmly. 'The leopard print shoes are on the draining board–'

'In the kitchen,' I said. 'I saw them there this morning.'

'Are you sure about that?' said Shawn sharply.

'Already bagged up, Shawn,' said Roxy. 'Dick's logged them and everything.'

'Would you identify them please, Kat?'

'I'll stay here and count the shoes,' said Roxy.

I followed Shawn downstairs where a young lad with terrible acne was seated at Vera's computer workstation.

'Thanks for coming, Alan.' said Shawn, adding by way of explanation, 'Roxy's brother. He's a computer genius. Found anything interesting?'

'A journal, hidden away in a folder on her hard drive.'

'Nice work,' said Shawn.

We continued into the kitchen. Just as Roxy had said, Vera's Louboutins were bagged and labeled on the draining board. 'Yes, those are the shoes.'

'Thank you.' Shawn beamed. 'Right then. Yes.'

'You had some questions for me?'

'Let's go somewhere private.'

Somewhere private turned out to be his grand-mother's cottage next door. It had the same layout as Eric and Vera's place, only there were a plethora of framed family photographs and a lot of lace doilies. Shawn made himself at home in the kitchen and put the kettle on.

I became aware of an unsettling electricity be-tween us. In the confines of the tiny kitchen it made me nervous. I suspected Shawn felt it, too. As he reached for the tea caddy, the lid fell off and the tin dropped to the floor scattering loose tea everywhere.

'Bloody hell,' mumbled Shawn, lunging for a dustpan on the top of a pedal bin. It hadn't been emptied. Fluff and dirt tipped down the front of his soiled white T-shirt. 'Oh dear, I'm hopeless.'

'Don't worry,' I said. 'I feel your pain. I do that all the time.' And the truth was, I did.

I found a broom behind the door and swept the

lot into the corner.

Moments later Shawn put two mugs of tea down on the table and gestured for me to take a seat.

He took out his moleskin notepad. 'We're trying to trace Vera's last movements.'

I repeated what I'd told William earlier at the stableyard, especially Vera's hysterical comment that she feared Eric might try to kill her.

'And why was that, do you suppose?'

'She took Eric's beloved tractor for a joyride.'

'Any idea why?' said Shawn.

'Vera was upset because she thought Eric had stood her up but in fact, she'd gotten the wrong day. I rang the restaurant to check.'

'And you saw her around what time and where?' Shawn licked his thumb and flipped to a new page.

'Ten-ish. I met Vera along the footpath in the pinewoods. She was barefoot, and carrying those leopard print shoes. Her dress was muddy.'

'Do you know what she was doing in the pine-woods?' asked Shawn.

'Just that she'd been to see my mother.'

'And what were you doing at the Hall on Saturday night?'

'My mother volunteered me to look after Harry,' I said. 'Lady Edith and Lavinia had a social engagement.'

'Yes, I've already talked to them – and William, too. He was in the field with a sick horse.'

'I waited until Rupert came back and then I went home.' I hesitated. 'Actually, I overheard a disagreement between Rupert and Eric. I got the

236

impression that Gayla had something important that belonged to Rupert.'

'Go on.'

'I don't know...' I hesitated again. 'It could be just my imagination but I felt that Vera was somehow involved.'

Shawn's pencil stopped in midair. 'Eric has an alibi.'

'And you believe him? Who else could it be?' I said, surprised. 'Everyone was out and Rupert would never leave Harry alone in the house. Unless – what time do you think this happened?'

'Just answer the questions for now,' Shawn said. 'I know this must be difficult.'

I thought of Vera lying on the floor of the grotto. 'She was hit on the head, wasn't she? The way her hands were folded across her chest–'

'We're almost positive that the incident took place elsewhere–'

'You mean someone *deliberately* took her body to the grotto?' I said. 'If I hadn't lost Harry I may never have gone there. No one ever would have known–'

'Well ... not for some time,' said Shawn.

'But that means–'

'Yes,' said Shawn. 'Someone knew the garden well.'

The implication that it might not be Eric but someone local – someone *here* was too horrible to contemplate.

Shawn flipped to a new page. 'Let's go back to your mother. Were she and Vera friends?'

'They hardly knew each other,' I said, 'Mum's only lived here a few weeks.'

'But you said they saw each other on Saturday night?' said Shawn.

'Apparently Vera asked Mum for a loan but she refused – obviously.'

'A *loan,*' Shawn exclaimed. 'Do you know how much and why?'

'One thousand pounds, but as I said, Mum–'

There was a tap at the kitchen door and Dick poked his head in. He seemed excited. 'Sorry for the interruption but I think you should come and see what we've found.'

Shawn sprang to his feet. 'We'll finish up later. Let's go.'

Back in Vera's cottage a pile of neatly labeled Ziploc bags were on the dining room table. One contained yellow Post-it Notes. Dick picked it up and gave it to Shawn who slipped it inside his trench coat pocket.

'And Alan's found something interesting,' said Dick.

Alan was still seated at Vera's computer workstation. 'A lot of e-mails sent on Friday night to someone called Trudy Wynne – and again, on Saturday.'

My heart sank. 'She's a tabloid journalist who focuses on celebrity stories.'

'I thought I recognized the name,' said Alan. 'Doesn't she have a new reality show on the telly?'

'That's right,' said Dick. 'She also writes that column in the *Daily Post – Star Stalkers* – or something.'

'For which good money is paid,' said Shawn. 'And we know that Vera was short of cash.'

'Got something interesting here, Shawn.' Clive

238

appeared from the kitchen. He was carrying two boxes of Marks & Spencer sausage rolls, a box of *vol-au-vents,* and a metal keepsake tin shaped like the Eiffel Tower with PARIS emblazoned on the lid. 'Found this lot in the freezer in the potting shed out the back. You'll never believe what's inside.'

Clive emptied the contents from the two sausage roll boxes onto the table. 'Credit card statements,' he said. 'Obviously hiding them from Eric. If my Janet did this, I'd feel like killing her.'

'Not funny, Clive.' Shawn poked around the statements and picked up a couple at random. His eyes widened. 'Vera's been paying off the balance in chunks. Not just the minimum payment, either.'

'And get this.' Clive removed a wad of notes from inside the box of *vol-au-vents.* 'One thousand quid in fifty-pound notes.'

Shawn turned to me and said, 'One thousand pounds.'

'Mum told me she didn't give Vera any money,' I protested.

'There's your motive,' Clive went on. 'Clear as day. Eric told me that if he caught Vera using her cards again she'd live to regret it.'

'Well, she didn't live, did she,' said Shawn grimly.

'Eric must have known she was getting the money from somewhere,' I pointed out. 'The shoe collection alone is worth thousands and I can't imagine Vera got paid much as a housekeeper. And what about the new tractor Eric bought? Where did he get the money for that?'

The three men looked at me with surprise.

'*And* I saw Lady Lavinia here this morning, too,' I went on. 'She was in the potting shed.'

'What were you doing here on a Sunday morning?' Clive's voice was heavy with accusation. 'Covering your tracks?'

'Of course not!' I exclaimed. 'I came to deliver those parcels.' I pointed to the boxes on the dining room table. 'They were sent to the Carriage House by mistake – actually, they were *addressed* to the Carriage House. There are shoes and lingerie from Ann Summers...'

'Took a good look, did you?' said Clive.

'No,' I said, exasperated. 'The brands are marked on the side of the box. Obviously, Vera did not want Eric to know what she was up to.'

Shawn picked up the Eiffel Tower keepsake tin. 'Let's see what's in here.'

'Nothing much,' said Clive. 'I already looked.'

Shawn ignored Clive and removed the lid. Inside was an EpiPen and an expensive Waterford fountain pen engraved with the letters L.M.C.H. The tin reminded me of Gayla's bamboo keepsake box I'd found in her rubbish bin.

Shawn picked up the EpiPen and inspected it closely.

'That's for people who have allergies,' I said.

'Yes. I am aware of that.' Shawn frowned. 'Why would Vera put the tin in the freezer?'

'Is there anything I can do?' Mrs. Cropper stood in the doorway looking pale and drawn.

There were warm greetings all around and it was obvious that these men had grown up together and were fond of Shawn's grandmother and she of them. Clive steered her over to the dining room table and pulled out a chair but Mrs. Cropper waved him away. 'Don't fuss, so.'

Mrs. Cropper gave me a nod of acknowledgement and said, 'And you can tell your mother that I didn't appreciate being woken up on Saturday night.'

'When was this?' Shawn cried. 'Yesterday? Last night?'

'That's right,' said Mrs. Cropper. 'She was hammering on Vera's door demanding to be let in.'

Shawn regarded me with suspicion. 'But you said your mother didn't leave the house–'

'I knew she was lying,' muttered Clive

'I – we – sorry, I didn't know...' I finished lamely, thinking I could throttle my mother.

He turned to Mrs. Cropper and presented the metal tin. 'Do you recognize this, Gran?'

'Oh yes,' said Mrs. Cropper. 'It belonged to that tart, Kelly. It was a keepsake from her honeymoon in Paris when his lordship took her to the Eiffel Tower.' Mrs. Cropper's expression filled with distaste. 'I'd be lying if I said his lordship wasn't better off without her – God rest her soul.'

'It was in Vera's freezer, Gran.'

'Kelly's keepsake tin was in Vera's freezer?' Mrs. Cropper's jaw dropped. 'How did that happen? The two girls hated each other.'

'And these pens were inside.'

'Oh, my heavens!' Mrs. Cropper clutched at the table for support and sank onto the dining room chair. Her face was ashen. 'It's Kelly's EpiPen.'

'Wasn't Kelly allergic to bees?' I said. 'Why would Vera hide it in a tin?'

'My cherry brandy,' she whispered. 'Oh Vera! Vera!'

'Vera, *what*, Gran?' said Shawn urgently.

'No, no, I can't believe it. I won't believe it!' Mrs. Cropper got back on her feet, pushed Shawn aside with surprising force, and hurried out of the cottage.

We all looked at each other in confusion.

'Gran was very fond of Vera,' Shawn said finally.

'Two hundred and three,' Roxy announced as she entered the room. 'What have I missed?'

'Everything,' said Clive.

'Shawn? Are you alright?' Roxy asked.

'Yes. No. Excuse me, I must see if Gran's okay and Kat–' Shawn turned to me, his expression grim, 'Please tell your mother we will need to take a statement from her.'

I walked back to the Carriage House thoroughly disturbed. Yes, I could quite see Mum giving Vera a thousand pounds and lying about *that* but I couldn't see her hitting her on the head with a blunt object and dragging her – with one hand – down the steps and into the grotto.

But after all of today's revelations I realized I didn't know my mother at all.

Chapter Nineteen

'I have a horrible feeling that my mother might be involved in Vera's death,' I said to David as we were tucking into a delicious steak and kidney pie at the Hare & Hounds.

It was a busy Sunday night thanks to the arrival of the local Morris Men who were now raucously telling jokes.

'What a noisy rabble,' David exclaimed. 'And why are they dressed as chimney sweeps?'

'They're Morris Men.'

'With blackened faces?'

'Didn't you hear what I said, David?'

'Of course I did. I've always thought Iris capable of murdering me.'

'I'm serious!' I cried.

David turned to me. 'Why? Do *you* think she did it?'

'Of course not,' I said hotly. 'Mum's only got one hand.'

'You only need one hand to lift a hammer.'

'Who said anything about a hammer?'

'Don't get in a fizz,' said David. 'Your mother would have to have a motive.'

'Well...' I hesitated. 'Vera asked my mother for a thousand pounds.'

'So she said no. Big deal.'

'They found one thousand pounds in Vera's freezer.'

243

'Why the hell would Iris give her the money?' said David with a sneer. 'What a fool.'

'She's not a fool!' I exclaimed. 'My mother...' I hesitated again. 'My mother is a successful romance novelist and values her privacy. She was afraid of being blackmailed.'

'Your *mother?*' David gave a snort of disbelief. 'Would I have heard of her?'

'Krystalle Storm? It's a pseudonym, *obviously.*'

David's eyes widened. 'You're kidding. *The* Krystalle Storm? Trudy read her for a joke but liked her so much that she told all her friends.' He laughed. 'Krystalle Storm is supposedly a recluse. Trudy's wanted to interview her for months. Can you ask your mother if she'll do an exclusive?'

'This isn't about Trudy,' I said as alarm bells began to ring in my head. 'I shouldn't have told you.'

'So Vera found out who your mother really is. So what?'

'It's a bit more complicated than that.' I told him about the villa in Italy, the manor house in Devon, and my father's untimely demise.

David roared with laughter. 'No wonder she wanted to keep Vera quiet.'

'Don't say that!' I said angrily. 'It's not funny.'

David reached over and took my hand. 'Hey. I'm sorry,' he said gently. 'Iris will be fine.'

'Promise me you won't tell anyone. Please David.'

David shrugged. 'I promise. Pity though. Trudy would have gotten a kick out of that. Anyway, enough of your mother – I've got something far more important.'

'More important than my mother being a murder suspect?'

'I'm just trying to take your mind off things,' said David soothingly. 'Tell me about Lady Edith's snuff boxes. Does she have anything else of value?'

I described the collections in the museum room in great detail. 'The Polyphon music box is extremely rare. Oh – and there's also an early nineteenth-century taxidermy giraffe and a huge polar bear.'

David nodded. 'Very interesting. Very interesting indeed.' He reached into his blazer jacket pocket and withdrew a thick sheaf of papers. 'Here is a list of items stolen from the Hall on June twenty-first, 1990.'

I grabbed it. 'Clever you. That *was* fast.'

'I thought you'd be pleased.' David's eyes gleamed with excitement. 'I called in a few favors.'

I skimmed the list. There were a couple of paintings by John Collier, some pocket watches, silverware, and a handful of Victorian toys. 'Wow,' I said. 'The insurance claim was for one million pounds.'

David pulled out a handful of color photographs and handed them to me. 'Is this the necklace you were interested in?'

The seed pearl parure was displayed in its blue velvet case. There was a necklace, two bracelets, a pair of earrings, three brooches, and an elaborate corsage ornament. Up close, the workmanship was exquisite. Each piece was made of gold filigree that featured a leaf motif with a curved apex, midrib, margin, and veins, all depicted by strands of seed pearls sewn into the design.

'Yes! That's it!' I cried.

'It's officially known as the Honeychurch Suite,' said David. 'A complete set such as this is extremely rare and a collector's dream.'

'It's beautiful.'

'Elizabeth Taylor's Daisy Parure by Van Cleef & Arpels went under the hammer in New York in December of 2011 and fetched a staggering seven hundred and fifty thousand pounds,' said David. 'The Honeychurch Suite is in the same league.'

'Do you think it's been broken up?'

'I'm coming to that,' said David. 'When Lady Edith's husband died just two months later, the death duties – as they were called at the time – were just over one and a half million pounds. Convenient, eh?'

'What do you mean?'

'The family sold off a place called Home Farm and some land for around five hundred grand. With the money from the insurance claim, they were able to cover the death duties and keep the Hall.'

'Are you saying you think it was an inside job?'

'Take a look at the list again,' said David. 'Recognize anything?'

I stopped at one unexpected entry – a Steiff *Titanic* mourning bear, valued at fifty-thousand pounds. My stomach did a funny lurch. I'd seen such a bear in Harry's bedroom. It was highly unlikely that the family would have owned two.

'No,' I lied.

'Don't you think it interesting that there were no snuff boxes included?' David went on. 'They're small, valuable, and easy to steal. They're also easy to sell on the black market.'

I didn't answer because I had a horrible feeling that David could be right.

'The items reported stolen were cherry-picked,' David went on. 'Your Lady Edith didn't want to give up her snuff boxes or museum artifacts–'

'You can hardly smuggle out a polar bear–'

'Instead she picked a few things that she could live without.' David grinned. 'Yes, I'm convinced it was an inside job.'

'Are you turning this into one of your pet projects?' I said suddenly.

David grinned. 'You bet I am.'

'Wouldn't there have been an insurance investigation at the time? A police report?'

David reached into his pocket again and handed me another document. 'According to this, the intruder came in through the french windows in the middle of the night. No alarm. No broken windows. No witnesses. Apparently all the family was away, except for the servants who live on the estate but don't live in.'

I read the report and my stomach gave another lurch as Shawn's father, Detective Chief Superintendent Robert Cropper was confirmed as the investigating officer.

'We'll need to talk to Cropper,' said David.

'If he's still alive. It was over twenty years ago.'

'I want you to do some sleuthing. You already have access to the family–'

'I don't know if I want to,' I said quickly.

'You don't *know?*' David's eyes widened. 'Come on, Kat, this is for us, for our future–'

'I've met these people. I like them – and for

247

heaven's sake, their housekeeper just got murdered.'

'So? What's that got to do with the robbery?'

'And what about my mother?' I said. 'When Dad reported one of their neighbors for tax evasion she got hate mail for months.'

'You surprise me,' said David. 'Your father would be disappointed in you. I'm convinced that a crime was committed here. Fraud was committed here. This is my job. This is what I do. I work on commission, Kat. I will have university fees to pay and Trudy's alimony. Now that you're determined to drop out of *Fakes & Treasures* the pressure is on me to support–'

'I'm not asking you to support me,' I said angrily. 'I just don't want to do your dirty work.'

There was a horrible silence. I reached out for David's hand. He let me take it but acted all hurt.

'I didn't mean it quite like that,' I said. 'I just don't want to ask questions.'

'You don't have to ask questions,' said David. 'I just want you to take the list and look around the house.'

'I really don't feel–'

'Just see if you recognize anything on the list,' David pleaded. 'That's all – a painting, a candlestick – anything that was reported as being stolen.'

'Okay. I will,' I said reluctantly. 'But that's all.'

'Good.' David broke into a smile and gave me a warm hug. 'I think this calls for a little celebration. Excuse me!' He called out to a young woman clearing plates off a neighboring table. 'Do you have champagne here–' David took note of her name badge. 'Suzi?'

'Yes, we do,' she said. 'But it's expensive.'

'What brand? I don't expect Dom Perignon in this establishment but give me something close,' said David. 'We're celebrating, aren't we, darling?'

'Aw, that's lovely.' Suzi grinned. 'Be right back.'

She returned with two champagne flutes and a bottle of Moët & Chandon in an ice bucket. 'Compliments of the house. I hope you'll be very happy together.'

News travels fast. My attempt to clarify the situation was lost as the cork popped and a ragged cheer reverberated around the bar followed by a chorus of congratulations. I waited for David to make a joke about the misunderstanding but instead he looked smug and pulled me closer and allowed everyone to toast our health.

'How embarrassing. I hope that wasn't your idea of a proposal,' I said.

'Of course not, but it won't be long. I promise.' He grinned. 'And we got a free bottle of bubbly.'

A series of ear-splitting crackles and whistles stopped any further conversation as a voice came over the PA. 'And here tonight, for our Sunday karaoke we have the one, the amazing, the incredible... Toooooommmmm Joooones!'

There was a round of applause and catcalling as a perfect Tom Jones look-alike complete with his signature rockabilly quiff and tight leather trousers, stepped up onto the raised podium.

'Come on.' David stood up and took my hand. 'I'm not staying for this rubbish. Let's get out of here.'

We stopped at the bar to pay the bill where a large framed photograph of Vera was sitting on the counter. She was laughing at the camera and looked happy. The frame was draped with tiny white plastic rosebuds. A small placard – VERA: R.I.P. WE MISS YOU – was cellotaped to a plastic bucket marked CONTRIBUTIONS.

'So this is Vera.' David studied the photograph. 'Not how I imagined a housekeeper at all.'

As David settled up with the barmaid he gestured to the bucket. 'Add on thirty quid from us. We're sorry for your loss.'

I began to protest, 'David–!'

'Thirty!' The barmaid's eyes bugged out. 'Her husband Eric will be touched. Vera was one of our regulars. Who should I say–?'

'David Wynne.' He flashed her a winning smile and produced a business card from his wallet. 'Here, keep this.'

'I'm Doreen – oh!' Doreen looked at David's card and shrieked, 'You're that famous art investigator!'

'And this is Kat Stanford,' said David. *Fakes & Treasures.*'

'I *thought* you look familiar,' Doreen said. 'It's your hair!'

'Hello,' I said politely, wondering what on earth David was doing. He was usually so private.

Doreen beamed with pleasure. 'What an honor! My husband and I own the place. Vera was always one for the celebrities. Friends, were you?'

'Sorry!' David snatched his mobile out of his top pocket and clamped it to his ear. 'Must take this. Nice to talk to you,' and David propelled me out of the door.

'You never fail to surprise me,' I said as we walked back to the car. 'I take it that the phone call was just a ruse to get us out of there?'

'Of course.'

'Well ... that was a nice thing to do anyway,' I said as we headed to the car park. 'Very generous.'

'You've got to butter up the locals, Kat. As you said, this is a close community where everyone knows everyone's business. Doreen won't forget us in a hurry.'

I was stunned. 'You mean your generosity had nothing to do with contributing toward Vera's funeral?'

'I'm not that heartless,' said David. 'Let's say it was a way to kill two birds with one stone – no pun intended.'

'That's not funny!'

I slid into the Porsche feeling troubled. True, I'd always known David to be ambitious. His reputation for recovering stolen art and antiquities was world famous but I had never been remotely involved before and it didn't sit well with me.

David gloated all the way back. I couldn't stand it.

As we drew close to the gatehouses at the main entrance to the Hall I said, 'You can drop me here.'

'You'll have to walk through all that mud.'

'I need some fresh air.'

'If you insist.' David swung into the gateway and cut the engine. He took my hand and kissed it. 'I'll need you to stay down here for a while so I can build a case. That should make Iris happy having you for a bit longer.'

I didn't answer.

'The Honeychurches are one of the oldest families in England with connections to the royal family,' David went on. 'Trudy's going to love—'

'*Trudy* ... what?'

'Nothing,' he said sheepishly.

In the console, David's iPhone lit up and began to vibrate.

To my intense fury, I saw Trudy's name flashing up on the screen.

'Why don't you answer it?' I snatched my hand away. 'She is still your *wife*, after all.'

I flung the door open. David grabbed my arm. 'Don't end the evening like this. You know I love you.'

I pulled free and got out.

Chapter Twenty

I was upset – more with myself than anything else. The fact that David was staying with Trudy and their children was such a big red flag that I could no longer ignore the obvious. He was never going to marry me. I was just as naïve as Gayla.

David always had an excuse not to finalize his divorce. '"Oh, just a little longer, Kat,"' I mimicked aloud. '"Sam's got a big cricket match coming up and I don't want to upset him. Oh, now isn't a good time – Chloe's got her period. Oh! Trudy's stubbed her toe. You can't expect me to ask her *now*. But I *do* love you.'" I wanted to scream.

Even though I'd had nothing to do with their separation, I felt as if I was turning into the 'other woman' cliché of women's fiction.

Perhaps that was why historical romance novels were so popular. The male heroes were always strong and sure. They were prepared to fight duels to the death to claim the woman they loved. They weren't bogged down by modern-day responsibilities. I was quite certain that Shelby the gamekeeper didn't tell Lady Evelyn he needed more time to find himself or that he couldn't risk upsetting the family dog. No, Shelby was willing to risk his life so they could be together forever and to hell with the consequences.

As I stormed down the main drive my eyes smarted with tears. The last thing I wanted was to see my mother and hear her say I told you so.

I passed the wrought-iron archway and paused. I craved privacy and solitude – somewhere to pull myself together and sensed this was the place.

As I suspected, it opened into the family cemetery.

Set on a gentle slope and enclosed on three sides by a thick, ancient yew hedge, the fourth side lay open affording a spectacular view of the River Dart shimmering in the moonlight under a canopy of stars. I took a deep breath and inhaled the scent of flowers and the heady smell of mown grass. Given the state of the rest of the grounds, the cemetery was surprisingly well kept.

I drifted through the headstones to read the epitaphs.

Mr. Manners
May 1958–December 1970
A Real Gentleman

Intrigued, I moved to the next:

April Showers
February 1914–January 1935
Always Gracious

I soon realized this was an equine cemetery and not a family plot at all.

Each one-line inscription revealed the personality of a much beloved horse. There was Sky Bird, Nuthatch, and Braveheart – 'Adored Mud,' 'Unstoppable!' and 'Never Beaten: A True King.' Old horses from the Carriage House were laid to rest here, too – Fiddlesticks, China Cup, and Misty.

A flash of blue caught my eye as a figure emerged from the shadows. I gave a cry of alarm fearing this could be the famous ghost of the blue lady but to my relief, it was Lady Edith wrapped in a blue pashmina shawl.

'Sorry,' she said. 'I didn't mean to frighten you.'

'I thought you were a ghost.'

'That would be my Royalist ancestor, Lady Frances,' said Lady Edith with a low chuckle. 'This isn't her turf. She prefers the sunken garden.'

'Have you ever seen her?' I asked.

'Of course. Many times.' Lady Edith gestured to a wooden seat halfway down the hill. 'Shall we sit awhile?' She didn't wait for a reply and assumed I'd follow – which I did.

We sat down.

'My father started this cemetery the day Queen Victoria died,' she said. 'I come here every evening just to be with my old friends. So many friends, all gone now.'

'I'm really sorry about what happened to Vera–'

'Yes, very sad but life goes on.' Lady Edith cut me short, implying that the subject was closed. 'Do you know there are over thirty horses buried here?'

'What about your other pets?'

'The dogs have their own special place, too.'

'Where is Mr. Chips tonight?' I asked.

'With Harry,' said Lady Edith. 'That dog drives me absolutely mad.'

'Harry is a lovely boy.'

'Isn't he?' Lady Edith beamed. 'Thank God he's nothing like his father.'

I didn't know how to answer that. 'At first, I thought this was the family plot.'

'The mausoleum is at St. Peter's Church in Little Dipperton,' said Lady Edith. 'But I intend to be buried with my brother. We're sitting on him right now.'

'Oh!'

'Look.' She leaned aside to reveal a gold-plated plaque on the back of the wooden seat inscribed with the words RUPERT – MY BROTHER, MY BEST FRIEND.

'It's all arranged.' Lady Edith said with a hint of defiance. 'I've already talked to Carrow, the butcher. He's promised to cut out my heart and bury it here.'

'Oh!' I said again. 'Is that legal?'

'I don't care. I can do what I like.'

Perhaps Rupert was right to worry about his mother's sanity. As if reading my thoughts, Lady Edith added, 'My son is trying to get me committed, you know – sent off to that disgusting home for mad people. He steals my things. Tries to make me think I'm imagining it. I know his little game. He wants power of attorney so he gains control of the estate.'

Again, I wasn't quite sure how to respond and decided to change the subject. 'My mother loves living here.'

'Good. I'm happy to hear it. Does she come from this area?'

'No, although Mum did visit Little Dipperton when she was a child.' I was longing to tell Lady Edith that Mum had been part of the traveling boxing emporium that camped here every summer – but I kept my promise.

'Your mother *will* stay, won't she?'

'Hopefully not long term,' I said. 'She's too far away from me and I live in London.'

'London! Who could possibly prefer London to here?' Lady Edith turned to me and studied my face in the moonlight. 'You look like a nice gel. I want you to promise me ... promise me that your mother will never sell the Carriage House to my son or that dreadful Eric Pugsley.'

'I ... I ... can't promise that,' I faltered. 'I'm sorry.'

'Then all is lost.' Lady Edith looked away. Her shoulders slumped. 'Rupert will win, after all.'

'I know it's none of my business, but if you

wanted to keep the estate together, why did you sell the Carriage House to my mother in the first place?'

'When you are as old as I am and have had as many adventures – or should we say, lovers, as I have,' said Lady Edith with a wry smile, 'one tends to be in the know a lot.'

Recalling Cropper's comment about the dowager's beauty as a young woman, I asked, 'And what do you know?'

'I have a friend on the district planning committee. He told me all about H & P Developments – Honeychurch and Pugsley. Pugsley! I can't believe my own son would go into business with that wretched man. Rupert has hired a company called PlayScapes to develop the estate – to build an adventure playground, go-kart track, convert the Hall into twelve luxury flats, and–' Lady Edith began to tremble. 'Most wicked of all – tear up this sacred cemetery and turn it into a caravan park.'

I realized that Lady Edith had known all the time. 'After all these years of struggling to keep it together,' she went on bitterly. 'I'm betrayed by my own son.'

I'd seen the mailing tube marked PlayScapes in Rupert's bedroom but it was empty. I distinctly remembered Eric's reaction to the phone call he'd received the evening I arrived. Eric had called someone 'a stupid bitch' and dashed off. Then, there was the argument I'd overheard between Rupert and Eric last night at the Hall. Was it possible that Gayla had stolen the plans? It certainly would explain why Rupert had been so desperate to get them back and Eric's role in their safe recovery.

'Do you think Vera knew about the proposed development?' I suggested gently.

'No. Never. Absolutely not,' said Lady Edith firmly. 'Vera would have told me.'

'Why is the Carriage House so important?'

'The location is key to the development,' said Lady Edith. 'Without it, the builders can't lay drainage pipes, put in sewer lines, or build a road.'

'But when you put the property up for sale, how could you be sure that an outsider would buy it and not your son or Eric Pugsley?' I asked.

'Laney, my land agent, engineered the sealed bid. Rupert hasn't a bean to his name.' Lady Edith's voice grew heavy with contempt. 'It's all Lavinia's money.'

'What about Eric?' I asked. 'He seems to have money. He just bought a new tractor.'

Lady Edith laughed. 'The money came from one of his so-called investors – that's what Laney told me,' Lady Edith said. 'Eric Pugsley put in a high bid but your mother offered more–'

'And Eric spent that money on a tractor,' I finished.

'Believe me, Rupert will stop at nothing to get what he wants – whether it's seducing the nanny or getting rid of me. If it weren't for darling Harry, I'd throw him out.'

'And Lavinia?'

'She turns a blind eye,' said Lady Edith. 'Besotted with him. I'm glad I'm old. I don't want to be young again, all those feelings, all that heartache.'

We fell quiet for a moment, soaking up the peace

and beauty of a summer's evening. I began to understand Lady Edith's love for Honeychurch Hall. If Rupert ended up having his way, all this would be gone. I'd been to my own fair share of estate sales; seen cherished furniture and valuable paintings displayed outside on the front lawns for the viewing public to feed on like vultures, leaving the house an empty shell with no heart.

'There must be some way to keep it all together,' I said and realized I meant it. 'Can't you transfer the property to Harry?'

'He'll inherit when he's twenty-one. But by then it may be too late. But there is another option,' said Lady Edith. 'Something that would put the cat among the pigeons. Yes, Rupert is set to inherit upon my death but I can still change my mind. I can leave it to whomever I choose. I could even leave it all to William.'

'Did I hear my name?' William seemed to materialize from thin air. I wondered how long he'd been listening. 'Edith, you'll catch your death of cold out here at this time of night.'

'Stop fussing,' she said but I could tell she liked his attention.

We both stood up. William enquired after my mother's health then gently draped a tartan woolen wrap around Lady Edith's shoulders. 'I thought you wanted to check on Jupiter tonight. The vet said she's doing much better.'

'That's because of your magic touch,' said Lady Edith.

'And then we'll have hot chocolate and marshmallows.'

Lady Edith took his arm and paused. 'By the

way, I know all about you, dear,' she said to me. 'I read the newspapers. I enjoy the gossip columns. They make life more exciting but I will tell you one thing...'

I braced myself for a derogatory comment about *Fakes & Treasures*, 'Yes?'

'If he hasn't divorced his wife by now, he never will.'

I felt my face grow hot.

'I don't doubt he loves you,' Lady Edith went on. 'But does he love you enough to give up everything?'

Back at the Carriage House I dreaded bumping into Mum. She'd take one look at my face and guess I was upset.

I needn't have worried. On my bed were a pile of blotch-marked pages to type up and a note saying, 'Exhausted. Have gone to bed.'

I retreated to my own with my laptop and Mum's imagination.

Irene hid the letter behind her back. She was frightened. She'd always been afraid of the earl but now she was terrified.

'Give me that letter,' he commanded but the gypsy girl shook her head. The earl seized her arm and, with his other hand, slapped her hard across the cheek. Irene staggered slightly, allowing him the chance to snatch the paper out of her hand.

As he devoured the contents, the earl's face turned ashen. 'Is it true she's with child?' he demanded.

Irene shrank back. She didn't answer

'Tell me!'

Still she said nothing.

The earl thrust Irene aside and in three quick strides

reached his horse, mounted and galloped away.

Irene was frantic. She knew she had to find them. She knew she had to warn them.

She flew along the track toward the sunken garden. Two shots cut through the still night air

A woman began to scream hysterically.

Irene froze in her tracks, her heart thundering so hard she feared she would faint. The woman kept screaming and suddenly, Irene knew. She was too late. This was all her fault.

I turned to the next page but Mum had scribbled 'discarded cartridges, cordite, nostrils, and macaroni cheese.' Other words were illegible because of smudged ink and watermarks. I wondered if Mum had been crying.

I sank back into the pillows deep in thought.

If the Lady Evelyn in Mum's story was based on the Lady Edith of Honeychurch Hall, was the 'wicked' earl supposed to be her beloved brother, Rupert, or her own husband? Had the real Lady Edith been pregnant? Who fired the fatal shots in the sunken garden and who died?

Most telling of all, was Irene the gypsy girl my own mother?

Chapter Twenty-one

William's voice woke me after a restless night of horrific dreams. Instead of finding Vera dead in the grotto, it was my mother lying there dressed in gypsy clothing.

I looked out of my bedroom window. William was sliding a railway sleeper under the chassis of Eric's Massey Ferguson. A winch and chain were attached to the axle of the tractor and connected to a battered old blue T-Ford. Rupert sat in the open cab.

'Let's have one more crack at it,' shouted William. He planted his feet firmly apart like a Sumo wrestler, squatted, and yelled, 'Ready on three!'

'On the count of three,' Rupert shouted back.

'One, two, three!' shrieked a familiar voice. Harry stood below watching as Rupert floored the T-Ford. The engine roared and William lifted the sleeper a few inches, straining so hard that I could see his eyes popping and veins bulging on his forehead.

The tractor shot out of the gulley accompanied by cheers all around.

William dragged the sleeper out of the hole and laid it to one side. I threw open the window and cried, 'Bravo!'

'Yes, bravo!' Harry exclaimed as he dashed over to join his father who had turned off the engine and jumped down.

From my vantage point I was able to make out an exposed brick wall.

'Looks like the foundations of an earlier house,' said William, peering into the void.

'Well, I'll be buggered.' Rupert gave a laugh of delight. 'I don't believe it!'

'Yes, I'll be buggered!' Harry peered down. 'Is it a cellar to keep German prisoners?'

'It's part of the old secret tunnel that runs underground back to the Hall,' said Rupert.

'A tunnel!' shrieked Harry. 'Can we go down? *Please!*'

'Not today, it's flooded and far too dangerous,' said Rupert.

'Tomorrow–?'

I left them all to it. By the time I was dressed and downstairs, Mum was chatting to William, Rupert, and Harry in the kitchen about the tunnel.

'Kat! Guess what?' cried Harry as I entered the room. 'Father used to go down there all the time when he was nearly seven. He had a sword and everything.'

'We played Roundheads and Cavaliers,' said Rupert. It was the first time I'd seen him genuinely smiling. 'A lot of kids lived on the estate in those days. I was a Royalist – of course – and Eric always played the role of Oliver Cromwell.'

'Where is Eric?' I asked.

'Still at the police station but apparently, he has an alibi,' Mum declared.

'What's an alibi?' said Harry.

I gave Mum a warning look and hoped she got the hint not to talk about Vera in front of Harry.

'What would you be, Harry?' I said, changing the subject. 'A Roundhead or a Cavalier?'

'A Cavalier of course!'

I turned to William. 'And you?'

'William wasn't born here,' said Rupert. 'He's not one of us. He's from the north. Blackpool.'

'I thought I detected an accent,' I said. 'Mum's got family connections in Blackpool. What brought you here to Devon?'

'Yes,' said Rupert with an ill-disguised sneer. 'Why don't you tell them? It's a fascinating story.'

'William was the strongest man in the world,' Harry chimed in. 'He worked in a circus.'

'Not a circus.' William laughed and patted Harry's Biggles helmet.

'Yes, you did,' said Harry, batting William's hand away. 'You did! You told me so.'

'And there lies the mystery,' Rupert said.

A flicker of emotion crossed William's features, something hard to describe – irritation? Alarm? His eyes darted over to the oak dresser as if looking for something, and then returned back to me.

'I was lucky,' he said. 'A few years ago I met Edith at a horse show and she took a shine to me. Offered me a job.'

'And now she can't live without you,' Rupert said dryly.

'Who can't I live without?' came a crisp voice followed by a tap on the kitchen door. Mr. Chips bounded in followed by Lady Edith dressed in her usual riding habit.

'Mr. Chips!' cried Harry, hurling himself at the little dog and chuckling as he was covered in slobbery kisses.

William snapped to attention and fumbled for his pager in his top pocket.

Lady Edith was carrying a large padded brown envelope. 'This was delivered to the stables by mistake.' She gave a heavy sigh. 'Our new postman is absolutely hopeless.'

'I'm sorry Edith,' said William. 'My pager didn't go off.'

'I didn't page you,' Lady Edith replied. 'Oh, Rupert, I trust you were successful pulling out Pugsley's tractor?'

'I know you'll find this hard to believe, Mother, but yes, I was successful,' said Rupert. 'Come along Harry, let's take the tractor back to the barn. Do you want to drive?'

He headed to the door followed by Harry shrieking, 'Yes! Yes!'

It was nice to see father and son enjoying each other's company. I found myself changing my earlier opinion of their relationship. Rupert clearly adored Harry.

William headed for the door, too. 'I'll tack up Tinkerbell.'

'Not *now*. I told you I wanted to ride at eleven,' said Lady Edith. 'Tinkerbell hates standing around tacked up.'

'Right.' William stopped in his tracks and walked back to the kitchen table where he seemed uncharacteristically agitated. Again, his eyes darted over to the oak dresser. There was an awkward silence.

'A cup of tea, your ladyship?' said Mum suddenly.

William pulled out a chair for Lady Edith. 'Would you like to sit down?'

'No, thank you.' Lady Edith scanned the kitchen. 'I thought I'd come and see what you've been doing to the place, Mrs. Stanford. You still look a fright.'

'Yes, m'lady.' Mum gave an awkward curtsey.

'Goodness, I haven't been in here for decades,' said Lady Edith. 'What are you going to do with the carriageway and stalls?'

'I'm keeping them as they are – just a coat of paint,' said Mum. 'I was thinking that perhaps

265

the stables could be used again.'

Lady Edith nodded thoughtfully. 'What do you think, William?'

'I don't see why not,' he said.

Lady Edith seemed pleased. 'Of course you'll put in new plumbing.'

'I'll keep as much of the original fixtures as possible,' Mum enthused. 'The only structural work will be in the grooms' quarters – a new kitchen, bathroom, central heating – that sort of thing. I don't want to change the exterior at all.'

'So you *have* decided to stay. Your daughter felt you'd be returning to London.'

Mum shot me a filthy look. 'I don't know where she got that idea,' she said coldly. 'I plan on leaving here feet first.'

Lady Edith showed a yellow-toothed grin. 'As do I–'

'And me,' William put in.

'There are so few carriage houses in Great Britain these days that aren't hideous conversions,' Lady Edith went on. 'Your plans, Mrs. Stanford, make me very happy indeed.'

'I love it here,' said Mum.

'Yes, Honeychurch Hall tends to get under one's skin,' said Lady Edith. 'Your daughter tells me you came to Little Dipperton as a child?'

Mum shot me another filthy look. 'Yes. That's right. I've always loved Devon.'

'Where did you stay?'

'Um – well – here and there,' stammered Mum.

Lady Edith walked around the kitchen. She took in the coronation china neatly arranged on the shelves above the dresser. 'You've got quite a collection there. Is that a coronation snuff box?'

'It's nothing fancy,' said Mum. 'Just King George V and Queen Mary.'

Lady Edith inspected the painted china snuff box featuring the new monarchs dated June 22, 1911.

'It's nothing like your snuff box collection, m'lady,' said Mum.

'No, quite.' Lady Edith picked up the photograph of the boxing emporium on top of the dresser and gave a cry of delight. 'Good heavens. Where on earth did you find this?'

Mum turned pale. 'I ... I ... can't remember. A jumble sale?'

'Tell her that's you!' I hissed.

Lady Edith studied the photograph closely. It was obvious that she did not recognize my mother – hardly surprising given the fifty-year gap and Mum's bruised and swollen face today.

'This was taken in the park,' said Lady Edith. 'Yes! I'm sure of it. I recognize the old cedar tree.'

'Wait ... I think ... yes ... I found it lying about in the old tack room,' Mum mumbled. 'That's right.'

'The traveling boxing emporium came here every summer.' Lady Edith turned the photograph over and studied the backside. Her eyes widened in surprise. 'Good heavens!' she said excitedly. 'This is a photo of *you*, William.'

'What? That's not–' Mum began but snapped her mouth shut.

'*Do* look.' Lady Edith gestured for William to come over. 'Someone has written on the back, 'Summer, 1954 – Alfred, Billy, and me.'' A shadow passed over Lady Edith's face. 'You were such a sweet boy, Billy–'

Silently, William appealed to us for help. It was obvious that Lady Edith was having some kind of memory lapse.

'Do you remember the cedar tree?' she said wistfully. 'It was struck by lightning, you know.'

'Come along, Edith,' said William briskly. 'Let's go and see Jupiter. Remember that we need to give her medication the same time every morning.'

'Yes, yes, of course.' Lady Edith gave one last look at the photograph before putting it back into the charger plate. I followed them out into the hallway and bid good-bye.

Lady Edith turned to me. 'Did you enjoy your ride on Tinkerbell this morning?' she asked. 'She's quite a handful, isn't she?'

Taken aback I said, 'I didn't ride–'

'Something came up at the last minute,' said William quickly. 'Kat changed her mind, didn't you, Kat?'

'Yes, that's right,' I said. 'But I'd love to ride out another time.'

William shot me a grateful look.

I returned to the kitchen. 'I think Lady Edith really *is* losing her mind–' I stopped in my tracks. 'What's wrong? You look as if you have seen a ghost.'

Mum was sitting at the kitchen table staring at the mail Lady Edith had brought in. Her face was ashen.

'Look,' she whispered and pushed a white envelope toward me. 'It was stuck underneath that brown one.'

The envelope was addressed to William Bushman, The Stable Yard, Honeychurch Hall, Little Dipperton. The return address was from a Mrs. Joan Stark, Sunny Hill Lodge Residential Home.

'Isn't Joan Stark, Vera's mother?' I said. 'William must have broken the news. I must say he seems very–'

'Don't you see?' said Mum sharply. 'Bushman. Billy Bushman? No, not possible – not possible at all.'

'You mean – Bushman as in Bushman's Traveling Boxing Emporium?' My jaw dropped. 'William is your *stepbrother* Billy?'

'No, of course he's not!' Mum cried.

'Mum – it could be Billy,' I said slowly. 'You told me that Lady Edith gave you and Billy each a toy mouse. Billy's has badges on the cardigan – badges of piers. One is Blackpool Pier. How else could the Ella Fitzgerald mouse end back here?'

'Billy was smaller. Whippier,' said Mum. 'He was a boxer, not a tug-of-war kind of man – I need a gin and tonic.'

'So do I,' I said and quickly made two.

'He's trying to pass himself off as my Billy,' Mum exclaimed. 'And it's *not* him. I'd know!' Mum shook her head vigorously. 'It's not him. It can't be. When Billy turned professional, his nose was squashed flat in the boxing ring and he had a cauliflower ear – the left one.'

'Well, there's always plastic surgery,' I said doubtfully.

'Why can't you be serious,' Mum snapped.

'I am. I'm trying to make sense of it all,' I said.

269

'When was the last time you saw Billy?'

Mum shrugged. 'I don't know... 1962.'

'And how old would he have been?'

Mum shrugged again. 'Fifteen.'

'So you haven't seen Lady Edith or Billy for over fifty years.'

Mum shook her head vigorously again. 'I would know Billy anywhere and besides, his brother Alfred said he died of an aneurism on Blackpool Pier. Remember? Hardly something you'd make up.'

I had to admit she had a point – and then I recalled the conversation I'd had with Lady Edith in the equine cemetery the night before. 'Lady Edith mentioned she might even leave the estate to William and frankly, I wouldn't blame her.'

'That's a terrible thing to say!' said Mum.

'Does it really matter if William is – or isn't her son?' I said. 'It was all so long ago.'

'Of course it matters!' Mum cried. 'He's an imposter!'

'Why don't you talk to Alfred again?' I said. 'Wouldn't there be a grave or something?'

'Alfred told me that Billy's ashes were scattered off the end of Blackpool Pier.'

'Then ask William,' I said. 'It's too much of a coincidence, Mum. Surely you see that.'

'I refuse to discuss this anymore. The subject is closed.' She jabbed a finger at the large brown envelope that still lay unopened on the table. 'Now you can make yourself useful and open that.'

'I don't understand you,' I said. 'Don't you want to know?'

With a heavy sigh, I ripped open the large

brown envelope and withdrew several large sheets of paper folded into quarters. 'What on earth–?'

A handwritten note fell out and Mum bent over to pick it up. Her eyes widened in shock. 'Well, I'll be blowed!' she cried. 'Look, it's from Gayla!'

I grabbed it. FOR LADY EDITH. URGENT. CONFIDENTIAL. 'When was this posted?'

Mum studied the postmark on the brown envelope. 'Dartmouth. Stamped Saturday morning,' she exclaimed. 'I thought you said she was going to Plymouth railway station?'

'That's what she told me,' I said.

'What a naughty girl. Crying wolf and causing all that fuss! Why would she do that? What are these papers?'

My stomach sank. 'They're drawings.'

Mum looked at them blankly. 'Who are H & P Developments? What is PlayScapes?'

'They're plans to develop Honeychurch Hall,' I said and squeezed Mum's shoulder. 'And the Carriage House is slap bang in the middle. See?' I pointed to the blueprints. 'Right there.'

It was exactly as Lady Edith had described. The Hall itself would be divided into twelve luxury flats. Cromwell Meadows would house a go-kart track. The parkland would become an adventure playground called Wizard Wonderland and Lady Edith's beloved equine cemetery was earmarked as a caravan park *with spectacular views over the River Dart.* The Carriage House was labeled RESTAURANT: OFFICES: PUBLIC CONVENIENCES.

Mum's eyes welled up with tears. 'Did you know about this?'

271

'Lady Edith told me last night,' I said. 'I was going to tell you.'

'How nice of you,' Mum said bitterly.

'Gayla must have found out,' I said. 'My guess is that when Rupert dumped her she decided to get her revenge by stealing the plans and telling Lady Edith so she'd disinherit him for good.' Quickly, I filled Mum in on the conversation I'd had with her ladyship in the equine cemetery.

It all made sense – Gayla's panicked reaction upon seeing Rupert's car at the top of the driveway on Friday night and Eric's role in trying to retrieve the plans that hadn't been destroyed after all. But what still puzzled me was how Vera fit in and how she ended up dead in the grotto.

'If Lady Edith knew all this,' said Mum, 'why doesn't she disinherit Rupert anyway?'

'I asked her the same question. Lady Edith told me that Harry would get everything when he turns twenty-one but of course, Rupert would manage the estate until then – unless she decided to leave it to someone else–'

'You mean, William,' said Mum flatly. 'No wonder Rupert wanted me to move to Sawmill Cottage–'

'And Eric's role was just to make your life difficult so that you'd do just that,' I went on. 'We should inform the police. These are vital clues in Gayla's disappearance. She may well have posted these plans from Dartmouth but we still don't know if she is safe.'

'Yes, you're right.'

'Let's take these plans straightaway. Perhaps we can even get the sale of the Carriage House

voided because you bought it under false circumstances.'

'I'm not moving, *now*,' Mum said stubbornly.
She gestured to the blueprints. 'It's obvious that
without the Carriage House they can't really
develop Wizard – whatever it's called.'

'Mum, you know as well as I do that eventually,
the developers will get their own way,' I said.
'They always do.'

'I can't – I *won't* betray Lady Edith again,' said
Mum hysterically. 'I let her down all those years
ago. I was tricked. He tricked me.'

'Who tricked you?' I said gently. 'Who?'

'I didn't tell him about Billy,' she said. 'He
already guessed he was her son.'

'You're Irene, the gypsy girl in the story, aren't
you?' I said. 'The go-between Lady Evelyn and
Shelby.'

Mum nodded. 'You guessed.'

'And *was* there a love child?' I asked.

Mum nodded again. 'Yes. It was Billy but of
course I didn't know until ... until...' She bit her
lip. 'I was five when Billy suddenly joined our
family. Aunt June said that the stork had brought
a baby to us.'

Mum was visibly upset. I reached over and took
her hand. 'I carried Lady Edith's love letters for
years. I thought it terribly romantic – very Lady
Chatterley and Mellors the gamekeeper.' Mum
went on, 'It was a different time back then. They
could never marry.'

'And then Lady Edith's brother found out?' I
prompted.

'Yes, it was my fault,' said Mum. 'He was very
273

protective of her – especially after their parents died in the Blitz. At least that's what Aunt June told me.'

'How did it end?'

Mum fell silent at the memory. Tears filled her eyes. 'I was taking a letter and the earl – that would be her brother, Rupert – stopped me.'

'How can it be your fault? How old were you?'

'Fifteen,' said Mum. 'Oh Kat, Honeychurch Hall was the only place I ever felt happy. I feel as if I have come home.'

'At least now I understand why you chose here and want to stay.'

'They were wonderful summers,' said Mum. 'It was only later I realized we were allowed to camp here so that Lady Edith could see her son.' Mum wiped away a tear. 'And then I ruined it. His lordship challenged Stark to a duel.'

'Good God,' I said. 'In this day and age?'

'Both of them died,' said Mum. 'Lady Edith blamed me. I was devastated. We were told never to come back to Honeychurch Hall. Frankly, I was surprised no one questioned me at the time. It was reported as a tragic shooting accident and hushed up.'

'Did Billy know Lady Edith was his mother?' I asked.

'Those things were kept quiet. Illegitimate children were shameful secrets in those days.'

'And she never saw Billy again, either?' I asked.

'I don't know.' Mum shrugged. 'When I married your father, I lost touch with everyone.'

'Did Dad know about all this?'

'Of course he did,' Mum said. 'It was your

274

father who found the newspaper clipping of Lady Edith in the first place just before he died. I suppose Frank wanted me make my peace with her. It's haunted me for years and now I find I just can't do it. It's best to let sleeping dogs lie.' Mum looked up. Her eyes filled with tears again. 'He said that the only thing that mattered in this life was love and forgiveness.'

'Tell her,' I said. 'Tell her everything. No more secrets, Mum. Promise.'

'You don't understand,' said Mum. 'Lady Edith does not forgive.' She abruptly switched gears. 'I think I'd better file that complaint against Eric Pugsley – especially if he is really trying to get me out,' she said suddenly. 'Do you think the police station closes for lunch?'

With a sigh I said, 'Fine. I'll get my things together and we'll go.'

Chapter Twenty-two

'Is this *it?*' said Mum, taking in the tiny police station on the outskirts of Dartmouth. 'How can anyone solve a crime from this cupboard?'

The police station was just one room with a sparsely furnished waiting area comprised of an uncomfortable-looking bench seat and two hard chairs. A round table held a handful of leaflets – Devon Recycling, Neighborhood Watch, and a few flyers for an upcoming Morris Dancing extravaganza.

A narrow counter kept the general public at bay. A large notice board covered the wall behind it with various pertinent police matters – and a black-and-white poster of Gayla. The photograph showed her standing in front of Nelson's Column in Trafalgar Square pulling a goofy face for the camera.

'We'll soon wipe the smile off her face,' said Mum. 'What a little minx.'

An old-fashioned bell was on the counter alongside a plaque saying YOUR DESK SERGEANT TODAY IS: MALCOLM.

'Malcolm? Shawn? Clive? Everything is so informal these days,' muttered Mum as she gave the bell a rap.

A uniformed police officer in his fifties – presumably Malcolm – with a hooked nose and wire-rimmed spectacles, emerged from a door that I'd assumed was a cupboard. I caught a glimpse of a kettle and an easy chair.

Malcolm was holding a cheese and pickle sandwich. 'Sorry,' he said through a mouthful of bread. 'Just making a bit of lunch. We don't often get walk-ins. Lost a cat, have you?'

Gesturing to Gayla's poster, I said, 'We've got important information regarding the missing nanny.'

Malcolm shoved the rest of his sandwich into his mouth and turned to the notice board. I could just about make out, 'Should have taken this down,' and 'bloody foreigners.'

'You've found her!' Mum and I chorused.

We waited for Malcolm to finish his mouthful. 'Yep. Got arrested for shoplifting on Saturday afternoon and spent the night in Dartmouth. They're a full-service police station. We don't have the facilities here.'

'Oh really? I thought this was a cell,' said Mum.

I was stunned. 'But Gayla was declared missing. There were teams of police out looking for her and no one thought to inform the Honeychurch family?'

'We only have a skeleton staff at the weekend – oh – my – God!' Malcolm gasped. His eyes raked in my appearance. 'Are you on the telly?'

'*Fakes & Treasures*,' said Mum. 'Yes, you have a celebrity in your midst.'

'Kat Stanford!' Malcolm beamed, exposing the urgent need for a toothbrush. 'My wife loves your show.'

'I'm so glad.' I beckoned Malcolm closer and said in a low voice, 'So what happened to the bloodstained turquoise bandana?'

'Can't tell you, sorry.'

'Come on, Malcolm,' I said, flashing him my best smile. 'Not even for me?'

'Red paint,' said Malcolm flatly. 'Something about building a model airplane. Shawn's pretty pissed off, I can tell you.'

'Is he here?' I said.

'And if so, where?' said Mum, scanning the room. 'Under the table?'

'Morning!'

Malcolm's demeanor immediately changed as WPC Roxy Cairns strolled through the front door accompanied by identical twin boys of around five years old dressed in matching shorts and dinosaur-emblazoned T-shirts. They each had a

277

coloring book and packet of crayons.

'We've just heard that you found Gayla,' I said.

'Yes. She took us all for a ride,' said Roxy. 'There was no wealthy father or agency called Nannies-Abroad. Why Vera hired her is a mystery to me. Fancy not doing proper background checks on a nanny!'

I handed her the brown envelope. 'Gayla sent this to my mother to give to Lady Edith,' I said. 'I thought Shawn should take a look at it. We think there could be some kind of connection to Vera's death.'

'I'll make sure Shawn gets it,' said Roxy. 'As a matter of fact he just called in to say there have been some new developments in Vera's case. He was actually looking for both of you and wants you back at the Hall ASAP.'

'Cute kids,' I said as the boys tipped out crayons and opened their coloring books on the coffee table.

'Aren't they?' Roxy said. 'They don't look like Shawn, do they?'

'They're Shawn's children?' I was surprised.

'It's tough being a single parent,' she said, 'But he's a wonderful father and we all chip in, don't we, Malcolm?'

'That's right,' said Malcolm.

'What happened to his wife?' said Mum bluntly. 'Run off with the postman?'

Sometimes my mother could be so tactless.

'She died,' said Roxy. 'Cancer.'

'Oh, I am so sorry,' mumbled Mum. 'We'd better be going. Come along, Katherine.'

'I'll be along shortly,' said Roxy. 'Be careful

278

what route you take back to Little Dipperton. Avoid Totnes. There's a huge demonstration over the new railway line.'

'Don't worry. I know a back way,' said Mum.

Ten minutes later we flashed past the welcome sign: TOTNES: TWINNED WITH NARNIA.

'We're supposed to avoid Totnes, Mother,' I said. 'Give me the map.'

'Do they mean the same Narnia from *The Lion, the Witch and the Wardrobe?*'

Rounding a corner we came to a large group of people chanting and marching in small circles blocking the road and waving banners – VOTE NO TO HS3 and WE DON'T NEED TRAINS. Two traffic cops were standing next to a West Country ITV news van.

'Darn. We can't get through.' I looked in the rearview mirror. 'And there's a ton of traffic behind me. You're a hopeless map reader.'

Mum pointed to a narrow alley. 'Go down there. It's a shortcut.'

'Shortcuts are not my specialty and that is a one-way and we're facing the wrong way.'

'Go on. There's nothing coming.'

For all of one minute things went well. But then the alley made a sharp right turn and to my horror, my Golf came face-to-face with a silver Porsche SUV driven by – David. Even worse, Trudy was sitting in the front passenger seat.

'Bugger,' I muttered.

Mum gave a cry of alarm. 'Good God! Isn't that *David?*'

'No.'

'Yes, I distinctly recognize his registration plate

– WYN 1. That's his new car.'

'Then it is David, isn't it,' I snapped.

'But wait! Who is that in the passenger seat?' Mum gasped. 'Good grief! Isn't that Trudy Wynne? I always think she looks like Cruella de Vil.'

Our car front bumpers stopped just inches away from each other. I tried to stem the tide of boiling fury that was consuming me. 'I'm not reversing. Let him bloody reverse.'

'It's his right of way, dear.'

'Be quiet, Mother.'

I'd never seen David and Trudy together and when two figures leaned forward from the rear seats – namely Sam and Chloe – that was the final straw.

'Quite the family outing,' Mum put in.

Trudy leaned over and hit David's horn with a gesture that clearly implied that I was in the wrong. Which of course, I was. She wound down her window and leaned out yelling, 'Reverse! Reverse, you idiot.'

I wound my window down, too, and screamed back, '*You* reverse!'

David sat motionless. Trudy turned her anger on him, her mouth opening and closing like a stranded fish. David must have said something because he began to reverse – erratically. There was a sickening crunch of metal as he backed into the car following.

'Bloody hell,' I said.

Mum started to laugh.

I was close to tears. 'It's not funny.'

'It is, it is,' she gasped. 'Look!'

The driver – presumably from the car behind the Porsche – got out. He was bald with a handle-bar mustache and dressed in shorts and a wife-beater T-shirt. The man hammered on David's window.

Mum squealed. 'He's going to punch him.'

Trudy flung open her door and got out. Mum was right. With her tall, angular frame and sleek black bob she *did* look just like the Disney villain from *101 Dalmatians.*

'No, *she's* going to punch him.' Mum was practically in convulsions. 'Oh, *no!* She's coming this way. Reverse! Reverse!'

I thrust the car into reverse as Trudy stormed toward us, delivered a perfect three-point turn in someone's open – and fortunately – empty garage, and we sped off. By the time we joined the main road the protesters had moved on.

I was shaking with fury.

'You should have seen her face,' Mum chortled. 'It was purple. So unattractive.'

'I don't want to talk about it.' A tear rolled down my cheek. I brushed it angrily away.

'Oh Kat, my love,' said Mum, seemingly con-trite. 'David is too weak for you. Did you see how he backed down?' She gave a snort. 'Literally.'

'This isn't a romance novel,' I shouted. 'People have responsibilities. His father-in-law is dying. It's hard for David.'

'Yes, poor man,' said Mum. 'We must pray for him.'

'You're *impossible!*'

We drove on in silence but my mind was whirring furiously. Why did this matter so much?

It wasn't as if David had told me a lie. I knew he was with his family.

I couldn't possibly understand the intricacies of a broken marriage but I was beginning to understand that divorce was never really final. Screenwriting legend Nora Ephron was right when she said, 'Marriages come and go, but divorce is forever.'

It was only when we turned into the courtyard to the Carriage House and saw Detective Constable Clive Banks waiting that Mum broke the silence between us.

'What is it with these Devonshire men and their facial hair?' muttered Mum.

We got out of the car and Clive hurried over. 'You're needed at the Hall,' he said grimly. 'Everyone is waiting.'

'Why, what's happened? We know that Gayla has been found,' I said.

'There have been a few new developments.' Clive paused dramatically then said, 'Shawn is going to make an arrest.'

Chapter Twenty-three

'What a grand room,' said Mum as Cropper ushered us into the drawing room. 'And how very *Downton Abbey*.'

It certainly looked like it. Everyone had taken their positions and seemed to be waiting for the word, *'Action!'* The 'gentry' were seated and the staff – Mrs. Cropper, Eric, and William – stood stiffly in a formal line with their arms by their sides.

The atmosphere was tense.

Rupert was in front of the fireplace beneath a magnificent portrait of Charles I – a vivid reminder of Honeychurch Hall's role in the English Civil War. He did not look happy.

Mum hesitated then whispered, 'Where should we go? Over with the servants?'

Lady Edith patted the seat beside her. 'Do sit down, Mrs. Stanford.' There was a general murmur of surprise at my mother's unexpected leap across the void to join the upper classes.

Two Knole sofas faced each other across an antique ebony and mother-of-pearl coffee table. Mum joined Lady Edith on one sofa and Lavinia and Harry sat on the other. It was the first time I'd seen Harry without his goggles or white scarf. It made him look older.

'Kat!' he said, bouncing happily. 'Sit next to me.' So I did.

'What are we waiting for?' said Lavinia.

'God knows,' Lady Edith muttered.

'The police, of course,' snapped Rupert.

No one spoke again, giving me the opportunity to take in my opulent surroundings.

The drawing room, with elaborate cornices and decorative strapwork, was exquisite. Red silk wallpaper shared the walls with tapestry hangings. Damask curtains fell graciously from the four casement windows that overlooked the park. The furniture reflected the Hall's various incarnations from seventeenth-century oak court cupboards to an ugly twentieth-century drinks cabinet. There was the usual plethora of side tables, lamps, and gilt-framed mirrors as well as an overwhelming number of miniatures that took up almost the entire wall to the right of the fireplace. A copper Gibraltar gong stand stood in the corner.

A very fine eighteenth-century French tulip-wood and parquetry display cabinet contained more porcelain snuff boxes and some early glass-ware. David's comment about the robbery being an inside job struck me anew.

With David's determination to expose the fraud, Rupert's plans to break up the estate, and the horror of Vera's murder, things did not bode well for one of England's greatest families.

Clive had said Shawn was going to make an arrest. Since Lady Edith and Lavinia had solid alibis, that left the four men in the room – Cropper, Rupert, William, and Eric – one of them was responsible for Vera's death. Cropper didn't seem physically capable, William claimed to be with a horse all night, and Eric had a firm alibi. That left Rupert.

Sensing my eyes upon him, he looked up. I expected to see defiance or even guilt but instead Rupert just looked sad.

Shawn walked in followed by Clive who was carrying a Tesco plastic shopping bag and the large brown envelope I'd given to Roxy earlier. Shawn scanned the room, pointedly ignored my smile of greeting, and said, 'Are we all here?'

'Vera isn't,' chipped in Harry. 'Where is she?'

'I knew this would happen,' Lavinia declared. 'I told you I didn't want Harry here.'

'Vera's gone on holiday, my pet,' said Lady Edith. 'Can we *please* get this over with?'

'Roxy will be here any moment,' said Clive. 'She's gone to the toilet.'

'Mummy told me we can't say toilet,' said Harry. 'It's common. We say lavatory.'

'Hush,' hissed Lavinia but cracked a smile. The tension eased and a peculiar giggle – half snort erupted from my mother.

Roxy threw open the door and hurried in. 'I'm dying for a cuppa.'

'There will be no cuppas today,' said Shawn gravely. He perched on the edge of the coffee table in front of Harry. 'I just have a quick question for you, young man, and then Roxy is going to take you for an ice cream.'

'Okay,' said Harry.

'I want to talk about yesterday morning in the sunken garden,' said Shawn. 'You and Kat were playing–'

'We were on a mission.' Harry looked to me for reassurance. I gave him an encouraging smile. 'We were looking for one of our men who had been captured by the Germans.'

'We were looking for Flying Officer Jazzbo Jenkins, weren't we, Harry?' I said.

'Jazzbo Jenkins?' said Lady Edith sharply. 'Did you say Jazzbo *Jenkins?*'

Lavinia rolled her eyes. 'It's just one of Harry's silly games, Edith.'

'Jazzbo Jenkins is a Merrythought "Jerry" mouse, your ladyship,' I said. 'As you know, I deal in antiques. Jerry mice are quite hard to find.'

'I'm sure Shawn doesn't care about toy mice,'

285

said Rupert.

'Well, I do,' said Lady Edith. 'Tell me about Jazzbo Jenkins, Harry.'

'Jazzbo wears a blue cardigan,' said Harry. 'But he doesn't have any badges like William's mouse, Ella Fitzgerald.'

'Don't you mean your Granny's mouse, Harry?' I said pointedly. I tried to catch Mum's eye, hoping she'd understand the significance of the question but her own were fixed on William.

'No. It's William's,' Harry insisted.

'Where did you find Jazzbo Jenkins?' Lady Edith demanded.

'Jazzbo belonged to my mother, your ladyship,' I said. Lady Edith gasped. 'Your *mother?*'

I felt, rather than saw, Mum look daggers at me but I didn't care. I was getting fed up with all these ridiculous secrets.

'Can we just get on with this?' said Rupert. 'Seriously? Mice?'

'Of course, your lordship,' said Shawn smoothly. 'Master Harry, did you and Kat go to the grotto in the sunken garden yesterday?'

'I went there alone,' I insisted. 'I told you all this yesterday.'

'Let Master Harry answer the question, please,' said Shawn.

'No.' Harry shook his head. 'I don't like the grotto.'

'He doesn't like it there,' Lavinia echoed.

'So you're positive you didn't go anywhere near the grotto?' Shawn said again.

'He already told you he didn't,' said Rupert.

Shawn stood up and started pacing around the

room with his hands clasped behind his back. 'The exact location of the grotto is very hard to find,' he said in a pompous tone. 'I grew up here. I know the estate like the back of my hand and I *still* have trouble locating the entrance.'

Shawn spun on his heel and turned to me, 'So what were *you* doing near the grotto, Ms. Stanford?'

I was no longer Kat. I was now Ms. Stanford. With a sinking heart, I suspected where this line of questioning was heading. 'I stumbled upon it by accident.'

'And where was Master Harry when you stumbled upon the grotto by accident?' asked Shawn.

'Harry had run off.'

Shawn cocked his head. 'But weren't you supposed to be looking after him?'

'Tell them what happened in the sunken garden, Harry,' I said. 'With William's mouse.'

'I only borrowed it,' Harry whispered. 'I was going to put it back.'

'What did you take this time, Harry?' Lavinia demanded. 'You must *stop* taking people's things without their permission!'

'Don't shout at him,' said Rupert.

Harry's bottom lip began to quiver. 'I just borrowed William's mouse, the one with all the badges because Jazzbo wasn't where I left him.'

'Shawn, is this really necessary?' William hurried over. He appealed to Lady Edith. 'Whether Harry took one of my childhood souvenirs or not is irrelevant–'

'But I thought you said the mouse belonged to

Lady Edith, William?' I said.

A faint blush began to creep its way up William's neck. 'I said no such thing—'

'I don't see what this has got to do with Vera's death,' Rupert grumbled.

'Harry presented me with William's mouse probably hoping I wouldn't notice,' I said. 'When I questioned him, he became upset and ran off. I followed him and ended up near the grotto.'

Shawn and Roxy exchanged a look as if to say, *sure you did.*

I felt my temper rise. 'I saw something glinting in the undergrowth that looked like Morse code. I thought Harry was sending me a message but it was the sunlight bouncing off the snuff box.'

'Snuff box?' said Lady Edith. 'A snuff box?'

'As you know, Edith,' said William smoothly, 'Kat found the Meissen with the elephant on the lid in the sunken garden and she gave it to me.'

'The elephant!' Lady Edith exclaimed and then seemed confused. 'But why didn't you tell me?'

'I did tell you,' said William. He walked over to the tulipwood and marquetry display cabinet, reached far inside, and handed it to Lady Edith.

'You most certainly did not tell me.' Lady Edith examined it closely. 'Thankfully there doesn't seem to be any damage.'

Lavinia gripped Harry's arm tightly. 'Did you take that from Granny?'

Harry started to cry. 'I didn't touch it. I promise. I didn't.'

'Now, now, stop all this nonsense,' said Rupert. 'If he said he didn't touch it, he didn't touch it.'

'I think he's had enough, Shawn.' Roxy stepped

forward. 'Master Harry, would you like to come with me and get an ice cream?'

Harry allowed Roxy to take his hand and they left the drawing room.

Once everyone seemed to have settled down again, Mum suddenly spoke. 'Officer? When were you planning on telling us that the nanny – Gayla – has been found?'

There was a universal chorus of surprise. Good old Mum. I knew she'd done this to take the focus off me and I was grateful. Frankly, I was disappointed that Shawn could even begin to suspect I'd had something to do with Vera's murder.

'Yes, it's true,' said Shawn. 'Gayla Tarasova is alive and well.'

'Thank you for letting us know, Shawn,' said Lady Edith crossly.

'All that fuss for nothing,' said Lavinia. 'Where was she?'

'In Dartmouth,' Shawn said. 'Gayla was picked up for shoplifting with her friend Anna.'

'I told you she had a friend called Anna,' said Mum.

Lavinia frowned. 'But why would Gayla put us through all that worry? I don't understand.'

'I'm at a loss, too, Shawn,' said Rupert. 'What about her suitcase? Why leave all her clothes behind?'

'The suitcase was empty when we found it,' said Shawn. 'A fact I couldn't have revealed at the time.'

'There was *nothing* in it?' Rupert said incredulously.

'She had a second suitcase inside the first,' said

Shawn. 'Ms. Tarasova admitted abandoning the larger one in the hedge and cutting through the fields to the village where her friend was waiting for her. She never intended to catch the train.'

'I hope you'll charge her for wasting police time,' said Rupert.

'Gayla provided us with a full statement of what happened. It appears she was upset at being accused of theft. Apparently, she and Vera had a bit of a fight.'

Lavinia rolled her eyes. 'How tedious.'

'I'm afraid there was more to it, your ladyship,' said Shawn. 'Gayla had been having an affair with–'

'Me,' Eric shouted.

Mum and I exchanged looks of surprise.

'Eric's always been a bit of a ladies' man,' said Rupert with obvious relief.

Of course Eric was lying. He was also covering for Rupert – given their volatile disagreement on Saturday night. I wondered what had changed between them.

Still Lady Edith didn't comment. She seemed to be in a world of her own, mumbling incoherently, shaking her head, and stealing the occasional sidelong glance at my mother who, in turn, was watching William's every move.

Lavinia frowned. 'So you think it was Gayla who *killed* Vera?'

'My poor Vera.' Eric gave a strangled sob. 'We had our problems but I loved her.'

'I'm afraid not,' said Shawn. 'You see – Gayla couldn't have committed the crime because she spent the weekend at Her Majesty's pleasure in

Dartmouth Police Station.'

There was a ripple of shock.

Lady Edith finally spoke. 'It's time for the truth,' she said. 'I'm tired of all the secrets and lies.'

'I am, too,' I said, more loudly than I intended.

Mum scrambled to her feet. 'We'll be off then,' she said. 'This is obviously a family affair and you won't want us here.'

'On the contrary, Mrs. Stanford,' Shawn said. 'We need to go over Vera's last movements again and we want you *both* here. Very much indeed.'

Chapter Twenty-four

'The coroner informed us that Vera died somewhere between midnight and six on Sunday morning.' Shawn began to pace the room. 'She suffered a blunt force trauma to the side of her head–'

'Oh, how frightful,' said Lavinia. 'You mean someone struck her with a heavy object?'

'Possibly,' said Shawn. 'But she regained consciousness. The actual cause of death was by asphyxiation.'

There was a universal gasp of horror.

'You mean she was suffocated?' Eric exclaimed. 'How? With what?'

'I'm afraid I can't tell you that. We haven't yet discovered where the first attack took place,' said Shawn, adding apologetically, 'We're a bit short-staffed.'

'I thought it happened in the grotto,' said Rupert.

'No. Her body was taken to the grotto – possibly by car,' Shawn said. 'The service road runs alongside the property.'

Shawn flipped to a new page in his moleskin notepad and addressed Lady Edith and Lavinia. 'Ladies? Where were you on Saturday night?'

'Edith and I attended a committee meeting in Tavistock followed by a frightfully long, dreary dinner at Shipley Abbey,' said Lavinia. 'We go every year to finalize the details for next month's Honeychurch Hall Sidesaddle Championship. It will be our forty-fifth year. It's a tremendous tradition.'

'And what time did you get home that night?' Shawn asked.

'About two-thirty,' Lavinia replied. 'We didn't leave the hotel until midnight and as you know, it's across the moors and we got a little lost.'

'You let Mother drive, didn't you?' Rupert exclaimed. 'I told you she mustn't drive at night.'

Lavinia ignored his outburst and carried on. 'I remembered looking at my watch because we went to check on Jupiter – she's a frightfully valuable mare – and William was still there.'

'That's right,' said William. 'As I said, Jupiter had colic and Ian Masters – our vet – thought it wise for me to stay with her overnight. Do you want Ian's telephone number?'

'I've already spoken to him,' said Clive from the sidelines. 'He's a mate. We play rugby together. Ian confirmed that he gave Jupiter a dose of ketamine to alleviate her symptoms and left an extra shot with you in case she needed more.'

'Quite the old boys' club,' whispered Mum.

Shawn motioned for Clive to step forward and whispered the word, *'Paris.'*

Clive delved into the Tesco shopping bag and pulled out the Eiffel Tower keepsake tin I recognized from Vera's cottage.

'Just pop it on the coffee table where everyone can see, will you?' Shawn asked Clive.

Rupert inhaled sharply and turned pale. 'Good God!'

'Vera always dreamt of going to Paris,' said Eric.

'I believe this tin belonged to Kelly,' said Shawn. 'Isn't that right, m'lord?'

Rupert nodded but didn't speak.

'Do we have to talk about that frightful girl?' said Lady Edith. 'She died years ago.'

'No more secrets and lies, your ladyship,' Shawn said firmly. 'Isn't that what you said?'

'Where did you find the tin?' Rupert asked.

'At the bottom of Vera's freezer in the potting shed,' said Shawn.

'In our freezer?' Eric exclaimed. 'What the hell was it doing in there?'

'Do you want to open it and see what's inside?' Shawn said.

Rupert didn't need any encouragement. In two quick strides he snatched up the tin and removed the lid. 'My God. It's Kelly's EpiPen!'

'And I believe there is another pen in there, too,' said Shawn. 'A fountain pen with the initials L-M-C-H.'

Rupert frowned and turned to Lavinia. 'This is

293

your fountain pen,' he said. 'Lavinia Mary Carew Honeychurch.'

Lavinia opened her mouth and shut it again. She seemed unable to speak.

'What's going on?' Rupert demanded. 'Why was Lavinia's pen in Kelly's tin and what has this got to do with my wife?'

'I wonder which wife you are talking about, Rupert,' said Lady Edith coldly.

Lavinia reddened. 'Vera must have stolen my pen.'

'Is that why you were at Vera's cottage yesterday morning?' said Shawn. 'Looking for that pen?'

Rupert raked his fingers through his hair, clearly bewildered. 'Won't someone tell me what the hell is going on here?'

'Perhaps you'd like to enlighten us, Lady Lavinia?' said Shawn.

'Nothing is going on,' said Lavinia.

Mrs. Cropper stepped forward. 'If you won't say something, your ladyship,' she said gravely, 'I will.'

Lavinia sprang to her feet. 'Alright. Yes. It's true!' she cried. 'It was an accident. I didn't even know that a wretched bee had stung Kelly. She just collapsed I tell you.' Tears filled Lavinia's eyes. 'She went purple in the face and collapsed!'

'Take a deep breath now,' said Shawn. 'Tell us everything.'

'Kelly and I arranged to go riding. It was a hot summer day and the honeybees were acting up. Cropper asked me to make sure Kelly took her EpiPen with her in case she got stung–'

'Did you know Kelly was allergic to bees?'

asked Shawn.

Lavinia shrugged. 'Vera said Kelly was making it up to get attention.'

'Go on,' Rupert's voice was icy.

'So we both hid it.'

'Hid it,' Shawn echoed. 'Where?'

'It was childish, I know – and I changed my mind,' said Lavinia. 'I ran back to the Hall to find Vera but she'd disappeared – along with the EpiPen.' Lavinia appealed to Rupert. 'I swear it was an accident.'

'You were jealous of Kelly,' said Shawn. 'Because you and Rupert had been engaged before they eloped during a New Year's Eve dinner. Isn't that true?'

'You know jolly well we were engaged.' Lavinia recovered a tiny bit of her self-respect and added, 'Don't be so pompous!'

'But it all worked out for you in the end,' Shawn went on. 'Because just months after Kelly's death you fell pregnant and his lordship did the decent thing and married you after all.'

'I told you it was a frightful, frightful accident.' Lavinia was becoming hysterical. 'I made sure we didn't go anywhere near the hives. One moment she was fine and we were drinking cherry brandy and the next minute, she fell off her horse.' Lavinia turned to Rupert pleading again, 'You must believe me.'

He turned away and strode over to the window, gazing out – presumably – at the white marble angel on the banks of the lake.

Despite the seriousness of the situation, I was utterly gripped and I could tell Mum was, too.

She was leaning forward with her mouth open in awe. I could almost hear her mind working out a new plot for her Star-Crossed Lovers Series.

'I galloped back to the Hall to get the EpiPen,' Lavinia continued. 'Vera pretended she didn't know what I was talking about. She denied any knowledge of her part. She never liked me–'

'But she disliked Kelly more,' Shawn put in.

'You can't force a bee to sting someone,' said Mum suddenly.

'She wasn't stung,' said Mrs. Cropper quietly. 'If anyone is to blame for Kelly's death, it's me.'

Shawn looked confused. 'Gran?'

'*Apis mellifera* is the secret ingredient in my homemade cherry brandy.'

'Bee venom,' said Shawn flatly.

'It's what makes it taste so sweet,' said Mrs. Cropper. 'Vera knew that.'

Lavinia frowned. 'Vera gave me the cherry brandy–'

'Vera knew what was in it,' said Mrs. Cropper. 'And she knew Kelly was allergic.'

'So, I'm not to blame?' gasped Lavinia.

Rupert sat down.

'Kelly was a tart, Rupert,' said Lady Edith. 'Everyone knows she was sleeping with Detective Constable Banks.'

All eyes swiveled to Clive who turned beetroot red. 'It – it – only happened once,' he stammered. 'Or was it twice?'

'And – as you already admitted – with *you*, Eric,' added Lady Edith.

'That was before Kelly married his lordship,' he said defensively. 'It doesn't count.'

Bong! Bong! A deafening shimmer of sound silenced the room. Cropper stood next to the Gibraltar gong, hammer in hand.

'Thank you, Gramps,' said Shawn. When everyone had settled down he added, 'When did Vera start blackmailing you, Lavinia?'

Lavinia blanched. 'You *knew?* But how?'

Shawn motioned for Clive to step forward again. This time he withdrew the box of *vol-au-vents* and set it down next to the Eiffel Tower keepsake tin.

'We found one thousand pounds in this empty box of *vol-au-vents* in the bottom of the freezer. Did you put the money in there yesterday morning?'

Lavinia nodded.

I stifled a cry of relief. Thank God I'd been wrong about my mother succumbing to blackmail.

'One thousand pounds!' shouted Rupert. 'One *thousand!* Do you think we're made of money?'

'Oh shut up, Rupert,' snapped Lavinia. 'It's from my trust fund. I do have my own money, you know.'

'But why pay Vera?' said Rupert.

Tears welled up in Lavinia's eyes again. 'She threatened to tell you that I'd stolen Kelly's Epi-Pen. I was terrified you'd divorce me if you found out because ... I love you, Rupert. I always have.'

Rupert looked surprised. 'You do?'

'The silly thing is that I realize now that Vera couldn't have proved any of it. I panicked. I suppose you'll divorce me now.' Lavinia pulled a handkerchief out of her pocket and gently dabbed at her eyes. 'How frightfully embarrassing this all is. I am so sorry, Edith.'

'I don't get it,' said Eric suddenly. 'Why would Vera want to blackmail anyone?'

Shawn motioned to Clive a third time. He pulled out the two sausage roll boxes and put those on the coffee table, too.

'I told her I didn't like sausage rolls,' said Eric sadly.

'They are jammed with credit and department store statements,' said Shawn. 'Vera was heavily in debt but somehow she was able to make hefty payments to her credit cards.'

'What the hell was she buying?' Eric wondered.

Was he blind? 'Shoes!' I said, exasperated. 'Didn't you ever wonder how she could afford them?'

Eric's face darkened with fury. 'Bloody Vera. I warned her. I told her—'

'Told her what, Eric?' said Shawn. 'That you'd kill her?'

'I didn't say that,' shouted Eric. 'And you know I've got an alibi.'

'According to the landlord, he was very drunk, sir,' Clive put in. 'Unable to stand. There's no way he could have driven, let alone walked back to the Hall on Saturday night.'

'Well, that's strange because Ms. Stanford tells me that she heard you at the Hall with his lordship late on Saturday night,' said Shawn. 'Where did you get those bruises, Eric?'

'Ms. Stanford doesn't know what she's saying,' said Rupert. 'And as for the bruises, Eric tripped and fell into the suits of armor.'

'I wondered who did that,' Cropper said, speaking for the very first time.

'No more, no more, *please*,' said Lady Edith wearily. 'I've known all along about your little scheme to turn the Hall into flats when I'm dead and gone. I know you plan on building a ghastly adventure playground and go-kart track. But what disgusts me the most is your determination to tear up the equine cemetery and make it a caravan park.'

'What caravan park?' Lavinia said, bewildered.

Rupert turned on Eric, his expression thunderous. 'You bastard! You told her.'

'I didn't tell anyone,' jabbered Eric. 'And Vera didn't know. I swear.'

Shawn snapped his fingers and Clive stepped forward again holding the blueprints.

'Gayla mailed those plans to my mother,' I said. 'She wanted Lady Edith to know what was happening to her home.'

Lady Edith looked taken aback. 'Why would she do that? I hardly knew her.'

'She wanted revenge, m'lady,' said Mum with relish.

'Revenge on *Eric?*' said Lavinia blankly. 'Why?'

'Where *were* you on Saturday night, m'lord?' said Shawn.

Rupert bristled. 'With my son, waiting for my wife to return from Shipley Abbey. Harry loathes the dark. I would never leave him alone in this house. You all know that to be true.'

'Yes, I believe that to be true,' I chipped in. And I did.

'Thank you, everyone,' said Shawn. 'You've been

most helpful.'

'Is that it?' said Lavinia. 'I thought you were going to make an arrest?'

'So that just leaves our new neighbors,' said Shawn. 'Ms. Stanford, does the name Trudy Wynne mean anything to you?'

My stomach turned over. 'Yes, I already told you she's a tabloid journalist.'

'But she's also your fiancé's wife.'

'Actually–' I took a deep breath. 'David is not my fiancé.'

'But weren't you celebrating your engagement in the Hare & Hounds on Sunday night?' said Shawn. Seeing my look of surprise he added, 'Rumor has it that your so-called fiancé made a generous contribution to Vera's post-service shindig.'

'You're right,' I said. 'But we were celebrating something else – something business related.'

'But you let everyone believe they were toasting your good health.'

'I suppose it would seem that way,' I said, thinking that Lavinia was right. Shawn *was* pompous.

'Regardless of the *misunderstanding*,' Shawn went on, 'I'm sure you wouldn't want David Wynne's current wife to find out, would you? Did Vera threaten to tell her?'

'For heaven's sake, no,' I exclaimed. 'Vera did not and frankly, my relationship with Trudy Wynne goes back years. She couldn't do any more damage to my reputation than she already has.'

'But perhaps she could damage your mother's?' said Shawn.

There was a deathly silence. My heart sank. I

daren't meet my mother's eyes because I knew exactly what was coming next.

'Clive, the honors, please.'

Clive stepped forward a fourth time. He set a plastic Ziploc bag containing yellow Post-it Notes down on the coffee table. He withdrew all three and laid them out.

'Would you care to read what those notes say, Mrs. Stanford?' Shawn asked.

Mum leaned forward and said, '*Shotgun, murder,* and *meet me in the grotto.*'

'And is it in your handwriting?'

'Yes,' she said, rolling her eyes.

'My mother is always writing Post-it Notes,' I put in. 'The dashboard of her MINI is covered in them.'

'Do you know where we found these Post-it Notes?' Shawn asked.

Mum shook her head. 'No, but I suspect you're going to tell me.'

The room was so quiet you could hear the proverbial pin drop.

'In Vera's bathroom,' said Shawn.

'I've never been in Vera's bathroom,' Mum said coldly.

'But you *did* go to her cottage late on Saturday night, didn't you?'

'No,' said Mum.

'Are you quite sure about that?' said Shawn. 'Gran told me you were hammering on Vera's front door, demanding she let you in.'

'Yes, that's right,' said Mrs. Cropper. 'She was making a hell of a din.'

Mum reddened. 'Saturday night? Yes, sorry, I

thought you meant Friday night. Vera didn't answer the door and I came home. I assumed she was asleep.'

'You also left a message on Vera's voice mail saying it was urgent that you speak with her,' Shawn went on.

'This is ridiculous!' I cried. 'Anyone can see that my mother couldn't attack anyone. Look at her! Her arm is in a cast–'

'That cast could knock someone out cold,' chipped in Clive.

'I agree,' said Shawn. 'Can you vouch for your mother being in her bed all night, Ms. Stanford?'

'Well–'

'Answer the question.'

'No. Not really,' I said.

'And is it true that Vera asked you for one thousand pounds, Mrs. Stanford?'

'If you say so,' said Mum.

Shawn nodded at Clive who produced a navy polka-dot Wellington boot from behind a chair.

'That's my Vera's,' Eric cried.

'According to your daughter, Vera was only wearing one Wellington boot when she was murdered,' said Shawn. 'We found this one in your dustbin.'

'*My* dustbin!' shrieked Mum.

'Someone is trying to frame my mother,' I said angrily. 'If Mum *had* done it, she would hardly have disposed of the evidence in her own dustbin.'

'You have quite a few secrets, don't you, Iris – or should I say...' Shawn paused dramatically. 'Krystalle Storm.'

'Iris!' said Lady Edith sharply. *'Iris?'*

'Iris Stanford, born Bushman, your ladyship,' I said pointedly.

'Katherine!' squeaked Mum.

'Iris Bushman!' cried Lady Edith. 'Little Iris?'

'Krystalle who?' said Rupert.

Lavinia gasped. 'Krystalle Storm? The *writer?*'

'Vera found out who you were,' said Shawn. 'It seemed she was quite a fan of yours. She knew everything about you and was an avid member of the Krystalle Storm fan club. According to her journal she had already gotten through to the semifinals of some contest run by your publisher. She dreamed of flying to Italy but then perhaps ... she discovered she wouldn't have to travel very far at all.'

'It's not what you think,' Mum exclaimed.

'That's what everyone says when they are caught out.' Shawn seemed to be enjoying himself immensely and it would seem the other spectators in the room did, too. They were all gobsmacked.

'Your website made very interesting reading,' Shawn went on. 'Where exactly in Italy is your home? Presumably you own another manor house in Devon because we hardly put the Carriage House in that category – and as for your husband's career as an international diplomat–'

'All right, all right!' Mum cried. 'I can explain but I'd like to go somewhere private.'

'We can certainly accommodate you down at the station.'

'Good,' she snapped. 'Then let's go but I'll tell you one thing. I didn't kill Vera Pugsley. Yes, I have secrets but it would appear that every single person in this room has a secret, too.'

'Let's go,' said Shawn.

'I want a solicitor – and not someone who went to Little Dipperton Primary School or is related to anyone in this room.' Mum stood up. She was shaking with anger. 'And I *am* coming willingly nor am I under arrest. Is that clear?'

'This is unbelievable,' I said. 'I'm coming–'

'I'm afraid not, Ms. Stanford,' said Shawn.

'Let's get on with it, shall we?' Mum turned on her heel and stalked out of the drawing room quickly followed by Shawn and Clive. I stood there, stunned.

'Ms. Stanford!' Lady Edith hurried over to join me. 'There is something I must ask you.'

'Yes, your ladyship?' I said.

'Jazzbo Jenkins – the mouse with the blue cardigan?' she said, eyes bright. 'Where did your mother get him?'

'From you, your ladyship,' I said. 'From you.'

'Yes, I thought as much,' she whispered.

'Mother, please,' said Rupert. 'I must talk to you. Please hear me out.'

'I have nothing to say to you,' Lady Edith said acidly. 'You are never going to inherit this estate now. It's over.'

'Mother–'

'Let her be, Rupert. Leave her.' William took Lady Edith's arm and gently walked her away.

Even though my mother had lied to me about everything, I knew she wasn't capable of murder. It was too ridiculous for words. The whole ordeal had turned into a farce of epic proportions.

Once word got out about Mum's early nomadic life at the Hall as well as her current incarnation as

Krsytalle Storm, the newspapers would have a field day – Trudy Wynne in particular. My stomach lurched as I could very well imagine myself being featured on *Walk of Shame! Celebrity Family Secrets Revealed.*

My mother had been framed – first, by the Post-its and secondly, the Wellington boot. And then I remembered something Vera had said to me that fateful night when I'd found her hysterical in the woods. She'd said she was going back to her cottage to change into her Wellington boots.

The footage Mum and I had watched of Vera's joyride had been taken *before* I met Vera. Later that night I'd heard voices outside my window.

I just hoped – prayed – that Vera's return had been captured on camera. And most importantly, who had returned with her.

Chapter Twenty-five

I went straight up to Mum's office, ignoring the persistent ring on my mobile. I knew it was David and I was definitely not in the mood to talk to him.

Luckily, the surveillance camera had still been running all this time because Mum had not thought to turn it off.

I took the remote, dragged over the three-legged stool, and settled down to watch the screen. It didn't take long to find Vera's nighttime performance. There she was, driving manically around Eric's field on his brand new Massey Ferguson.

I paid close attention to the footage where Eric's tractor toppled into the old tunnel and Vera dropped the keys.

When Vera climbed down to get them, she disappeared from sight. The tunnel wasn't that deep. Now I realized I should have at the very least been able to see the top of her head.

Vera was gone a long time but because Mum and I had been laughing so hard at her expense, we hadn't noticed. The time code registered a full ten minutes before Vera reemerged, clambered out of the gulley with her muddy Louboutins in one hand, then hurried out of the frame.

Now, only the tractor filled the screen. The odd cow ambled into view. A solitary rabbit hopped on by but other than that, nothing.

I fast-forwarded five minutes, ten, and then one hour. Still nothing until two figures finally appeared at twelve-fifteen.

My stomach turned over.

Vera *had* brought William back with her. She was wearing a jacket over her dress and, yes, she'd changed into her polka-dot Wellington boots.

William strode into frame with a flashlight and a roll of black plastic dustbin liners. He helped Vera climb down first then – with some difficulty because of his size – followed her.

Both of them vanished from sight.

There was a bright flare as the flashlight was turned on and then, darkness. I waited for both to reappear. They were gone much longer this time – the time code registered twenty-five minutes.

When they finally emerged, Vera scrambled out and turned back to lift up two bulging black plastic dustbin liners from William's outstretched hands. William bent down and popped back up again to toss out a telescopic mailing tube – similar in shape and size to the one I'd seen in Rupert's bedroom. He then heaved himself out of the tunnel.

Vera seemed excited and happy. She was doing little bunny hops and William – towering over her – grabbed Vera around the waist and they danced an awkward jig in their Wellington boots. Whatever they'd found was obviously important and I was mesmerized.

William had lied.

He'd said he'd been with Jupiter all night but he hadn't. And there was something else that I remembered. This afternoon in the drawing room, William had told Lady Edith that I'd found the snuff box in the sunken garden. I knew that I had told him I'd found it outside, but not *where*.

What's more, William had access to Mum's Post-it Notes and could have easily placed them in Vera's cottage. And as for her Wellington boots–

'Hello, Katherine.'

'William! You startled me.' I exclaimed and realized the tape was still running. I hit stop on the remote control and added hastily, 'I was just watching a DVD to take my mind of things.'

William closed the door behind him. My mouth went dry and my knees turned to jelly. 'I can't believe my own mother has been arrested, can you?' I said lightly.

'The whole thing is ridiculous.' William seemed

nervous. 'But we'll sort it out. Don't worry. What are you watching?'

The DVD case of *Downton Abbey* was on the top of the television set. *'Downton Abbey,'* I said. 'Although I think Honeychurch Hall has far more intrigue, don't you?' It was a pathetic attempt at a joke and I knew it.

'That must be difficult,' said William. 'Because your mother loaned the DVD to me.'

'There were extra bits,' I said quickly. 'You know, outtakes.'

My heart began to thunder in my chest as I became aware of how enormous William really was – certainly large enough to carry Vera effortlessly to the grotto.

'I've never been in here before.' William scanned the room. 'Your mother always kept it locked.'

'She's very private.'

'I can't believe she's the author Krystalle Storm,' he said. 'I really enjoyed *Gypsy Temptress.*'

'Yes. It's brilliant, isn't it?'

'I lent it to Lavinia,' said William.

'Good.'

William ambled over to the corkboard and pointed to the newspaper clipping of Lady Edith. 'Isn't she an astonishing woman? It's hard to believe she's eighty-four.'

'Yes. It is,' I said.

Gesturing to the corkboard with all Mum's scribbles and Post-its, William said, 'What's your mother's new book? Is she – writing about the family? About Lady Edith?'

'I have no idea.'

He pointed to the Post-it labeled *Billy Bushman.*

'Is she writing about me?'

'I don't know who you are but I do know that you are not my mother's stepbrother,' I said boldly. 'Or Lady Edith's illegitimate son.'

William stood staring at me. 'And what makes you so sure?'

'Billy died of an aneurism on Blackpool Pier–'

'Ah. I see. Guilty as charged.' William looked sad. 'He was my friend, you know.'

'But you decided to impersonate him? Why? Did you know that Lady Edith was Billy's mother?'

'He told me,' said William. 'Billy and I did the circuit during that time when most of the traveling shows were being broken up in the late sixties–'

'Harry was right. You really were the strongest man in the world.'

'Billy told me all about his big sister, Iris, and how she ran off with some bastard who put their dad in prison for racketeering.'

'Oh,' I said.

'Billy told me some other things about this house, too.'

'So you just came south and asked Lady Edith for a job?'

'Not exactly,' said William. 'About eight years ago, just after Billy died, Edith comes to Blackpool asking questions. She was in a terrible state. Seems Rupert had eloped with one of the servants and she'd disinherited him. Billy and I used to joke about that stupid mouse mascot of his. He said if anything ever happened to him, I should have it because it would bring me luck – and it did, up until now. The old biddy assumed I was Billy and refused to believe I wasn't. She hadn't seen Billy for decades so I thought – no harm, no foul. Why not.'

'You fooled a vulnerable old lady!' I cried. 'So *who* are you?'

'Ralph Jackson.'

'But why pretend?'

'You just don't get it, do you?'

'No, I don't.'

'I'm sixty-six years old – no, I know I don't look it,' said William, pulling in his stomach. 'Life on the road is hard and these days my sort – carnies, circus folk, and gypsies – are herded onto traveler sites and treated like pariahs. Do you know what it's like to have no money? No pension plan? Just relying on the bloody government and the charity of people like Edith?'

'You're right, I don't know what it's like,' I said hastily. 'I couldn't even pretend to understand.'

'I'm devoted to Edith but when she dies, what's going to happen to me? Who is going to look after me if Rupert gets his way?' William's mood had darkened considerably. I could sense his desperation and that made him dangerous.

'I'm not going to say anything,' I said. 'We can keep this between ourselves. It's obvious Lady Edith is fond of you and I can see that you are of her, too.'

'But your mother knows the truth,' said William. 'She'll tell her.'

'Believe me, Mum doesn't care about stuff like that.'

'She doesn't care that I'm pretending to be her stepbrother?' he said with scorn.

William sank down into the wingback armchair

310

and put his head in his hands. 'No, it's too late. Edith has guessed. Did you see her expression when she was looking at that old photograph of your mother's?'

'What does it matter?' I said.

'I knew it was over, when Harry showed me Jazzbo Jenkins,' said William. 'I knew.'

'William—'

'You don't understand,' shouted William. 'I told Edith that Iris was dead.'

"What?' I cried.

'Yes! You see? *Now* do you understand? I told Edith that Iris had drowned and she was devastated.' William was getting agitated. 'She was guilty and upset because she never got a chance to say she was sorry for sending Iris away.'

'All these things can be sorted out,' I said soothingly. 'I'm sure of it.'

'It's too late,' said William.

A loud click sounded on the DVD and the screen fizzled and recalibrated to show the field outside my bedroom window. And then I remembered Vera lying dead in the grotto.

'*Bugger*,' I muttered.

William's jaw dropped. His eyes darted to the television set, the surveillance box, then followed the cables running out of the partially open window. 'You saw us Saturday night.'

'Saw what?' I edged toward the door, slipped Mum's Dictaphone into my pocket, and fumbled for the large record button.

William's eyes flashed and for the first time I felt afraid.

'You're not going anywhere,' he said grimly.

311

'I wasn't intending to.' I tried to stay calm but my knees were trembling so much I could hardly stand. I knew I had to keep him talking – wasn't that what people did on TV?

'What did you find in the underground tunnel, William?' I asked. 'What were in those two black plastic dustbin liners? Were they from the robbery?'

'Clever you,' said William.

'The cylindrical tube gave it away. It's used for transporting canvasses,' I said. 'Several paintings were stolen that night.'

For a moment William seemed taken off guard. 'How do you know that?'

'My boyfriend investigates stolen art, remember?' I said. 'I have a full list of all the items that were taken. You'll never be able to trade them on the black market.'

'We weren't intending to.'

'Oh!' Now I was really confused. 'We?'

'When Eric's tractor fell into the tunnel, Vera found a recess where the Royalists used to hide during the Civil War,' William said. 'The stuff was in there. I'd been looking for it for years.'

David was right. 'So it *was* an inside job. How did you know?'

'Billy stayed in touch with Shawn's dad–'

'Robert Cropper, the Detective Chief Superintendent,' I said.

'Everyone knew what had gone on,' said William bitterly. 'Shawn's dad the copper, Tom's folks, the Croppers, everyone except Edith. Vera's mother told me it was the old earl's idea. He knew how important the Honeychurch estate was to her. He didn't want Edith to have to sell up after his death. Damn Vera! She ruined everything.'

'She was going to blackmail you, too, wasn't she?'

'Blackmail?' William seemed incredulous. 'We couldn't wait to tell Edith that we'd recovered the loot – most of all, the seed pearls.'

'I don't understand,' I said. 'You were going to give everything back?'

'Yes. Of course we were.' William sounded impatient. 'I told Vera we'd give everything to Edith in the morning. I took the stuff up to my flat. Half an hour later Vera pays me a surprise visit – says she can't sleep for excitement and wanted to try the pearls on because she knew she'd never have another chance.'

'What happened?'

'I was packing up to leave this place. I knew it was only a matter of time before Edith discovered I wasn't the man she thought I was and that Iris was very much alive.' William's shoulders slumped. 'Vera – stupid cow – saw my suitcases. She thought I was doing a runner with all the stolen heirlooms. I told her I wasn't but she got hysterical – and then she saw that wretched elephant snuff box–'

'It was *you* who was taking Lady Edith's snuff boxes?'

'No!' William shook his head vehemently. 'I'm positive Rupert was responsible for that. Tormenting poor Edith by taking them out of the credenza and then putting them back. Trying to send her mad. But yes, I did take the elephant snuffbox because–'

313

'You needed the money,' I said gently.

'None of this would have happened if Vera hadn't come back,' William said bitterly. 'But she wouldn't listen. She wouldn't let me explain.'

I could easily imagine Vera's hysteria. I'd seen it firsthand myself.

'I gave her the snuff box. She tripped and hit her head on the corner of the coffee table. It knocked her out but I knew it wouldn't be for long.'

'Tell Shawn it was an accident,' I insisted but William didn't seem to be listening.

'I carried her to the grotto. I was just going to leave her in there so I could get away but she came around just as I reached the steps—'

'Vera threw the snuff box up on the bank?'

'I didn't know Vera was terrified of the grotto. She was screaming about the blue lady. I couldn't shut her up. I never meant to hurt her ... I just wanted her to be quiet.' William regarded his hands with bewilderment. 'I told you, it was an accident ... I just put my hand over her mouth ... but who would ever believe me?'

'I believe you,' I said quickly.

'I love Edith – she's been kind to me.'

I was about to point out that he had deceived Lady Edith but decided against it. As if reading my mind, William added, 'Not at first. No, at first I just wanted to find the loot. I saw her as someone I could easily fool but over the years...'

'You should tell her ladyship everything you've told me,' I said firmly. 'She cares about you. She doesn't need to know that you stole the snuff box.'

'Tell Iris, I'm sorry about the Post-it Notes.'

'It was *you* who tried to frame my mother?' I

said. 'And the Wellington boot?'

'Yes. I put it in the dustbin and yes, it was me who drove Vera's car to Totnes railway station and left it there,' said William. 'I cut across the fields and when I stopped to check on Jupiter, Edith and Lavinia turned up.'

'Tell Shawn the truth,' I said again. 'It's the only way.'

William shook his head again. 'No, I can't do that.' His expression of despair had been replaced with something more sinister. 'I'm so sorry, Katherine.'

Suddenly, he lunged out of the chair. I shrieked and tried to dive out of his way but tripped over a stack of *Country Life* magazines and fell down hard.

William was on top of me in an instant and pinning my hands above my head. I struggled, kicking my legs up violently but he was far stronger than me.

'Don't,' I gasped. 'Please. I won't say anything. Just leave. Please. Please!'

Holding my wrists in one of his massive hands, William pulled a syringe out of his jacket pocket. 'Stop fighting me.'

I saw the needle and screamed, 'What are you doing?'

'It won't hurt,' said William. 'I promise. It's ketamine. By the time you come around, I'll be gone.'

I struggled so violently William couldn't remove the cap.

'Lay still!' he shouted but I kept on wriggling and managed to jab my knee into his groin.

With a cry of pain, William rolled off me and

curled up in a fetal position. I got to my knees, tried to crawl to the door, but his hand grabbed my ankle and pulled me back toward him.

'Let me go,' I shouted and lunged for the winged cupid crystal award that Mum kept on the shelf of her bookcase. I smacked it down hard on William's head. He fell back, dazed but still conscious. I snatched the syringe out of his hand, tore off the cap, and plunged it into his neck.

William went out like a light.

The office door rattled, 'Open up! It's the police.'

There was a crack and crash as Clive shouldered the door and exploded into the room closely followed by Shawn and my mother who cried, 'I've brought the cavalry!'

Chapter Twenty-six

'I'm nervous,' Mum whispered.

We were standing at the gate inside the equine cemetery. 'Don't be silly. I'm sure Lady Edith is far more nervous than you. Why are you whispering?'

'It's a whispering sort of place,' we chorused and laughed.

'There she is.' I pointed to the small figure on the wooden seat looking out over the river. 'Are you sure you don't want me to come with you?'

Mum shook her head and set off down the hill alone.

Back at the Carriage House my heart sank when I spotted David's Porsche parked in the courtyard. He jumped out and hurried over.

'Kat!' he cried. 'I was worried! Why haven't you returned my phone calls?'

'I've been busy.'

'Is this *still* about Trudy and Dartmouth?' He pointed to his Porsche's rear wing that had substantial damage. Eric was right when he'd said cars weren't made the way they used to be. 'I think I came off worse in that scenario.'

'Really?'

'Look, I understand why you're angry and that you need to cool off a little but,' he paused, 'I need to talk to you. Not about us, but about your mother.'

My heart sank. 'What about my mother?'

'Trudy got an e-mail from someone called Vera Pugsley this weekend,' he said. 'She's the housekeeper here. Apparently this Pugsley woman told Trudy she had important information regarding the real identity of Krystalle Storm – and of course, given what happened to Vera–'

'Vera's death had nothing to do with my mother,' I said sharply.

David looked hurt. 'I didn't say it did. It just looks a bit suspicious, that's all. I know how much William – or should I say, Ralph Jackson, liked your mother.'

'You mean my mother was so afraid of being found out that she persuaded William to kill Vera off?'

'So what really happened?' said David. 'I couldn't get a straight answer at the Hare &

Hounds, only that Jackson got twelve months for involuntary manslaughter.'

'Isn't that all we need to know?' I said.

'Aren't you curious?' said David. 'Why did Ralph Jackson change his name to William Bushman?'

'I haven't the faintest idea,' I said, feeling my face redden. I had always been a hopeless liar. 'Why are you so interested?'

'I would have thought a story like this would have been in all the local newspapers,' said David. 'But it was hardly mentioned at all.'

'The family wants to keep it quiet.'

'Like they kept the robbery quiet?' David said mildly. 'Have you been keeping an eye open for me? Seen anything on that list?'

'Of course I'll keep an eye open,' I said but I hadn't and I didn't intend to, either.

David stepped forward and gave me a hug. 'So we're okay? You and me?'

'Yes. Why wouldn't we be?'

'Dinner. Saturday night. You pick the restaurant?'

'Can't,' I said. 'You're right, I should stay down here a while until Mum gets her pins out.'

David gave me a peck on my forehead. 'Do you want me to call you later?'

'Not really.'

David laughed, unaware that I was serious. With a wave, he sauntered back to his Porsche and in that moment, I knew it was over between us.

I went back to the Carriage House feeling liberated. Mum was staying and for now, so was I. It was time to unpack all those boxes and help

Mum make this her real home. I opened the sitting room door and surveyed the chaos.

Taking the box marked FRANK – DOCU-MENTS, I said, 'Let's start with you, Dad.' I knew this was the one chore Mum dreaded doing.

Removing the lid I saw a sealed letter marked IRIS – PLEASE READ. Dad had written the date on the outside of the envelope. It was the week before he died.

'Oh, Dad,' I whispered as tears filled my eyes. 'We miss you so.'

I put it down and knew I couldn't tackle that box, either, so focused on sorting towels.

Mum was gone a long time.

'What are you doing in here?' she demanded.

'Helping you unpack. How did it go? I was thinking about you *all* the time.'

'Look.' Mum handed me a blue velvet case.

'The pearls!' I gasped. 'You're kidding.'

'She said she hoped they would make up for what happened between us,' said Mum. 'She insisted I wasn't to blame and that she had made a terrible mistake in sending us away.'

I opened the box. 'They're beautiful – and wait ... one day they will be mine!' I gave her a hug. 'What about the rest of the spoils from the robbery?'

'I'm sure I don't know *what* you mean,' said Mum with a wink. 'Her ladyship – Edith – told me that you are welcome to look through the attics. Apparently there are a lot of Victorian toys up there for your shop – that is if you are still planning on having one. She'll even loan you the Steiff mourning bear.'

Gesturing to the pair of mice on the mantel-piece, I said, 'Well, you'll be happy to know that Jazzbo Jenkins is enjoying his reunion with Ella Fitzgerald.'

'Where was he?'

'Recovering from his ordeal behind the back of William's – or should I say, Ralph's sofa,' I said.

I went to give Mum a hug but she yelped, 'Pins!'

'So all's well that ends well,' I said.

'Not really.'

'Oh Mum,' I exclaimed. 'You're never satisfied.'

'The government is building a high-speed train line through the estate.'

'But that's terrible!' I said. 'We have to fight it.'

'Oh we will, don't worry,' said Mum. 'Rupert is distraught. He's sworn to help fight it, too, though I'm not sure if I trust his motives. Do leopards ever change their spots?'

'Mum, there is something you must see.' I opened Dad's letter. Her hand shook as she took it. 'No, I can't. Read it to me,' she said. 'I ... I just can't.'

My fingers trembled, too, as I held the paper and recognized his quirky spidery handwriting. *"'Iris, I know you were never happy living in the city. I know you gave up so much for me but I want you to know that never a day has passed by without me thanking God that we met. I will love you for all eternity."'*

'Dad loved you so much,' I said, trying hard not to cry.

'Do you think that's why Frank gave me the newspaper clipping about Lady Edith?' Mum asked. 'Perhaps it was his way of giving me his blessing – to return to a place I loved?'

'Yes, I think it was.' I put my arms around Mum's shoulders and held her tightly. 'But I have one more question for you,' I went on. 'If Vera had answered the door on Saturday night, would you have given her the money?'

'Of course. I'd do anything to protect you from that awful Trudy Wynne,' said Mum. 'Oh Kat, I was terrified you'd become the next victim on *Walk of Shame! Celebrity Family Secrets Revealed*.'

David's questions as to William's true identity suddenly hit me. Had Trudy put him up to it? What if she discovered the connection between Lady Edith, the real Billy, and my mother? She'd have a field day. I went cold at the thought.

'Did I mention that nice policeman wants to pop in later?' Mum went on.

'No, you didn't,' I said. 'Please don't play matchmaker, Mum.'

'Just be open,' Mum said. 'He has a ready-made family and you're not getting any younger.'

I bit back a stinging retort. 'Are you ready now?'

We stood on the banks of the River Dart watching the setting sun. Silhouetted above was Eric on his tractor, hauling away the white marble angel.

'They're moving Kelly to the family plot,' said Mum. 'Apparently Rupert didn't realize that Lavinia was besotted with him. He thought she was just doing her duty. The gentry have such strange views on love.'

I handed Mum the orange Tupperware box containing Dad's ashes and helped her into the rowing boat. Picking up the oars, I pushed off from the riverbank and we glided out onto the glassy water.

The publishers hope that this book has given you enjoyable reading. Large Print Books are especially designed to be as easy to see and hold as possible. If you wish a complete list of our books please ask at your local library or write directly to:

Magna Large Print Books
Magna House, Long Preston,
Skipton, North Yorkshire.
BD23 4ND

This Large Print Book for the partially sighted, who cannot read normal print, is published under the auspices of

THE ULVERSCROFT FOUNDATION